Crimson Bride

ANNALEE ADAMS

CRIMSON BRIDE

First edition. January 2023.
Copyright © 2023 Annalee Adams.
The moral rights of the author have been asserted.
Written by Annalee Adams.
This is a work of fiction. Similarities to real people, places, or events are entirely coincidental.
All rights reserved.
No part of this publication may be reproduced, transmitted, or stored in a retrieval system in any form or by any other means, without prior written permission from the author, Annalee Adams. No part of this publication may be circulated in any form of binding or cover than that which it is published in.
ISBN: 979-8-495-189997
This book has been typeset in Garamond.
www.AnnaleeAdams.biz

To Mark, my Husband and best friend.
Thank you for being my everything,
my Ethan.

Chapter One
Willa

"There's no chance in Hell I'm marrying that man!" I yelled, gripping the table.

Nora smirked, twirling her bleached blond curls as the pearl necklace encased her neck. "You will do what the duke demands." Her smile widening as she took another gulp of wine.

I sighed, staring down at my plate. The evening meal was usually when my adopted family came together. It was the only time they allowed me to sit at their table, showing me off to the masses, hoping to sell me as their princess of child birthing age. I shuddered, glaring at my evil stepmother. Nora said it was all I was good for. The fact it was the twenty-first century didn't seem to matter.

I watched as her expression softened. Her daughter Jenna smiled, placed down her mobile phone, and discussed her latest class. I listened, wrapping my arms around myself. I was only allowed to attend classes after I'd finished my chores; and assisting Chef took most of the day. So, I'd missed it. Hell, I'd missed most of them. English Literature always seemed to be when I was needed in the kitchen. It's almost as though Nora planned it. Knowing full well it was my favourite subject.

I never understood why Father didn't put a stop to her demands. But then he was rarely in attendance of late. I shrugged; lips pursed. Now I knew why. I bet he couldn't look me in the eye, knowing full well he'd sold me to another family. Why the hell I had to marry that vile Prince I don't know. I'm not even a real Princess, so what does that make this? A farce of two families? I smirked. They'd find out I'm sure… I just hope it's Nora that pays for the lies rather than me. Sighing I looked down, twirling my spoon in the bright orange soup. Spotty sixteen-year-old Harold walked over in his crisp white waiter's uniform. He'd not long started at the manor and seemed to enjoy working around the estate. "Is it to your satisfaction Princess Willa?"

I turned, dropping the spoon, tomato soup splashed out over his trousers. "Shit!" I said, grabbing my napkin to clean it off.

Harold squirmed. His fresh face bright red to match the soup. "I've got it, thank you," he said, backing away.

Jenna looked up from her phone howling with laughter. "Did you really just try to clean his dick?" Nora sniggered as I narrowed my eyes, gritting my teeth. Fists pummelled I scowled. She was such a spoilt brat at times. Jenna was younger than me, only by four years. She'd just turned thirteen and thought the world revolved around her. Which, it did. Since Father married Nora, I'd been cast aside. Their pristine baby girl taking centre stage. She lived to torment me.

I jerked forward, lips pursed, eyeing Jenna from across the table.

"Why doesn't she marry him?" I spat, as Jenna looked up, eyes wide.

"Ha, you're funny Willa! The duke is my father, not yours!"

"He is Jenna!" Well at least he used to be.

"Since when?"

"Since they adopted me. You know that!"

"Willa… father only keeps you around because he feels sorry for you."

"That's not true! The Duke and Duchess adopted me."

"The Duchess is dead," Nora stated. "I'm the new Duchess, and you were never part of my family."

"So why the hell did you keep me here then?" I asked, picking at my food.

Nora's eyes narrowed. "If I had my way, you'd have been living in the servants quarters years ago!"

"I do the chores anyway Nora," I huffed, staring down at my ragged dress.

She snarled. "What? It's not like you'll outgrow it anymore!"

"Does the Prince know he's marrying a slave?" Jenna questioned, smirking.

I stuck my finger up, flipping her off.

Nora took another sip of wine. "Well, we are going to have to at least wash and change you aren't we," she said. "He'll never even know!" she winked, smirking.

"Perhaps if he did know, I wouldn't have to marry him!"

Nora's face flushed; her eyes narrowed. "If you dare breathe a word of any of this, I will send the guards to bring me your head," she said, shaking her fist at me.

Raising one eyebrow I smirked. "I don't think murder is allowed nowadays Nora!"

"I don't think anyone would care Willa," Nora said, her fists pummelled as she slammed them down on the table. Hell, my whole life had been a tapestry of unspoken words, I sighed. What difference would another one mean?

Jenna watched, grinning. "Well, if you do breathe a word of this, I'm sure Gareth would happily make you disappear," she said. I flinched. Gareth was not a guard you'd mess with. I'd pushed his putrid advances away one too many times. He was an arrogant prick. A vicious fat, thick-headed man that stunk like a pig. He was the one Father used when he wanted people interrogated outside of the law.

Nora smiled, taking a sip of her wine. "You know we can make people disappear," she said, gloating. She was right. I'd seen it before. In this family, with their daily activities, you were living on the edge of a razor blade. If the threat wasn't Father's men, it was some obnoxious asshat from the Caputo family wanting to make a name for themselves. I sighed, looking down at my soup. At least our rivals looked out for another. They were a close-knit family based in the southern borough of London central. I'd witnessed the twins Valentina and Angelo get into a brawl with the local skateboarding gang. They came out on top of course. The skateboarders were later found in a ditch off West End Common.

I caught Jenna staring as I looked up. "It's either marry the monster or die at the hands of one… obvious really!" she snarled.

I narrowed my eyes. "You just want me out the way Jenna!"

"Yes," she nodded. "And what's wrong with that?"

Nora smiled, "nothing dear," she said, taking Jenna's hand from across the table. Jenna smiled. I fake gagged. Another servant brought over a second bottle of wine. Nora filled up her glass.

Jenna's eyes narrowed as she stared at me. "What? Jealous much?"

I feigned a laugh, folding my arms. "Of you? Never!"

She sniggered, pouting. "It's sad really, your own mother never wanted you and then you killed your adopted one," she said with a close-lipped smile.

I winced, snapping my head round to face her. "That's not true!" I yelled. Pushing my bowl away, I hammered my fists down on the table; tomato soup flying everywhere.

Nora's expression darkened, breathing heavy. "Don't be disrespectful!" she screeched.

I sat up straight, shaking with anger. "My mother did want me. She had no choice but to give me up."

"How would you know! You were only a mere babe!" Nora cackled, finishing her glass of wine.

My heart sank. She was right. My own mother never wanted me. I was lucky they took me in. Who knows what would have happened if they'd left me out in the cold? Tears welled in my eyes as I lowered my face to my hands. Gerrard, the head water walked over, bringing our main meals. He wiped the spilled soup and removed the bowl. Two other waiters delivered Nora and Jenna's.

Nora sighed, placing down her glass. "If Wilbert didn't find you on the hunting trip you'd have been eaten by those wolves," she said as she took a bite of potato.

"Maybe that'd been better," I said, biting my bottom lip.

She laughed. "Maybe it would have. But we can't hope for that now can we." She smiled. "Now you're of age, you will marry Prince Ethan James Bane."

I took a deep breath. My lips pursed. Hands clammy. "This isn't even legal you know!"

"Oh honey, we own the police force."

I sighed. I knew that. Here in the city Father had his hands in every dirty deal going. For saying he was the Barone of a high-end Meth kingdom was an understatement. He was known worldwide and pretty much owned every cop this side of the West County line. I couldn't get out of it, even if Nora wanted me to.

"Why would he even want to marry me?"

Nora shrugged. "Wilbert didn't tell me."

Jenna looked up. "Good riddance I say," she smirked.

My lips pursed, I stared down at my plate, picking up a roast potato and mushing it. Hmm, perhaps Father owes them money? Or maybe it's the Elder Vale. They own the land and it used to be theirs, it's entirely possible they want it back. I nodded. That makes more sense, Father was all about alliances. Maybe this was his way of cementing a new one?

"So, he's selling me to clear his debts?" Nora frowned. "Or is it the Elder Vale? Do they want it back?"

She sat upright. "You know your father won't part with the vale!"

"So, it's debts then."

Nora's expression darkened as she spoke through gritted teeth, "I would presume so." She stared at me, the edges of her lips curling into a sadistic smile. "You were always just a business investment my dear. You must have known your day would come?"

"Like hell I did! You've never seen me for who I am! I'd have been better off alone."

She slammed her hand down on the table. "Willa Rose, you owe us for the clothes on your back, the food on your table and the roof over your head. You will marry that man tomorrow or I will destroy everything you know and love." She stood up, her chair legs screeching against the oak floor. Glaring at me, she turned away and stormed out of the dining room.

My jaw dropped and I slumped down in the chair. Jenna laughed, sat up straight and threw a bread roll at me. "You've done it now. Father won't stand for your insolence anymore." She picked up an apple and I ducked ready for the next impact. Instead, Jenna stood up, took a bite, and glided out of the hall, swinging her hips as she left.

Gerrard walked over, placing a hand on my shoulder. He smiled, picked up my plate of uneaten food, then left. I was alone except for Harry and Luke, fathers' bodyguards, or my captors. I wasn't sure which.

My bottom lip quivered, eyes watering. I pulled my legs up and cradled myself. Even if I ran, who could I trust? They all wanted to use and abuse me. This was nothing new. I sighed, wiping my tear-stained cheeks. My body slumped in the chair. It was pointless fighting anymore. I was and would always be alone.

Chapter Two
Willa

Sitting up, I glanced down at the fresh stain of tomato soup that sullied my dress. Shit! I only had three to my name and there was no way I'd be able to wash that out! I groaned. Well not unless Chef had some white vinegar lying around.

I wonder if Nora meant what she said. Dressing me like a Royal and passing me off as a real Princess? In some respects, I hoped she would. I'd played the part for years, dressed up as a doll whenever she saw fit. Public appearances mostly, when they felt the need to parade us before the higher end of society. But with everything else I was broken down to rags and made to work the kitchens to pay my way.

I sighed. I'd always known this was a possibility. Especially since father made a big deal about me reaching a hearty child birthing age. I gagged. It wasn't right. None of it.

The thing was I thought I'd be wed to Prince William, or even perhaps Thomas or Edward. I could've learnt to love them. But to be forced to marry a man I'd never met. Especially a man with a blood thirsty reputation. The only reason our family still reigned, was at the courtesy of The Banes. The Grand Duke, Oswald Bane was a known tyrant, and his son Ethan was even worse. I highly suspected they owned the Meth empire; or at least had shady dealings in something secretive and illegal. I reached in my stained linen pocket and pulled out my phone, an old flip phone. It was all my friend Juliet had to spare, considering Nora took my last one away from me.

I must have tried four different search engines, there was nothing. Ethan was a ghost in the system. No social media. No selfies of endless parties and drunken disasters. Okay, so maybe that was all me. But what else could an orphan girl live for? I smiled. Because of my friends, life had been fun here, even with all the shit Nora caused. I knew I was lucky I lived in a manor house and had friends behind the walls. Okay so not like people actually living in the walls. I shuddered. That's serial killer creepy! But my best mate Juliet and I escaped through the secret passages many times. It was the only way to get round fathers men and sneak out after hours. She'd lend me a dress and shoes, we'd put on makeup, tie our hair up high, then sneak over to the South end of London and meet Valentina and Angelo at Lola's bar. A few unpronounceable cocktails later and all was right with the world.

Granted they were my family's rivals, but they were good mates and were as fed up as I was with the messed up city we lived in.

They'd even offered to put me up if I ever left the manor house. I'd thought about it time after time. Even packed my things on several occasions. But I couldn't go through with it. I couldn't trust them. I knew their father would try and use me as leverage in the Meth war. Then when I was seen as insignificant, he'd be rid of me just like everyone else.

I sighed, looking down at my glass of water. Shit. Seventeen and married. That's messed up! All other girls would be heading off to university soon. I would have loved that. Studying English literature and living through the stories of my playful foes. Heck I'd be able to write a biography by the time I hit my twenties; with all the screwed-up crap that's happened.

How could I tell Juliet? Then again, I was sure she already knew and would be on her way here right now. That girl was gossip central for the whole manor house. I wonder if she knew why I was being sold to the highest bidder. Surely, they know I'm not really a Princess, right? Their arrogant blood doesn't run in my veins. I sighed. Why would they even want to keep the vale anyway? The whole place was one disaster after another. After my adopted mother died there, father should have wanted the whole place burned down. But he didn't. He'd go out there every day, disappear into the forest for his afternoon walks. He never did say what killed her. But I knew for damn sure it wasn't human.

I'd been at the lake with Juliet when my mother died. We were swimming in the tranquil waters, shocked back to reality by her screams. She'd been taking a walk, heading over to join us to sunbathe under the midday sun. But she never made it. We couldn't stop the bleeding. There was too much blood, her abdomen ripped clean open. Father never looked at me the same after that. He said I reminded him of her. I always saw it as a good thing. But clearly it wasn't to him. After he remarried, they had Jenna. Then, I was merely a living memory. The face of his trauma; all I bought was pain. He couldn't even look at me anymore. The sweet part of the deal for him wasn't the debts, or the vale. It was the chance to be rid of me. To leave his horrendous past behind and move on with his new family. I didn't like it, but I understood it.

I sighed. Twirling the gold rose necklace between my fingers. I missed her. My mother. Heck, I missed them both. I wish I'd known my real mother. The one who left me this. I tugged on the necklace, sitting back in the chair.

Did Duke Oswald or his son even know I wasn't a blood born Royal? Maybe if they knew I wouldn't have to marry Prince Ethan? I stretched in the chair, leaning forward, platting my rose red hair. I could tell them. Send an email, a text or even a letter? But if I did. Would that mean I'd be cast to the streets to live a life of solitude under the watchful eye of the moon and the stars? Perhaps being alone would be better than to be married into the family of a tyrant?

What if they did know? Would they drag me to prison as a liar and a cheat? I had played the part of a Royal all my life. Smiled when told. Curtseyed when necessary. To find out the Princess was a fake would devastate the truce between both families. Either family would surely see me sliced and diced before granting my freedom!

There was no way out of this. I had to suck it up and dance. Perhaps I'd be lucky and have my own room and be able to roam free among their gardens. It was my only escape during the daytime. My mind wandered to the rose garden I tended to here at the manor. My closest friend Juliet had shown me how her family were the manors gardeners; I'd always been welcomed there. Although her parents were quite close with Nora's family, so I still had to watch my back.

The door opened as Juliet bounded in, banging into Harry as she tripped over the step. "Oops sorry," she said. Harry groaned, pulled her up and stood back at his station. "Is it true?" she asked. Her face a picture of utter dismay.

I nodded. My bottom lip wavering.

"Oh Willa," she said, pulling me up to stand, holding me tight. Salty tears cushioned my lips. "What can I do?"

"There isn't anything Juliet," I said as I pulled away from her hold.

"But to that tyrant? To his family? Why?" Her brow arched; eyes thinned.

"I don't know," I said, shaking my head. "But I have no choice."

Tears welled in her eyes. She shook them off, feigning a smile. "Okay." She took a deep breath. "You know what you always tell me."

I inhaled, held, and exhaled, shaking my body free of negativity. "I know. Smile and wave. Smile and wave."

"You can do this Willa. They may surprise you yet."

My lip quivered. "I hope so."

"So… when do you go?"

"Tomorrow."

She sulked. "New Haven isn't that far away," she said, wiping her eyes. "We can text and meet up on weekends. It'll be like you never left!" She smiled and I sighed. She was right. I had to make the best of this. Standing tall she took my hand and pulled me out of the dining room. "Okay, let's get you packed."

I nodded. Pulling her in for a hug as we went to pack away the only life I'd ever known.

Chapter Three
Ethan

    Danica's soft undercoat flowed through the breeze, her wild brunette bristles shimmering under the midnight moon as we galloped through the Elder Vale. Our wolves jumped about playfully as we entered a clearing, having known each other for the last four years. Danica bowed before me, submitting as she changed back to human form. Her voluptuous body craved my own. Standing over her I howled, my black wolf going into hiding as my human form took shape. Tanned and burned with the markings of the pack, I pushed her down. She opened her legs, revealing her brunette pubic hair as she gripped the fallen leaves beneath her and groaned. I reached down, feeling the warmth of her vagina. Deep. Hot and wet.

    Danica reached down, using her hand to guide me as I thrust

myself inside, taking her as my own. Pulling her neck back so I could scent the arousal all over her. Nails clawed at my skin as she cradled her legs around me.

Standing up, I held her, gripping her buttocks, slamming her up against the tree. She was my mate, my true love. Sweat cushioned my upper lip as her tongue licked off every bead. Gripping the back of her neck, I pushed her lips to mine. Delving deeper into her mouth, my tongue delighting in her taste. I pulled away, crashing my mouth to her neck, to what should be my mark. But I couldn't. Danica screamed my name as I thrust in harder. Deeper. I didn't understand why my wolf wouldn't mark her. She was mine. My mate.

Footsteps crunched over the Autumn leaves. "Alpha," Alaric said, coughing. "You're needed back at the Castle."

"Now?" I asked, pulling away from Danica. She fell to the ground, groaning in anger.

"Yes Alpha. Father asked for you immediately."

My eyes widened. "He's still up? But it's past midnight!" There must be something wrong!

He rolled his eyes. "Then you'll want to come quickly."

I growled at him as he threw me a pair of pants. "If you weren't my brother, I'd have had your head by now."

Alaric smirked; eyes drawn to Danica, who was brushing the leaves off herself.

"Eyes on me, Beta!" I demanded.

Alaric chuckled, "do you need a head start brother?" he yelled as he turned away and set off, racing me back to the castle.

Running up and over the bridge, past the dilapidated build of Old Tim's farm, the sweet fruity smell of Patrick's ale engulfed me. The Crescent Bar and Eatery were New Haven's answer to cocktails and fine dining. Turning the corner I took the lead, hurtling through the narrow-winding street beside the rose dipped oils and incense of Arias Apothecary. We finally entered the grounds, wolfing out as we sped through the darkened hedge maze, bypassing Darkwater lake and through the corridors down to the father's office. Alaric stood by the doorway. "Good luck!" he uttered as he grinned and left.

Father was sitting at his desk when I opened the door. His eyes ached as he strained through the darkness. A mere desk lamp lit the room, casting shadows over its architecture. Father was old-fashioned. He didn't enjoy the modern ways of this world, always against change. He'd even resisted the installation of a microwave oven, let alone central heating! Mother was quite the opposite. She welcomed change and new beginnings. I smiled. She also liked to wind my father up as often as she could.

"Ethan," he boomed. "Let me see you."

"Yes, father," I said, changing back. The guards passed me trousers and a shirt.

"It is time, Ethan. You must play your part."

I narrowed my eyes. What was the old man on about? "What part?" I asked, taking a seat. He set up the chessboard on the desk and moved his first piece.

"We need an alliance. More now than ever."

"Why?" I asked, moving my first pawn two spaces.

"You know why!" he boomed, standing up. "The Council will not sit on the side lines any longer. They want our land and they're coming to take it." He whipped out the knight, setting up the kill.

"Since when is Hela bothered about land?" has he lost his mind?

"Don't you get it, son! She's always wanted control."

"But why now?"

He shook his head. "I don't know. But we've had word that there are spies within our mists."

"What!" I boomed, slamming my fists on the desk. The chess pieces jumping on the board.

He growled. Moving them back to where they were. "I have dealt with them."

"Who was it?" I asked, sitting forward and moving my bishop, ready to attack.

"John, Deedee and Jolee."

"Jolee! Really!"

He nodded. How could I have been so stupid? She was the young wolf we'd taken in six months ago. So kind, fragile and trustworthy. Or so I thought!

He sat down again, slumping in his chair. "Yes son. I'm afraid James overheard her talking to John and Deedee. They'd been reporting back to the Council ever since they arrived." He took my pawn and was in position for his next kill.

"But why!"

He shook his head. "We can't trust anyone, son."

"We can trust the pack." I said, taking his piece.

"She was part of Tristan's pack, Ethan. Even he didn't know."

"She was new Father. The rest of the pack have stood by us for years."

He nodded. Moving his queen out.

My head lowered. I sighed. "It would have devastated James." I followed suit, moving my queen into a defensive stance.

"He was. I doubt he will ever trust another again."

My heart sank for him. He had cared for her like a little sister.

She was merely fourteen years old. I shook my head. They're training them even younger now. My lips pursed; fists clenched.

"Where are they?" We continued to play.

"James handed them over to FALCON."

My eyes widened; my jaw dropped. "What! Since when are we working with FALCON?"

"We're not son. But he couldn't bring himself to end her. Tristan offered to do it. But the entire pack is at a loss. It seemed the best course of action."

"What will they do to her?"

He shrugged. "I'm guessing extract information on the Council. Then lethal injection."

I shuddered. FALCON was a force to be reckoned with… for saying they were mainly human hunters. It'd been tough since Nathaniel left them. He'd been the voice of our kind. But now it appeared all wolves were fair game. It didn't help that one of the southern packs murdered one of their families. That was a damn stupid move. But since those packs had joined the Council. FALCON had left us alone.

My head lowered. "So, the Council knows what we've been up to?"

He nodded.

"So, what's the plan?"

He sat upright. "We need to increase our defences."

"But how? With the South gone, and the packs to the North being questionable. How can we?"

He pursed his lips, scratching his head. Using his queen to take my bishop.

I took a deep breath. "Our packs will fight, father. They're loyal to us."

The Grand Duke leaned forward in his chair. His eyes narrowed. "You're always too quick to see the blood of battle, son. You know since the Council gathered the packs to the South, we're severely outnumbered."

"Including the Amber Rose brotherhood?" He nodded. "I can't stand Darius and his brothers. Not after what they did to Layla." I studied the board. My mind wandered to sweet Layla Landon. A fragile ten-year-old that had so much life to live. As a new member of my pack, I was fond of her. She reminded me of an older version of my sister, Cleo.

She had not long survived her first change. New to the supernatural world. Then one fateful day in the Elder Vale she witnessed a horrific attack. She tried to help the victim, but the woman died, her abdomen half eaten. We'd heard Layla's call for help through a mind link, but none of us could save her. Darius and his brothers interceded, thought Layla had murdered her, and took her to the Council for execution. There were never any trials. No innocent till proven guilty. The witches could have heard the truth if they'd tried. But Hela wouldn't listen. She despised the fact we were the strongest pack out there and used Layla as punishment for that.

That was the last we heard of poor Layla Landon. They slaughtered Layla; we felt her fear as she succumbed to Helas torture. Heard her last goodbyes and wept as her mind link diminished, as she too died with it.

He growled. "They will get their comeuppance one day." He pushed forward, taking my queen. Shit! I frowned. How did I not see that!

My lips pursed. Hands gripping the desk. "We will not stand for it, Father!"

"I know, and we won't, but we must bide our time until our

armies are strong enough to destroy them."

I sat back, staring at the board, only three pieces left. "So, what can I do?"

He nodded, sitting up in his chair, making his next move. "It requires that we make an alliance with the human, Duke Wilbert."

"What? Why would you?" I frowned. "Humans are the weakest of all creatures." Well, except FALCON, they were the ninjas of mortality.

He nodded. "Yes, but they're also the only ones we can trust. You know the Council would never even consider them a threat."

I frowned. "Yes, because they're not a threat…" well not really.

"They would be if we changed them…"

My brow furrowed. Changing humans? That'd surely piss Hela off. She'd see it as a threat and come for us. I shrugged. Then again, it sounded like she'd already infiltrated our forces. Humans may be our only hope.

"But what about the odds of them surviving their first change?"

"It's a risk we have to take. We need an army. Duke Wilbert runs the Meth empire in London. He has an army of men and women at his disposal. By becoming allies, we would keep the Elder Vale, and wipe out his debt to us."

I pursed my lips, scratching my head. "He owes us a large sum of money."

He nodded. "We are the reason he has such an empire."

I frowned. I always wondered why Father had offered to assist him. "So, I presume this was your plan all those years ago?"

He smiled, his expression darkening. "It was always my backup plan, son. I knew Hela would come for us one day." He took my King. Check mate. I huffed, sitting back. He smiled and said, "Checkmate." No wonder I could never beat him at chess. He played the long game, whereas I rammed through every piece as quickly as I could.

Hot damn, though, he had a point. Hela and her bunch of supernatural devil worshippers wouldn't see it coming. I smirked. It'd be bloody glorious to see Darius's expression when we kicked their door down with an army of newly turned wolves on our side!

Father grinned. "So, are you game to give this old man a little fun before I hand over the reins?"

I smiled and nodded. "There's one catch though."

I narrowed my eyes. "What?"

"You've got to marry the human Princess."

"WHAT?" I gasped, wide eyed and frozen to the spot. "You can't be serious!"

"I am Ethan. Her name is Princess Willa Rose. She will be here later today."

"You can't demand this of me. I have my mate! I will marry no one else."

"I won't Ethan. But the fate of our people depends on you marrying that girl."

"Damn you father!"

The door opened. Mother walked in. "What is going on?" she asked, yawning. "Don't you two ever sleep?" She walked over and kissed my cheek, then sat beside Father. "What's wrong Oswald?"

"It's time Bernadette, their forces are growing, and several packs have already joined the Council. We no longer have the numbers to defend against them."

Mother's head lowered. She sighed.

My hands balled into fists. "But we're the toughest pack there is. Why should we falter?" I yelled, standing up.

"Ethan, lower your voice!" my mother said, arms crossed.

"Yes, mother."

Father sighed. "We cannot survive an attack. We must form an alliance and grow our numbers... Ethan must marry their first daughter."

Mothers' eyes lost their sparkle. She stood up and walked over to me. Wrapping her arms around my torso, she laid her head on my chest. "I'm sorry, son. We need to think of our people."

"But they're humans!"

"Humans may be all we have now. Our numbers are dwindling. If the Council wanted, they could take our land and destroy everything we've ever worked for or loved... Think of Danica," she said.

I frowned. "So, you want me to marry another woman to protect my mate?" I asked. She pulled away.

"I'm sorry, son." It filled her face with sadness as she looked up at me.

I sighed. There was no choice. My people came first. They were my responsibility now. I was there, Alpha. "Fine. But Willa will be a legality. Nothing more."

My mother nodded and sighed.

The Grand Duke stood up from his chair, yawning. "We will have the contracts drawn up in the morning." He kissed Mother on the forehead. Rested his hand on my shoulder and walked away. Mother left after him; her face sullen as she kissed my cheek when she left.

Shit. How do I tell Danica? She would never understand!

Danica... where is she? Did I leave her in the clearing? I winced. Shit. I did. She'd be pretty pissed by now, and with this news, I doubt she'd even speak to me again. This wasn't how it was.

Mates were for life. We meant everything to each other. Danica was who I should marry, not some obsolete human from a naïve city. I sighed, storming out of the office. My body ached and itched to release the wolf. I was angry, upset and felt a failure of a mate. All I needed now was to run. So, I did.

Chapter Four
Ethan

The following morning, I awoke by Darkwater lake. Stretching back into my body, as I gazed down at my reflection. Black curls, blue eyes with a tinge of green streaked over the right iris. Sun-stroked skin that was covered in the blood of my latest kill. A deer I believe. I smiled, splashing water over my face. Standing up, I could see the gardeners tending to the hedge maze. "Morning, sir," an older gentleman said, while holding a pair of clippers.

They were used to my naked strolls back to the Castle. Plus, it was indeed the day for it. Granted a tad on the cooler side of Autumn. But the longer I take out here, the less likely I will bump into Danica and have my balls handed to me. I growled. She's lucky she's my mate. No other person would dare speak to me the way she does.

Two boys ran past dressed in jeans and colourful jumpers.

"Morning, Mr Prince," one of them squawked, as the other ran off yelling for his mother.

I smirked as I walked past.

Tristan came into view. My best friend since birth. They had killed his family in a battle with another pack, so my father took him in. We'd been brothers ever since. Alphas of our own packs, and the closest friends we could be.

"Ethan, have you ever heard of clothes, man?" he asked, laughing at me, and throwing me a pair of blue shorts.

I gave him a snide look. "Thanks mate."

"You know it's past noon. Danica's been looking for you. She's doing that devil eyed angry expression."

I winced. "Does she know?"

He snickered and shook his head. "But she's about to. As that black Mercedes there has the Princess inside."

"Shit." I yelped as I ran toward the Castle, leaving him in hysterics. The car pulled up as Edward, our foots-man, helped the Princess out. My mother and sister Cleo were there to greet her.

"Ethan!" my mother yelled. Her eyes wide at the sight of me.

"Sorry mother!" I said, running past, looking back only to meet eyes with Princess Willa. Rose red hair fell down past her bosom. Pale skin cradled her fragile body as her olive-green eyes met my own. My heart pounded. I took a step forward, catching her as she tripped getting out of the car. My inner wolf growled. My body tingled as we touched, bathed in curiosity and arousal of her tender form. Who was she? She gasped; eyes widened as she saw me. I stopped. Breathed in her scent, lavender and roses.

Mother stepped forward, taking the princesses hand from mine. "Ethan, get changed!" she demanded. Cleo stood giggling next to her.

Reality hit me as I looked down and remembered the bloodied deer. I growled, angered at my appearance, disappearing to my room to bathe and change.

Damn it! What must she have thought of me? I huffed, shaking my head. Why does it matter? She's a mere human and a means to an end. My inner wolf growled. What? You can be quiet! You've got us both into enough trouble with that deer! He groaned and silenced himself. I took off the shorts, jumped in the shower, and cleaned up. Wiping the mirror and shaving my overgrown stubble afterwards.

Drying off, I found the suit that was laid out for me. Sighing, I got changed and looked in the mirror. I pulled off the suit well. Even Danica would approve, and she wasn't the easiest to please! I cringed, remembering. Damn! I was hoping to speak to her before the ceremony began. How was I supposed to explain this one?

Looked like I didn't have to. The door handle turned. Danica pushed open the door, slamming it against the wall. Hands on hips. Body shaking with anger. Spittle foaming at her mouth. Shit! I was about to be in prime position for her full-on rage fest. She was premenstrual as well. Fuck! This would not be fun!

I winced, stepping forward. "Danica… I can explain!" It was clear she already knew.

She walked in and slapped me. My inner wolf screamed for release. Sweat beaded on my brow as I fought to keep him in. She went to slap me again, but I grabbed her arm in time. "Don't you EVER do that again!" I yelled, baring my teeth. I know she's my mate, but who the fuck does she think she is? She backed off. The rage inside me battled at the surface. I pushed her to the wall, gripped her neck, closing the gap between us. Lips crashed into one another. Kissing, searching each other's mouths, desperate for more. I growled, pulling away, glaring at her. Even through anger, I still couldn't bring myself to hurt her. And damn, she made me angry! I needed a release. I Need it now. There was no time to shift. No time to run. So I gripped her arm, directed it to my hard-on, and pulled off her panties. Fingers wet and warm, I had Danica groaning in no time. Licking my way down her body, I took in her taste. She was my aphrodisiac, and I had to have more. Lifting her up, I threw her on the bed, whipped off my trousers, and mounted her from behind. Clasping my hands over her hips, I rocked back and forth, picking up speed as I drove harder, faster. Breasts swung below, mimicking my movement. Gripping the right one, I squeezed, playing with her nipple. She cried out in pleasure, and I spun her body over so she lay below me. Holding her hands in place, I thrust myself in deeper. Moving one hand down to her neck, gripping it as she whined for more. She liked it rough. Begged for more. Nails ripped at my back, gauging my skin like their life depended on it. Moments later, we were hot, sweaty, and in the throes of passion. Danica arched upwards, crying out, whining with pleasure. Every part of her tensed, squeezing me till I couldn't take any more. Growling I released. Total escapism took over, pure invincibility and a feeling like no other. I moved and slid off, panting, wiping my brow. Danica lay smiling, staring at the ceiling. She moved on to her side, eyes narrowed. "I've still not forgiven you; you know."

I smirked. She had. I kissed her lips, delicate red lips, her face flushed, hair swept back.

"So, is this what you're wearing?" she asked.

"Yes." I looked down at my trousers strewn across the floor. "Well, it will be." I said. Then sighed, kissed her forehead, getting up to re-dress.

She sat up, pulled on her clothes, and sat staring at me. Her expression darkened. "You're not actually going through with it, are you?"

"I have to Danica. I have no choice."

"You always have a choice, Ethan. You could choose me."

I lowered my head. "I am choosing you Danica. It's always you."

She growled. Fists gripping the satin sheets and she stormed out of the room.

I growled, zipped up my trousers and went after her, finding her leaning against the table in one of the old dining rooms. No one used this side of the castle much anymore.

She glared at me when she saw me. "You say it's always been me. It isn't. Not if you're marrying that whore of a princess!" she shrieked. "We're mated!"

Technically, we weren't yet, but I'm sure my wolf would get round to it! She stood up and put her panties back on.

"I know Danica. I'm doing it to protect you!"

Her eyes widened. "Do you even hear yourself… you're marrying another woman to protect me. For fuck's sake Ethan, you're delusional!"

"It is to protect you Danica, you know I'd never do anything to hurt you."

"What do you think you're doing right now?" she screamed. Her eyes welling up.

I growled, running my knuckles down her cheek. "I tried to get out of it!"

"I mean nothing to you! You should have said no!"

"Of course you matter to me! But you know how persuasive my parents can be."

"So, what now?" she asked, her heart wrenching as tears fell down her face.

"Nothing will change Danica. You will always be my mate. This is just a legality."

"It had better be!" she said, thumping her hands on my chest. I pulled her in close for a kiss, mounting her on the table.

This would not be the end. I would fight for Danica every day, so that my heart continued to beat.

Danica pulled back from me as I kissed the tears from her face. "Make sure you make her life a living hell, Ethan."

I nodded, kissing her once again.

Chapter Five
Willa

New Haven was a town with a lively crowd. Open seated bars full of tourists, a beach packed with families, broken sandcastles, and melted ice creams. From what good old Google told me, it was England's surfer central. Epic waves from sunrise to sunset. Which, thinking about it… is it even possible? Surely the tide would play a role in that during the day. I shrugged. Who knows!

The marina was packed with tourists. There were brand new Yachts, millionaires and scantily clad girls. No wonder Prince Ethan loved his hometown so much!

I sighed. Could I live here? Take in the rich lifestyle and be the princess I was meant to be? My head lowered. It was shit, though. It all was. I could never have the old-aged dream of marrying for love.

Living happily ever after. In my reality, those things didn't happen. Apparently forced marriage was all I had to look forward to.

Gazing out of the window, I watched as the world went by. It was a delight of colour. Juliet would love it here. I can imagine the nights out we'd have, ending with beach parties or dancing on poker tables on million-pound yachts. I never imagined that this gem of a town lived beyond the Elder Vale! At least I've got that to look forward to.

Sneaking out my phone, I took a video and sent it to Juliet. She'd be stoked to see it. I'd have to barter with the Husband to be so she could visit. I shuddered. He had better not try anything. Better yet, he'd better not come anywhere near me or else he'll get a face full of these fists. Shuddering again, I remembered back to my last encounter with the lowlife men of my town. Jeez. They're all asshats!

Taking a deep breath, I exhaled, staring up the hill towards New Haven's very own castle. It looked like it came straight out of its very own gothic fairy tale. One where you'd expect Snow White to live, with the Evil Queen plotting her demise. I smirked, looking at Nora. She snarled. Heck, it sounds like home to me.

The Castle was within several acres of grounds, all at the top of a tremendously winding road. They certainly had the views, as the castle looked down at New Haven's glorious seafront, with Elder Vale to the side of it.

My heart pounded as we reached the gate; turrets either side, topped with witch's hat roofs and held together by an old red brick building. It'd taken over an hour to travel through Elder Vale by car. The forest amassed old winding roads and captivating landscapes. It was a place I'd played as a child, swimming in the lake and picnicking by the hillside. It always felt warm there, no matter the season. Even after my mother's death, the Vale felt safe, like home.

"He's got to be ugly or stupid and cuckoo crazy!" Jenna spat, waving her finger by her ear.

Nora smirked.

"Now Jenna, let's not be nasty," father said. His balding head gleamed from the light from the car window.

"Sorry, father," she snarled, elbowing me in the ribs.

My brow furrowed. My new family couldn't be any worse than this!

I took a deep breath as we drove through the grounds, delighted by the display of spectacular gardens. There was a large lake in the centre, with an extravagant hedge maze to get lost around. This will be my escape. I thought, smiling.

Turning the corner, I saw a tall, muscular man covered in blood and gunk. He looked like he'd lost a fight to a bear, losing his clothes. Well, all but his tight shorts. I smirked. His tousled black curls enveloped his face, while his tanned body strengthened his muscular torso as he sped to a stop beside the car. I could feel his presence outside as I bit down on my lip, my stomach fluttering with nerves. Who was he?

We came to a halt, and the duke got out, helping Nora and Jenna. Jenna backed against the car. "What's wrong with that man!" she said, eyes wide. I clutched my bag and peaked out, finding my own way out. Jenna continued to point at the bloodied mess before her.

"Jenna, you know it's rude to point!" I exclaimed as I exited, tripped, and landed in the arms of the bloodthirsty male. I jumped up, covered in God knows what. He smirked as I gagged at the stench of him. Stepping back, he growled, turned, and left. The Duchess ushered over a servant to help clean my dress. "It's okay," I said, battering their hands away. "I'm fine."

"I apologise for Willa's mistake," Nora said. "She's quite clumsy."

My adopted father, the duke, had already left to discuss the contract of marriage with the Grand Duke.

"Nonsense. It was only the fault of my son, Ethan."

"Hell. That was Prince Ethan!" Jenna said, bursting out laughing. Nora smirked, hushing her daughter.

"Is there somewhere I can clean myself up?" I asked.

"Of course, Cleo. Can you please show Princess Willa the way?"

"Yes, mother," she said, attempting a curtsy. Cleo had wild black hair, a jewel ordained Disney princess dress and a pretend crown that was too large for her head, and a little wonky to the side. I smiled. She must have been six years old, at a guess.

I thanked the Duchess and followed Cleo through the serene courtyard and into the open corridor. Each pillar was adorned with climbing roses, their buds in full bloom, bringing out the beauty of sunshine colours inside the old build. I smiled as Cleo took my hand. We walked down the corridor past majestic stone carvings displaying an array of mythical beasts. I shuddered as my eyes met with a flying one. Cleo chuckled. "That's the Gargoyle, but we don't see them around these parts anymore."

"Pardon?"

She giggled. "They used to live here, but Daddy said we ate too many of them."

I smiled and nodded, my eyes widening. She certainly had an over-active imagination.

"Where did they live?" I asked, humouring the conversation.

She smiled, took my hand, and pulled me to a magnificent painting on the wall. "In here, our sacred lands." A golden Fleur de lis captured each corner, framing the piece.

I traced my finger over the lake, the waterfall, and the three rocks at the top of the cliff. "Do you mean Elder Vale?" I asked, smiling as memories flooded back to me.

"Yes, Daddy says it's sacred."

"Indeed. It is beautiful."

She nodded. I smiled as she grabbed my hand again, pulling me down the corridor and into the main castle. The extraordinary beauty of this place was breath-taking. It was more extravagant and luxurious than back home. Vaulted arches gave way to modern skylights, letting natural light fill the room. Inner corridors trailed off each side, leading to more discoveries of memories gone by. The entire castle was a delight of gothic architecture, brought into the twenty-first century with modern adaptations, enhancing every aspect of the castle's mysterious grandeur.

"It's here," Cleo said, pushing open the wooden side door for me.

"Thank you." I smiled.

"Want me to wait?"

"No, that's okay. I should be able to find my way back."

"Okay." She walked away, then spun back and said, "Willa… I've always wanted a sister." She grinned and skipped off down the corridor. I smiled, watching her go.

Even this bathroom was magnificent, and I say this as I presume there were many more. I smirked. I'd upgraded to a life of luxury. Looking at this place!

After I'd finished freshening up, I left the bathroom. A maid, dressed in black, showed me to my bedroom. Think turn of the century gothic chic and you'd be somewhere nearby. A dark mahogany four-poster bed, satin sheets, luxurious red velvet curtains and cream walls. It was beautiful.

Hanging on the wardrobe was an off-white crystal ordained wedding gown with a crimson belt covered in crystals. Behind it hung a deep red cloak to match. I walked over, my shoes tip tapping over the sparkling wooden floor. This wasn't for me, surely? It was stunning. The dress felt heavy in my hands, intricate beading, delicate crystals, and a low-cut v neckline to show off my assets. At the back the lace up matched the cloak with its deep crimson colours and red crystals. The cloak was gorgeous, made from a lush fabric with lace trimming. They had spared no expense having this designed and crafted in record time. I was uncertain how such a feat had passed. It was certainly much more extravagant than the flimsy white gown Nora made me wear. The maid watched me, smiling. "Do I wear these?" I asked.

She nodded. My lips curled as I thanked the maid, requiring no help to change. I always preferred to do things myself. When she had closed the door, I ran to the dress. I had never seen something so exquisite! Granted, I wasn't marrying the man of my dreams. But I was bloody marrying the dress of my dreams! It was magnificent; every crystal shone a display of rainbows across the entire room.

Slipping off my bloodied linen dress, I used the en-suite to wash myself. Drying and fixing my hair, I stepped into the slinky crystallised gown. Pulling it up to my shoulders, I caught myself staring in the mirror as it cascaded over my hips, gently caressing my fragile figure. It was perfect. The cloak shaped the look, protecting me from the cooler Autumn nights and giving me an air of security as I fastened it below my neckline.

Straightening my hair in a bun, curls flowed past my bosom. I smiled, taking a deep breath, and remembering things could only get better. Taking one last look in the mirror, I smiled, blew myself a kiss, and walked out of the bedroom to find the rest of the family.

I could hear voices further down the corridor. That must be them. I hadn't been this way yet; it was a little darker and creepier, a tad on the haunted side of the castle. But still full of mystery; and I suspect an array of hidden passageways somewhere along the way. The voices grew louder as I walked further forward, hoping to locate the ceremony room and not get lost on my first day in this enormous place. There were only two voices speaking. Raised and angry, arguing about something.

I was close enough now to hear every word they spoke.

"Whore of a princess," wow! That's awful! Wait... Did she mean me? No! She doesn't even know me! I stopped. Huffed. Lips pursed. I have you know that I'm far from a whore. Well, I mean, my best mate, she'd been around the block one too many times, but for me... I was still waiting for the right guy. Backing into the corner, I listened to more of their conversation.

"Nothing will change Danica. You will always be my mate. She is merely a legality." I heard the male say.

I peered around the corner and gasped. It was Prince Ethan; he had another woman in his arms, and they were full on making out on the table! Seriously! What an ass... it's our wedding day. Who makes out with some floozy on their wedding day? I sighed. Shoulders dropped; arms crossed. I could see this marriage was going to be hard work right from the start.

Nothing more than a legality. Wow... I'm only a legality? I should have guessed it was too good to be true. I'm going to live in a stunning old castle beside the sea, and have a new and hopefully loving family. But I'm stuck with this poor excuse of a man as he swings his dick all over town, making out with whoever he wants. This was not the path I'd expected my life to walk through. I huffed. My head lowered as I watched them. Shit. Why do I even care? It's not like I know him. Perhaps I am just a legality to him. After all, isn't that what he is to me? Tears welled in my eyes. What the heck is happening? My hands clammy, heart pounding, I felt sick, so I did what any self-respecting female would do. I turned and ran.

Chapter Six
Ethan

Being alone with Danica was a delight. We rarely spent real time together. It usually involved sex or training. Both of which I fully enjoyed. Granted, she was part of Tristan's pack, but I enjoyed training together, and our quick rough rumbles in the woods. She took my hand and smiled as we entered one of the dusty rooms. This part of the castle was unused and unkempt. I hadn't been down here in quite some time. Even Cleo rarely ventured into these parts. Except perhaps to visit the library or the torture chamber. I smirked. I wasn't sure which was worse… a library of old books or a chamber of torturous devices. It had been a while since I'd picked up a book. I thought back. Four years, in fact. Before my mate enchanted me. Smiling, I looked over at her. Danica sat herself on the table, calling me towards her. "Come here, handsome," she said. Smiling, I walked over. "A penny for your thoughts?"

I laughed. She hadn't heard her say that in a while. "I've got a tough decision to make."

Her brow furrowed. I smirked. "I was contemplating if the dungeon was worse than the library."

She laughed, slapping me playfully. "What do you mean? The dungeon is far worse!"

"But you don't even like books!"

She smirked. "The worst they can give you is a paper cut!" I nodded. She had a point. "But the dungeon, well…" she cradled her legs around me, pulling me in closer. "We've not been to the dungeons before." She smirked. "Want to try some roleplay?" Her smile curved like the Cheshire cat.

I grinned. "Oh baby, you know I would. But I need to leave soon."

She huffed; fists pummelled. I grabbed her wrists, held them behind her back, then leant in for a kiss. She obliged, biting her bottom lip as I pulled away.

"I can't believe you're leaving me for that whore of a princess!"

I sighed. "I'm not leaving you Danica. It's something I have to do."

She growled under her breath. "She had better not sleep in your bed, Ethan!"

My eyes widened. "Of course, she won't! I'll arrange a separate bed."

"Or a separate room?"

I smiled. "Anything for you."

Her expression lightened. "You promise nothing will change between us?"

"Nothing will change Danica. You will always be my mate. She is merely a legality."

I nodded, kissing her again. Turned on by her taste, enchanted by her scent and in the need for more. Much, much more.

Then something changed. I felt her before I heard her. My future wife. Her fragile figure sneaking down the corridor, catching me in a passionate embrace with Danica. My mate. I winced. But why did it matter? Danica was my mate. Not Princess Willa. My wolf didn't seem to think so. I'd lost control over my body. My wolf forced me away, growling, angry as he raged inside of me. It took all my self-control to stop him from shifting and running after the girl. My human side urged me to caress Danica at that moment. But my wolf forbade me to touch her. Was it developing a conscience now?

That's when I saw her. My bride. Her dress, a sparkling array of rainbow delight. Her delicate frame casting light through the darkness in the room. In that moment, she was the light in my life, whereas Danica stood beyond the shadow. It overjoyed my wolf to have Willa so close. Such innocence, such purity. She was the most beautiful person I had ever laid eyes on, and right now I felt an utter bastard for her catching me this way. Her expression saddened when she saw me, tears falling as she fled. I almost ran after her until Danica pulled me back, overpowering the urge to protect every ounce of her being right now. The need to take away Willa's pain was unbearable.

"So that's the whore you said you'd marry?" Danica spat; her eyes narrowed. "She looked like a scared little girl," she laughed.

Danica's insults continued as I silenced her snarling voice in my head. What was it about Willa? My wolf wanted me to run over and take her in my arms. How does it not see Danica as my mate right now? He's normally so quiet when Danica's around; until today. I've never felt him push for control as much as he had right there.

It makes little sense. I shook my head. Danica stared at me. "Are you even listening?"

"Of course, Danica. You know I only have eyes for you."

She frowned. "I know," she said, moving in for a kiss. I kissed her hard, and fast. But with each flick of my tongue or suck of her lip, I pictured Willa before me.

Chapter Seven
Willa

How could he? My head lowered; my lip quivered. I would be nothing to him. My palms fisted as I fought back the tears. Shaking my head, I ran. I'd clearly lost my mind. Why did he matter so much? I hardly even knew him! Wiping my eyes, I wrapped my arms around myself, holding tight. Taking a few deep breaths, I relaxed. Every time he came close, I felt a pull towards him. It unnerved me. Took my breath away.

Mate! A voice screeched inside my head. My eyes widened. I looked around. Who said that?

Panting, I escaped from the castle and made my way into the gardens. Tears fell once again. What was wrong with me! Was it the shock of all the changes over the last twenty-four hours? Or was it seeing Prince Ethan in the arms of another woman that hurt so badly? But why? What did it matter that I was to share my marriage with this other woman? I felt sick at the thought of it. Juliet would be dumbstruck at my clear emotional breakdown. I shook my head as I stopped beside the lake.

It must be the stress of the last few days. I stretched out my body, one limb at a time. Wiped my tears and womanned up. I needed to get a grip. I'd made this into something it's clearly not and never will be.

Walking beside the lake, I came to the entrance to Elder Vale. An enormous forest of tranquillity. I smiled. I loved nature. It always eased my pain when I needed it. Granted, I'd needed it a lot throughout my life. I'd hid in the gardens for the majority, keeping out of Nora's way as much as possible. I smiled. Thank the lord that facade was over!

Entering the forest, I took a deep breath. It was calm here, peaceful. I sighed, wiping my tear-stained cheeks. Everything would be okay. Look how far I've come with no family, no love, nothing. My bottom lip quivered. But will I be, okay? I'd lost the only good thing in my life, my friend Juliet. Tears welled again. Maybe I'll make new friends. Maybe this marriage will mean more freedom. I could travel back, meet Juliet by the lake, like old times? There's always a way, she'd say. I had to believe it to be true.

I fell back against a tree, laid my cloak over the cleanest rock I could find, and sat down. Taking a deep breath in and out, I gave myself a talking to. Come on Willa, you can do this. Smile and wave, smile and wave. I'd put on the face of royalty all my life. This wouldn't be so much different.

Opening my clutch bag, I pulled out my phone. The bars were red. "Bloody hell, seriously!" I said, laughing through my tears. This day was getting better! Not even 3G around here. It'd damned well better work in the castle or I'm off. You'll find me in the town, drunk on the beach. I smiled, wiping my tears away. That certainly sounded better than being stuck in a threesome with the handsome asshole that was Prince Ethan.

Sitting beneath the tree, I stared into the vibrant green before me.

A mass of flourishing trees stood tall; moss-covered stones framed the road we had recently driven on. This place was the Vale. Old-fashioned, but a tranquil delight that intensified every sense of my being. I took a deep breath, sat back, closed my eyes, and relaxed. Every part of my body, from my toes to the top of my head, eased in relief. This here. This would be my safe place. I smiled, opening my eyes, staring up at the snout of a huge, yellow-eyed wolf.

To say I jumped would be an understatement. I backed into the tree trunk further, hoping by some miracle it would absorb me into it. My heart pounded, eyes wide. The wolfs salivating mouth bared sharp canines as it growled, ready to rip me apart. Every ounce of my being bled out of me as my skin paled. I froze as it padded forward, its cold snout rubbing against my neckline. Tensing up, I cried out, kicking at the ground and trying to blend deeper into the tree. I screamed when it snarled, hot breath misting over me. Bracing for its first bite, I wept, tears flooding down my face. The heat from its breath disappeared as the wolf stepped back. Opening my eyes, I saw how it stood calmly, staring at me. Yellow eyes lowering to the ground. In the distance, another wolf howled, followed by several more. The grey wolf howled in return, then ran off, jumping over a fallen branch as it went.

I stayed like that. Stiff in the moment. My hands were covered in mud as I'd clawed at the ground. Panting for breath; I realised I'd held mine the whole time. I stayed like that, purely frozen, for what felt like hours, yet mere minutes must have passed. Finding my feet, I pushed myself up to stand. Shaking. My eyes red raw from crying. Finding the path back, I entered the gardens, stumbling on the rocky path. Cleo saw me, she'd been playing by the lakeside.

"What's the matter?" she asked, staring at me with narrowed eyes.

"I saw a wolf.". My hands were still shaking.

She nodded and smiled. "Wolves aren't allowed here today, Willa!" Cleo said.

"But when I saw it, it went to bite my neck!"

"Oh no, they're not allowed to do that, Willa. I'll tell Daddy. He'll stop it."

I nodded as Nora, Jenna, and my adopted father walked down the steps into the gardens.

"What on Earth Willa! Get up this instant!" Nora said. Jenna laughed at me.

"What happened Willa?" my father asked.

"A wolf," I said. He helped me up as I brushed myself off.

Two men ran down the path. "We will contain the threat princess, do not worry."

I nodded. Nora's expression darkened. "Now come on, Willa, hurry and marry this man. I'd like to be home before dark!" she shrieked.

I sighed. Wiped my tear-stained cheeks and made my way to the ceremony room.

Much like the rest of the castle, the room where my forced marriage would take place was a mixture of old and new entwined together. Ornate gold chairs with cream cushions, a deep red aisle runner over oak wooden flooring. Light fixtures steeped in black ironworks and twisted Fleur de lis designs. It was beautiful! Lush fabrics hung from the vaulted arches. The walls held candles, bleeding wax down black metal fixtures. I stood for a moment, taking it all in.

"Are you okay, my dear?" the Duchess asked, walking over.

"Yes, thank you," I said, feigning a smile.

"What happened?"

Jenna sniggered. "A wolf apparently."

The room fell silent as the Grand Duke stopped mid-conversation with the priest.

"A wolf?" The Duchess said, raising her eyebrows.

I nodded, biting my lower lip.

She took a deep breath. "Not to worry. We will deal with it." She smiled, ushering a maid over.

The maid handed me a damp cloth so I could wipe my face and clean my hands. She tutted as she cleaned my gown, then excused herself.

The Duchess smiled. "We will find the culprit. But I advise you not to walk alone in those woods until we do, Willa," she said, pulling me in for a hug. "Your part of our family now, we wouldn't want anything to happen to you."

I pulled back. "Err, thank you," I said, dumbstruck. It had been years since an adult held me like this.

She let go, stood back, and swirled me around. "You look stunning, my child. I knew the crystals would light your hair the way they have." She smiled. "Have you seen?" I nodded. "No, have you seen?" she smiled. "Come here." She pulled me over to an ornate gold-framed mirror, lit by natural light from the skylight above.

As I looked before me, I could see precisely what she meant. Every crystal that encased my bosom was glowing under the light of the sun. My rose red hair lit up with every shimmer the crystals offered. I was alive in this mirror, impeccably ferocious in design. Soft skin, delicate long red hair, olive green eyes as vibrant as the forest that surrounded them.

I caught a gasp as Prince Ethan walked in, his eyes hungry and needy. His body stiffened when he saw me. The Duchess directed him to the aisle and smiled. Taking my hand, walking me to stand beside him. I shook as she placed our hands together. Gasping as my body jerked at the intensity of emotion stirring within me.

He turned, watching me. His gaze burned into my body as I forced myself not to look at him. Our hands heated as our grip of each other tightened. Ethan breathed deeper. My heart pounded harder.

"Can we hurry?" I heard Jenna say, tapping her foot on the ground.

I saw the Grand Duke give his wife a confused look. "Let us begin," he said, taking his place.

The priest stood before us. "Do you Prince Ethan James Bane take Princess Willa Rose Paignton to be your lawful wedded wife?" Ethan gripped my hand tighter. His chest rising rapidly. He nodded. "Yes." Sweat dripped from his brow. I bit my bottom lip as he pulled my hand closer.

The room closed in, and I tried to calm my breathing down. Heavy panting escaped me as we continued with the vows. "Yes," I said, agreeing to take the prince as my husband.

The Priest continued, ushering us to place the rings on one another's fingers. My hand shook as he caressed it, gently placing on the ring. A spark zapped my finger. I jumped, gasped, and locked eyes with him. His face pained beyond belief. Was this really so hard for him? I huffed, eyes narrowing. This wasn't exactly a picnic for me either! I let go of his hand. He turned to face me, a puzzled expression elevating his face. I felt betrayed. It was clear he hated me and didn't want me here. As soon as the Priest declared us husband and wife, he let out a harsh breath and stormed off.

Jenna laughed as Nora inspected her fingernails. Father remained silent. Whereas Ethan's family appeared somewhat disheartened by his behaviour.

Cleo ran over and hugged me. I smiled. It was nice having a loving sister. I glared at Jenna as she scowled back.

"Goodbye," my old family said, declining all attempts from my new family to stay and enjoy the celebrations. Their immediate dismissal of me should have been something I expected. But to not even stay to check, I was going to be okay. That hurt.

I waved goodbye, the usual smile and wave technique I'd aced through the years.

The Duchess walked over, put her arm around me and squeezed me. "You will like it here Willa," she said. I smiled. "Just know you can come to me. Should you ever need to talk?"

"Thank you, your majesty," I said, smiling.

She chuckled. "There will be none of that here. You may call me Bernadette, and his name is Oswald," she said, pointing to the Grand Duke.

"Your family now," he said, walking over. He was tall, weary, and looked older than he probably was.

I returned their smiles, thankful that they did not suit their reputation of murderous tyrants after all. It was a blessing to be around such a loving family for once. Well, all except Ethan. This was going to take some getting used to.

Chapter Eight
Willa

After the farce of a wedding, I followed the Duchess; I mean Bernadette, through to another room. This one full of colourful chairs. A sitting room, I believe. I wouldn't exactly know, considering I had never been allowed in the sitting room at my home. That was for Nora and her family, of which I wasn't part of.

Walking past another picture, I could see a blueprint of the grounds. It was huge. There were even rooms underneath us, as well as above! They literally had room after room here. I was guaranteed to get lost!

Bernadette saw me staring and smiled. "You will get used to the castle, Willa. It will become your home too."

I smiled. "Thank you," I said.

She smiled in return, then sighed. "You will also get used to Ethan. He can be a little hot-headed… but he means well."

Like heck he does. I smiled and nodded.

She walked over to one sofa and patted the space beside her. I'm guessing she wants me to sit with her. I smiled, walked over as gracefully as I could, and sat beside her. "So, did you like your room?"

"Yes, thank you."

"It is Ethan's room as well."

My eyes widened. "Oh."

"We thought that now you two are husband and wife, you would like some alone time together." Is she seriously going to talk to me about sex right now?

I pursed my lips, eyes wide, and nodded.

"If you need any advice about anything, then please come and find me."

Lips still pursed, eyes wider. I nodded again.

Oswald walked over and I dismissed myself, stood up and walked over to view their works of art.

Just then, the door hit the wall. Ethan stormed in, his eyes undressing me as he walked past me. The supple, woody smell of the forest surrounded him. "Mother, what's this I hear about a party?"

She smiled. "So, this evening," she said, "we will host several guests to celebrate your union and introduce Princess Willa to the family."

"Oh," I said, turning to face them. My eyes widened. I wasn't expecting that.

"WHAT?" Ethan's body stiffened; fists pummelled.

The Grand Duke Oswald stepped toward him. "Lower your tone, son," he said, then whispered something in his ear. Ethan shot a glance at me and nodded.

"Ethan, your father and I think it's best. We need to introduce

Willa as yours and yours alone."

Ethan groaned at the news. "Fine. I will make an appearance," he huffed, staring at me with contempt.

My eyes narrowed. "I can go on my own if it's too much trouble," I spat, clenching my jaw.

His body stiffened with my words. "It's fine." He glared.

What an asshole! I huffed, folding my arms. I hated the thought of a party. They were always so fake, so unimpressive… fake people living fake lives. I'd had enough back home. I sighed. Ethan's brows furrowed as he watched me. My spine tingled as I straightened up, standing my ground before him. He wouldn't win again. I'd never shed a tear for that man again.

I could feel the heat rising through my body as he took a step towards me. The entire room disappeared from view as our eyes met and I envisioned our bodies entangled. If only. I sighed, watching him from across the room. What was with the sexual tension between us? He smirked, upped, and left.

Bernadette looked over. "So, Willa, you will find a wardrobe of new clothes for you in your bedroom. I will have a dress hung out for you for tonight."

I smiled, catching my breath. "Thank you. Where can I go to freshen up?"

"Of course," Bernadette said. "Cleo," she said, ushering her over. "Can you show Willa please?"

"Yes Mother," she said. Taking my hand and pulling me out of the sitting room.

Cleo pulled me down the corridor and past two doors, entering one on the right. It was the same room I'd dressed in earlier. And the same room I had to share with the obnoxious asshat Prince Ethan. They had taken my old dress away and replaced it with a whole new wardrobe of clothes laid out for me.

"Here we are," she said. "This used to be Ethan's room, but Mother said you will share now you're married."

I smiled and nodded. I'm still not sure how I feel about that!

I looked over, taking in the design in the room. Masculine, but with the sordid woman's touch of luxury through the red velvet curtains and satin sheets. To the side sat a mahogany desk, a gold ornate mirror, and a shelving unit full of books. Hmm, so it appears we have something in common at least. My hand brushed over the spines. A fair few classics, as well as older fantasies by Tolkien and Pratchett. Granted not my favourites, I was more into the grisly thrillers that Stephen King spurted out. Lucky for me, though, there were a few of his older titles.

"If you like books, Daddy has a library in the North tower." Cleo grinned, as did I.

I turned to take in the rest of my surroundings. Two paintings adorned the walls, one of the sun setting, with several eyes escaping the forest. The other of a battle, a victor holding a sword and shield. The symbol of a red wolf carved into it.

After Cleo left me to adjust to my new surroundings, I sat on the bed, fingers entwined in the red satin sheets. I kicked off my shoes and laid down. Inhaling, then exhaling, I breathed. My body relaxed as I calmed myself. Today had been a mishap of unfortunate events. One inescapable situation after another. This day alone would take me weeks to process. It was a lot, and I wasn't anywhere near the fact of accepting I was married to an ass of a husband. I sighed, curling around on the bed, holding myself. Breathing deep, I snuggled into the pillow. It'll get better. It will, I promise. I told myself. My mind a mess of thoughts and feelings. I breathed in, my body relaxed, and Ethan's woody masculine scent caressed me. Intoxication took over, and I pulled the sheets closer, cradling them in my arms. Burying my head in the satin, inhaling deeply.

Mate. The inner voice said, causing me to bolt upright. What the hell?

The door flew open as Ethan stormed in. He stopped when he saw me, watching as I cradled his sheets. Shit!

He growled under his breath. What was with that?

His entire movement screamed menace as he walked over to the bed.

Ethan walked over and tugged the sheets from my hands. "Stay away from my bed," he spat. Anger inflicting his tone.

I sat up straight, backing away from him. "So where am I supposed to sleep?" He bared his teeth. "Fine." I huffed. "I'll sleep on the floor!" Like heck I would!

"Let's get something straight. There will only ever be one woman in my life and you're not it," he hissed, anger straining through his voice.

"Err, okay," the cocky shit. Did he really presume I was laid there for the taking? I wasn't, err, was I?

His fists clenched; vein throbbed in his neck. "We will never sleep in the same bed." He stepped closer. "Do you understand?"

"Fine," I said, arms crossed. Who the hell does he think he is shouting at me like that!

He turned abruptly and stormed towards the door. "So why the hell did you marry me?" I shouted. "You already have a lover."

He turned around, his eyes solemn. "I had to."

My eyes widened. Really! That's the reason. Because he had to? I shrugged. To be fair, though. I was in the same predicament. They had pushed me to marry a complete stranger, too.

Mate. "What the actual hell!" I yelled.

Ethan's eyes widened.

"Oh no, not you," I muttered, clearly looking insane. "I've got to get changed Ethan," I said, ushering him out the room.

"FINE," he boomed, storming out and slamming the door behind me.

I stuck my finger up at him after he'd gone. Asshole. Heck, he was arrogant. Bloody mardy too! I'd married a child. A pure, hot headed and god damn gorgeous boy child. I groaned, lying back on his forbidden bed.

Chapter Nine
Ethan

Damn it, she was insolent! I sighed as I walked down the corridor and across the grounds. What was it about her! She made me so tense, so hot damn hungry for more. Her scent was like a drug, and I was addicted, needing more. Growling under my breath, I envisioned her laid there, wrapped in my satin sheets, her soft, supple skin, innocent and pure, her body writhing below me, her cries bellowing my name. My inner wolf growled. He agreed. We needed her, and I don't know why.

Marching through the grounds, I entered the pack house. They had already been forewarned. No wolves allowed on the grounds while she was here, at least for today. After that, hell if I know. It was a tough ask. But she was human, and until I was sure she could handle the truth, there was no way anyone was telling her.

Everyone hushed when I walked in. Alaric lifted his head from his hands. "I don't know what happened, Alpha!" he said, standing up.

I growled, standing at the top of the table. "Who was it?" I demanded. I only knew three grey wolves in this pack, and it'd better not be one of them!

Nicholas huffed, sitting back in his chair. "Don't look at me, brother!"

"That's Alpha to you!" Alaric said.

Nicholas stuck out his tongue. I sat down, shaking my head at him. "What about Ricky or Aaden," he said, selling them out.

Ricky gulped, lowering his head. Aaden sunk into his chair. "So?" I asked, body tense, hands gripping the edge of the table.

"No, Alpha," Aaden said. His eyes narrowed as they met my own.

I nodded. "Ricky?"

"I swear I didn't Alpha." He fidgeted in his chair. "I haven't even met the Princess yet!"

I growled, sighed, and took a seat. They would never dare lie to me. We were the closest any pack could ever be. "So, who was it?"

Alaric sat forward. "What about Tristan's pack?"

"No, Tristan doesn't have any grey wolves."

"What in the entire pack?" Alaric asked, frowning.

I nodded.

Nicholas sat forward, smirking. "He prefers the gingers," he grinned.

I narrowed my eyes and smirked. "Indeed."

The whole pack burst into laughter, easing the surrounding tension. I picked up a glass, and Aaden poured me a drink.

"So could it be a rogue?" Aaden asked as I took a sip.

My brow furrowed. There had been no rogue wolves in these parts for generations. Not after Hela had all the deserters killed. A lone wolf didn't last long in these parts. "We must find whoever it is and question why they were on our land."

Alaric, my beta, nodded.

I narrowed my eyes, staring across the room. "And if it's a bloody Council member, I want their head!" Hela had better not be sending her damned spies again. I was sick of all the shit she had caused. I'd even had to marry a total stranger because of her. Danica had put up with so much as my mate. And for her now to accept another woman, to know she would never be my wife. I don't know how she can stand it. I sighed, swirling the drink around before gulping it down. If it were me, no man or wolf would ever come anywhere near her, let alone marry and share a room with her. It's all fucked up. Nicholas walked over and grabbed the bottle, pouring me another drink. "Hard day?" he said, smirking.

I growled, and he grinned. "So, tell me, brother. How are you going to manage two women and keep them both happy?"

Growls erupted out of me, and Nic burst out laughing, holding his hands up. "I joke Ethan," he said. "It's a joke."

My brow furrowed, and I gulped down the drink. "But if you want a hand…" he said. I stood up and roared at him, slamming my glass down on the table. It smashed and shards splintered across the room. Nic laughed, backed up, and ran from the pack house.

"The little shit," Alaric said. "Want me to bring him back?"

I sighed, sitting down, wiping the glass from the table. "No, he will learn eventually." Alaric nodded and brought over another glass, pouring me another drink. I thanked him. "Now go, find this wolf and teach him what happens when he crosses into our territory."

"Yes Alpha," Alaric said. Standing up and ordering the pack members out on the hunt. Aaden, Ricky, Nicholas, Gabriel, Michael, Wyatt and Xander followed him out of the door.

I sat in silence. Body tense, gripping the glass in my right hand. Whoever the fuck it is, better stay away from my wife. I growled, gripping harder. The glass smashed, and I groaned. Picking out the shards from my hand. Fuck. It'd heal. But damn, they won't when I get hold of them!

Chapter Ten
Willa

After Ethan left, I sat back on the bed. What was his deal? He constantly ran hot and cold. One minute he appeared to want me. The next he despised me. I shook my head, taking a walk over to the window. Ethan was storming through the gardens, waving over to two other men, and ordering four others to join him. They disappeared into the Vale. Surely, they know there's a wolf in there. He needs to be careful. Damn, what's wrong with me? Why did he affect me so much?

I sighed and looked around the room. Set my sights on a gorgeous slinky red dress that hung on the wardrobe. My cheeks inflamed. Surely, they didn't want me to wear that. It was a low-cut red velvet dress with a slit all the way up to what I can only presume would be my crotch. It was the tightest, sexiest dress I'd ever worn. I was shocked at how seductive it was. It reminded me of something Jessica Rabbit would have worn.

I went over to the wardrobe to see what else there was. An array of deep colours and lush fabrics greeted me. Closing the door, I felt the fabric of the red dress they'd hung out for me. I sighed. I've got to wear it. Or Duchess Bernadette will be disheartened.

Slipping it on, I checked myself in the mirror and gasped. This couldn't be me! Could it? One maid entered, smiled, and I sat down as she curled my hair into an updo. I thanked her and finished the rest myself. Applying a little tinted face cream, blusher, and apple lip balm.

I smiled. Fastened my shoes, took a deep breath, and left the room.

My shoes tip tapped down the corridor as I headed towards the main hall. The sensation of butterfly wings fluttered through my tummy as I swallowed down my anxiety. What would I be walking into? I could hear the chatter of several people up ahead. I turned the corner and walked towards the entrance. Two doormen were stationed outside. I smiled, and they nodded. But I wasn't ready yet. Not for this. Standing outside at the side of the door, I took a breath.

"Would you like to be announced?" the doorman asked.

"No, no thank you," I said, taking a step back. He nodded and looked straight ahead again.

I peered around the open doorway and immediately fell back. Hell! There's nearing fifty people there. My palms clammed up. Heart pounding. I hate being in crowded places. It was hard enough back home. At least there I could hide in a corner with a good book. Here I only knew the royal family, and I was now the centre of attention. I sighed, straightening myself up and plucking up the courage to go inside. I put on a fake smile, urged my feet to move, then stepped into the limelight.

The music quietened as all eyes fell on me. My face flushed. I gulped as bile wretched at my throat. Biting my bottom lip, I stepped further inside. Yet every part of me screamed to turn and run.

A loud growl detonated my false composure. My eyes widened, body tensed, jaw dropped. The last time I'd heard that growl, I was face to face with the wolf. Every ounce of self-control drained out of me. I turned to run. Coming face to face with the perpetrator.

My Husband.

Ethan.

Ethan stormed over and grabbed my arm, pulling me towards him. I gasped at his touch. Warmth flowing through my body as he closed the gap between us. His eyes narrowed, brow furrowed, sweat beaded on his top lip. He spun my body around, hiding my fragile figure from our audience, shadowing me under his thick, masculine frame.

Anger filled his face. An innate primal urge appeared to have control of him. He breathed harder. Pulled me closer. I gripped his arms as his hands moved to my waist. Our bodies touching. He growled again. A deep, ferocious growl that enticed me further.

Mate

What was that? Why did my inner voice urge me to mount him right there and then? I wanted him. Needed him. The closer he held me, the more his woody scent curled through my nostrils. Face to face. Lips almost touching. I gasped. His tortured eyes battled as he breathed harder. Faster. Shaking his head, he came to his senses, pushed me back, picked me up and over his shoulder, then walked down the corridor, enraged.

He opened the bedroom door and slammed it shut, hurling me onto the bed.

"What the fuck are you wearing?" He demanded.

"W-what?" I stuttered. Shaking, adrenaline surging.

His expression darkened; nostrils flared. "You don't know how dangerous that was!"

My eyes widened, body tensed, hands gripping the bed sheets. "Dangerous! Don't you think throwing me across the room was dangerous!" I stood up, angry as hell. Moved towards him, teeth bared, eyes narrowed. "How dare you manhandle me like that?" I screamed. Pushing him back. "Hell! I didn't choose this dress. They hung it out for me."

Ethan's eyes widened; fists pummelled as he growled under his breath.

"Don't push me Willa," he said, his lip trembling.

I pushed him again. "What, so you can push me about, but I can't push you?"

He took a step back, his body shaking. "Get back," he said, growling.

I stepped forward. The door flung open. The Grand Duke's eyes widened. "Willa, step back," he demanded, taking my arm and pulling me behind him. Bernadette rushed in, her face paled. She took me by my arm and pulled me towards the door.

"Let go of me," I yelled. Anger still surging through my veins.

Bernadette instantly let go. "Willa my dear, we need to leave Ethan to calm down."

"Why? I'm the one who should be angry! He had no right to carry me away like that! Who the hell does he think he is!"

Bernadette winced. "He does not mean any harm Willa."

"You could have fooled me. He threw me on the bed! What is it, caveman times?" I yelled, crossing my arms. Bernadette stayed silent. Taking a few deep breaths, I looked over and saw Ethan in a raging conversation with his father. Looking back, Bernadette smiled and nodded at me. I nodded back. It wasn't her fault. "I'm sorry for shouting at you Bernadette," I said. I hated upsetting anyone. Especially if they didn't deserve it. She pulled me in for a hug.

"You have nothing to apologise for, my dear."

Moments later, Ethan growled at his father and barged past me. Leaving the room.

What an asshole.

Chapter Eleven
Ethan

Fuck, why did she do that to me? She's mine. Mine alone. The dress showed every curve, every fragile feature. It left nothing to the imagination. Every wolf in that room stirred. I felt them. Felt their hunger. It was dinnertime, and she was the meal.

I stood seething as I held her body close. Roses and lavender engulfed me. Hot damn that scent! I pulled her closer. Tighter. Our bodies merged as one. Her lips parted as she gasped at my touch. Growling, my wolf pushed harder. Straining to rip itself out of me and ravish her right there and then. She was mine! I wanted her. Needed her. Picking her up, I slung her over my shoulder and carried her to my room, throwing her on the bed, hungry and ready to pounce. Growling, I went to war with my inner wolf. Pushed him back as far as I could. It took all my strength to keep him at bay. Gripping the bed frame, I growled. Shaking my head, trying to remain in control. Hands pummelled. Eyes narrowed. She did this to me. Angered me, played with my emotions, uncaring about how it'd make me feel.

Didn't she know how dangerous her games were?

That's when she stood up. I was shocked at first. No-one but my mate had ever stood up to me. But she knew no fear, walking towards me with bared teeth and anger in her eyes. Fists gripped tighter I backed off. Body tense as the vein in my neck strained. What's she doing? Get back! No-one challenged me. "How dare you manhandle me like that!" her voice screeched. My eyes widened. Her hand rushed forward, connecting with my torso. I snarled. What the actual fuck! "Hell, I didn't choose this dress. They hung it out for me!"

My jaw dropped. What did she say? My eyes narrowed; head lowered. So, this wasn't her doing? I growled, low and menacing. No matter how hard I tried to push the wolf back, he kept on coming. "Get back!" I shouted as she took a step towards me. Her face confused, yet angry. My voice trembled as I fought the change, afraid I'd rip her to pieces the moment my wolf let loose. I backed away. It pained me to be close to her. I needed her. Wanted her. Panting heavily, I screamed inside. Control your breathing. Damn you! She did not know the effect she had on me. No idea how hard it was to hold back. She would be my kryptonite one day. I was sure of it.

Father stormed in; eyes wide as he rushed over to me. "Son. Back away," he said. "Control the wolf," he whispered.

"What do you think I'm doing," I cried.

"Remember what I taught you. Breathe deep and slow. Close your eyes."

"This isn't a training session, father. He wants out, and he wants out NOW."

Father gripped my shoulders, lifted my chin, my body sweating, straining to hide myself away. He looked at me, searched in my eyes, then nodded. "Go take a minute, Ethan. Now!" he whispered, stern and direct. I took a deep breath, glared at Willa, and left the room.

As I left, I screamed inside. How could she hit me like that? Why did her body enchant me so much? Every cell of her body screamed out to be fucked. I could smell her damn arousal from here. There was no way to describe it. She was mine, I had to make her so.

But what about Danica? My mate. Damn, I was so confused. My wolf never came out with Danica. Not like Willa. But I knew it. My human side knew it. Danica was my mate. Not Willa. I stormed down the corridor. Stood right outside the hall and slammed my fist into the brick wall. Shit!

Blood and red brick merged. I threw another two, then three punches. I needed the release. A way to let myself go without the shift. There was no way I could go running right now. Thanks to my mother I had a room full of guests to attend to. Shit… Willa would be there, too. I groaned, looking down at the bulge in my trousers. Damn it! Keep it together, man. Keep it together!

Chapter Twelve
Willa

"I'll be out in a minute," I said as Bernadette smiled and left the room.

I nodded and sat on the bed alone. Why had he been so possessive of me? We'd only just met! He was really taking this Husband-and-Wife thing one step too far. Granted, we're now stuck together, and like he said, I'm only a legality to him. I sighed; head lowered. If that's the case… then what does it matter what I wear? If he thinks he can tell me what to do all the time, he's got another thing coming!

A few minutes later, Cleo entered the room, her face etched with dismay. "My big brother's mean sometimes. Are you okay?" she asked.

I nodded my head. My bottom lip quivering.

Cleo jumped on the bed and sat beside me. "Didn't he like your dress?"

I smiled, my voice wavering. "No, I don't think he did."

"Oh," she said, her head bowed. "I thought it was prettier than the one Mummy put out for you."

Oh no, Cleo. Bless her. She was only trying to help. "I'm sure he really loved it," I said. Placing my hand on her shoulder. "He must have been surprised when he saw it."

"Okay, well, I like the colour," she said.

I smiled, pulling her in for a hug. "Me too."

Bernadette walked into the room. "Are you okay?" I nodded. "I don't know what came over Ethan."

"It's okay. But… does he usually growl like that?" I asked, brow furrowed.

"I didn't hear him," she said. Her eyes widened. I frowned. She must have heard him! His deep throated musical number was louder than any voice in the room!

Cleo jumped off the bed. "We can't talk about it," she said and skipped out of the room.

I stood up. Puzzled.

Bernadette feigned a smile. "How about we make use of that stunning dress and introduce you properly this time?"

"Should I change?" I asked.

"No, Willa, wear anything you want. Never let a man push you around," she said. Then smiled. Interlocking arms with me, she directed me out of the room. We walked down the corridor and saw Ethan waiting outside the door. His body tensed as I came closer. The Grand Duke Oswald had gone in. Bernadette smiled, nodded, and placed my hand in Ethan's, walking into the room to announce us.

Ethan looked uncomfortable. I glared at him. "Aren't we supposed to smile?" I asked, sarcasm being a familiar coping mechanism.

He growled. "Fine," he said, smiling sarcastically. "We wouldn't want people to suspect this wedding was a farce would we."

"You're the one that wanted this," I said, hurt.

He looked at me, eyes narrowed.

"Guys." Cleo cut in. "Mummy is waiting."

Ethan nodded. Gripped my hand tighter, smiled, and we walked into the hall. The Grand Duke and Duchess started clapping, and the entire crowd joined in. Each person watched as we paraded. Curiosity, admiration, and a few glares met me as we walked to the centre of the room.

The Grand Duke stepped between us. "Ladies and Gentlemen, we invited you here tonight to meet Prince Ethan's enchanting wife Princess Willa. I know every one of you will give her the wholehearted welcome she deserves." He raised our hands high, and cheers erupted throughout the room.

As soon as the Grand Duke let go, Ethan disappeared, and crowds started gathering around me. They fired questions, ambushing me over and over. My palms clammed up. It was getting hot in here. I couldn't see a way out for the rings of guests surrounding me. Breathing heavily, I wavered. My gaze darted from the room, looking for solace. I found it there in Ethan. He had stood with his back to the wall, talking to another man. His eyes met mine as I became dizzy from all the questions. Ethan darted forward, pushed through the crowds, and pulled me into him.

"Overcrowding my wife will not earn you any points," he said.

Guests mumbled and dispersed. The Duchess came over. "I'm so sorry Willa, I was caught up with Oswald."

Ethan let go of me. "She does not look well," he said to his mother.

"Indeed," the Duchess said.

"I'm fine," I said. "Just a little light-headed."

"Perhaps some food?" she said. Her brow furrowed.

I nodded. She took my arm and directed me to a seat in the corner. Waving over a waiter and ordering a plate of food from the banquet to be bought for me. "Here, rest. It's been a long day," she said, smiling.

"Thank you," I said. Taking the food from the waiter. She nodded and left to greet her guests. They had given me a plate of raw cuts of meat, pastries and what looked like sausage rolls.

Cleo bounded over. "Burgh," she said, pointing at the sausage roll.

I smiled. "Don't you like those?" She shook her head and stuck her tongue out. I laughed.

"Mummy said I should keep you company. She said you felt poorly."

"I did a little," I said. Then took a bite from each of the delicious pastries.

"What's wrong?" she asked, pure curiosity forming over her face.

"I'll be okay. It's been a hectic day, Cleo… don't you think?"

She nodded. "Especially as the rogue attacked you!"

"What rogue?"

"I don't know his name Willa. Mummy said he's one of the bad wolves."

"There's more?"

She laughed. "You'll see," she said, skipping off.

Great. Either that kid has an overactive imagination, or I'm surrounded by a forest of ferocious wolves. I sighed, then carried on, tucking into the plate full of food. A young guy with blond hair and brown eyes stood towering above me. He coughed.

I looked up. "Any better?" he asked.

I smiled, "yes thank you."

His eyes widened, and he took a seat next to me. He watched as I took another bite. Moving in closer, he whispered, "You'll find there are a lot of vultures in the inner circle," he said, chuckling. I smirked. "You'll get used to them." he grinned. "I'm Nicolas, but most people call me Nic." I smiled and nodded, finishing the pastry. "You don't talk much, do you?" he grinned.

I laughed, wiping my mouth on the serviette. "I never know what to say at these parties."

"Well, you'll find in a weeks' time you'll be old news."

"Ha, thanks," I said, then lent forward. "Although secretly I'm glad."

He smirked. "How are you doing since Ethan's melt down?"

I laughed. "Oh fine. I've met men like him before."

"Oh, I doubt that!" he said, eyes wide.

I smiled. "He can't be that bad?"

"Oh no, not at all, he's the most loyal person you'll ever meet. He's the strongest of us all, that's why he's the Alpha, oh, erm..."

"What?"

"Oh, nothing."

Ethan walked up to the table and lifted Nicholas up by the arm. "Nic, don't you think you should go by now?"

"He's fine Ethan," I said, standing up.

"No, he's right," Nic said. "I've got to watch Cleo, anyway."

"Oh, okay."

"It was lovely to meet my sister-in-law, anyway." Ethan growled, let go of him, and he scampered off.

"He's your younger brother?" I asked.

"Yes, he's quite the troublemaker!"

"Well, he was fine with me. He was making sure I was okay."

"As long as that was all he was doing." His voice strained.

I sighed. "You're quite the possessive type, aren't you?"

Ethan growled and walked off.

Sitting back down, I smirked. I liked him; I don't know why. But something about him attracted me… and it wasn't only his mouth-watering body. I smiled, lost in thought, picking at the remainder of my food.

Chapter Thirteen
Danica

Staring out over the balcony, the night sky had found its sparkle. Dad had said the sky lost its light years ago when we first joined the Council. But he'd never had a choice. Mum had left him and shacked up with a shifter by the name of Lance. Then the barn burnt down in some freak accident, and we lost all our savings when the market crashed that year. Dad had literally gambled away every penny we had. So, he had no choice; we had nothing left. I was only a tiny teen back then, new to the world of werewolves, and recently experienced my first shift. Dad had to sell the farm, and we ended up homeless, living in a cave down on Council property. Jeffrey must have seen our make-shift fire that night, as he and his guards stormed in and pulled us in front of the Council the next day.

I watched from the balcony as a young couple found solace by the lakeside. Throwing a picnic blanket down, lighting candles and watching the world go by. I envied them. It was so simple for the normal folk in this town. They could live and do what they wanted. Be with who they wanted. I sighed, taking a long breath. It wasn't Ethan. He was gorgeous and way out of my league. But knowing he really didn't love me, that the whole thing was a bloody lie, it made it hard. Living like that for four years has aged me more than anything ever could. Gripping the handrail tight I looked over. We were two floors up. The cold hard concrete laid below, lit by garden lights. Illuminating the black railing, with pointed tips, sharp and deadly right below me. It was sitting there, waiting for my body to crash down on top of it. Looking down at my feet, there was a ledge, a small one, but one big enough for me to stand on. Easy enough to climb over. It wouldn't take much. I sighed again. A little jump and this could be all over.

The problem wasn't my nerves. I would happily jump if I knew my false life would end. The issue was with my father. Hela would blame him for my death. They would arrest him and take him to the Council. Hela would take his head that very same day. She quite liked to collect the heads and have them embalmed. Their hideous screams displayed for all time. Rooms and rooms of perfectly dead props all laid out. A Rocky Horror show in the making. I sighed, looking down at the freedom that lay below me.

When Hela first saw me, she took me into her bosom like a mother to a child. She embraced my kind heart and hardened it through the years, showing me the truth of the cold, hard world out there. She taught me to be an enchantress, to use men for what we wanted, and for her… she wanted the most powerful pack, the strongest Alpha of them all. Prince Ethan James Bane.

Hela was never interested in a life of love or lust. She said those were pointless human notions. All Hela ever wanted was power… and she had it. But never enough of it.

Since Edwina cast her spell of deceit, Ethan took me in his

arms, made me his own. Hela delighted in the fact. She pictured his family joining her, pushing the supernatural realm to the top of the food chain, where it should be. She wanted the humans to work for us. We were the pure, the just, and the deadly. Why should we hide any longer? I understood her goal and bloody believed in it too. Why should we hide in the shadows?

Was it ludicrous that I missed her madness? Every day a dance of delight, a symphony of song as the music filled the room, her charismatic display winning the hearts of every friend or foe. She won me over with her first embrace, and ever since she's been the mother I never had. Especially after she allowed me to end the life of my biological one. That bitch shouldn't have left me!

I grinned, staring up at the stars. I'd never realised at first, but each star up there… it told a tale. Every twinkle late at night was viewed by a thousand eyes, captured in a thousand memories. If only those stars could talk. I wonder what they would say. Do they see our world as one worth saving? I sighed. Exhausted from years of lies and betrayal. It's worth it… I know. But it's hard not to slip up, and I miss my home. My Dad being here doesn't make up for the slightest ounce of affection Hela had shown me.

"There you are!" Ethan said as he wandered out onto the balcony. I smiled, holding my arms wide so he could join me in an embrace. He was as much a victim in this as I was, perhaps even more so? If I could even be called a victim. After all, I knew what I was doing, didn't I. I sighed, holding him tighter.

"What are you doing?" he asked. Pulling back and ruffling a hand through his wild, black hair. I loved the way he grinned at me, his eyes sparkling like the stars above. Soft, supple skin. A chiselled jawbone. He was both handsome and cute, all in one. I was sodding lucky… I knew that. But I also knew it was all a lie, and one day it would come back to bite me in my not so royal arse.

"I was taking a moment before joining in the celebration," I said, sighing.

Ethan pulled back; his eyes saddened as he searched my face. "I'm sorry this has been hard for you Danica. You know you are the only girl for me."

I leaned forward and kissed him. "I know. But it's hard to see that when all eyes are on her."

He cupped my face in his hands. Kissed me hard and pulled me into his powerful arms. Lie or no lie. All was right with the world once again.

Chapter Fourteen
Willa

I looked up to see an older man staring at me, studying me intently. His eyes narrowed as the Duchess walked over. They chatted for a few minutes, then both looked down at me. What? Who is he? They walked over and I stood up, ready to greet him. There was something about the way he stared at me. It made me uneasy.

"Willa, this is Lucius Daventry. He is a highly esteemed friend of the family. I am sure you will both delight in each other's company." She smiled.

"Thank you, my Duchess," he said, bowing.

"Oh Lucius, you're practically family, there's no need for that."

He smiled. Stood upright and nodded. "Princess Willa, it is lovely to meet you," he said, feigning a smile, looking me up and down. "When my Danica told me that her Ethan had gotten married. I was shocked." He snarled. Bernadette stiffened beside me; brow furrowed. "But I must say Princess, that I can see why he chose such a bride."

"Err, thank you." I think.

"You are lucky Princess, for my Danica had her eyes set on the prince."

The Duchess gave an uneasy chuckle.

"Danica," he shouted, waving her over. She turned around, and I felt sick to my stomach.

It's her. She's the one Ethan is in love with!

She had long brown hair that wrapped around her bosom, deep brown eyes that made her pupils almost insignificant. A voluptuous hourglass figure, covered in a sexy short black dress. She was undoubtedly one of the most scantily clad people in the room and considering my dress… that's saying something!

Danica glared; lips pursed as she walked over. She feigned a smile and pretended to courtesy before me. "I have never met a Princess so beautiful," she spat, sarcasm apparent in her tone.

Bernadette glared at her. "Danica, this is Princess Willa," she said, "Ethan is now her Husband."

"Yes, my Duchess," she said. Lucius glared at her.

"So, speaking of Prince Ethan," Lucius interrupted. "Where is he?"

"Oh, he was outside with me a moment ago, father." My body stiffened. "I'll get him." So that's where Ethan rushed off to. To be with his lover Danica again. I should have guessed. Danica turned to face me. "It is lovely to meet you, Princess Willa," she said, offering out her hand. I warily accepted it. She gripped tight as she shook it. So tight it took a while for the colour to return. Curtseying, she left.

Lucius smirked as I shook my hand. Bernadette smiled nervously.

"Those two have such a lovely bond, don't you think, Bernadette?"

he said, waving goodbye to his daughter. He turned to the Duchess. She nodded, clearly uncomfortable.

"Well, not always." Nic cut in, arriving beside me. "When Danica arrived, Ethan thought she was quite arrogant, if I remember right," He smirked as Lucius growled.

"It isn't nice to call people names Nicolas," the Duchess said, although clearly not a fan of Danica herself.

"Sorry mother, but it's quite true." He smiled at me. "It's almost like Ethan had fallen under the strain of a love spell, perhaps." Her eyes widened as he smirked.

"How preposterous!" Lucius said. His expression darkened. He shook his head, muttered something under his breath, then excused himself and left. Bernadette sighed, smiled, then excused herself to find the Grand Duke Oswald.

"Thanks for that," I said, relieved he had gone.

Nicholas grinned. "Anytime Willa."

I smiled. "I wish I could repay you for saving me," I said, smiling. It was nice to have a brother looking out for me.

"A hug will suffice!" he suggested, holding his arms out.

A low, menacing growl came from behind. I turned to see Ethan glaring at Nic. The look on his face was deadly. Nicholas pulled away. "Wow brother, you can't blame me!"

I stood back, perplexed. What's wrong?

Ethan stepped forward, grabbed his brother by the shoulder, and growled in his ear. Nic stepped back, narrowed his eyes, and smiled. "Fine. Just be grateful it was me asking her for a hug, and not any of the men staring at her right now."

"Ethan! "Danica shouted. Her face was a picture when she saw Ethan step in again. Her eyes wide, mouth open.

Danica's voice appeared to snap him out of it. He seemed

in control of himself once again. He glared at me. I gave him a perplexed look. What did I do?

His eyes moved from me to scan the room, and a scowl formed on his face. I followed his gaze and saw a few hungered looks staring in my direction. All male and hungry to meet me.

A muscle ticked in his jaw, and it appeared he was fighting to control himself.

"Where is my father?" Danica asked.

"Well, he seemed upset Danica. Perhaps you should run off and find him," Nic said with a smirk. It was obvious he didn't like her.

"What did you do?" she asked, angered.

He smiled. "Ask him," he said.

"Nic!" Ethan warned. Not happy with his brother's tone.

Danica rolled her eyes and took Ethan's hand. "Let's go find my father."

My stomach flipped as she took his hand. Skin paled. That should be me holding his hand, I thought. Danica smirked, turned, and pulled Ethan along. Nic watched me. "Do you need to sit down again?" he asked, his expression uncertain.

"No, I need some air," I said. He nodded. "Want company?"

"Although that would be lovely, I think some alone time would do me the world of good," I said, and smiled. He nodded, smiled, and walked away.

I walked out of the room and down the corridor towards the gardens. It hurt, it hurt like hell to see them together. It made little sense, how I could feel so much for a man I'd only just met. But I did. He was infuriating, obnoxious, possessive, and a general prick most of the time. But my heart longed for him. Why? I entered the gardens; it was magnificent here, pathway after pathway of marvel and delight. All the colours of the rainbow lit under the moonlit sky.

Lanterns of garden lights coloured the shadows as I slowed my pace to enjoy the enchantment before me.

For the first time since I'd reached here, I actually missed home. Missed Juliet and her wild ideas as we played in the gardens chasing butterflies. Granted, I was barely seven back then, but it was still one of my fondest memories of her.

Walking over the gravel path, I smiled, reminiscing. I missed chasing boys in the town, tourists with too much money, fast cars, and plenty of drinks. Summer solace in the rose garden, pruning the yellow roses and capturing their beauty on camera. That was when I had a camera phone. I sighed. But what I miss most is our midnight margaritas under the moonlit sky, watching as the world slept, dreaming their blissful dreams. My old family had treated me awfully, but it was home, and what I knew. At least when I was there, I didn't have to worry about my heart breaking every time I saw my husband in the arms of another woman. Is this what my life will be like now?

Sadness cradled my heart as tears escaped me. It was a new pain I was experiencing. Grief. Grieving over the loss of my old life and the anxiety I felt at starting this new one. I walked beside Darkwater lake, staring down at my reflection. An unwanted bride in a living nightmare. I sighed, wiping my tears. Sod it. These were the cards they had dealt me. I'd suck it up, make friends and live out my married life down in the town with every Jack, Jim and Elijah I could get my hands on. I licked my lips, remembering the bottle of Jim Beam Juliet used to sneak out for us.

I carried on walking, taking in my surroundings. The three headed horseman statue was another of the monstrosities this place displayed. I shuddered. It was enough to give anyone the creeps at this time of night. To the right was the entrance to the Hedge maze. A mass of lush green hedges enticing the weary traveller to partake in its extravagant trails. I could get lost here. I smiled. A simple thought that gave me an element of escapism. It was a wish I almost hoped would arise as I entered; my right hand flowing across the hedgerows as I delved deeper in.

I wandered down the first path, taking a left, then a right. Every hedge way appeared the same. My only company was my shadow that cast from solar powered floor lights. The moon was strong tonight, almost full, but nowhere near strong enough to grace every corner, turning or dead end. Of which I'd found a few of late. I stood staring at the next dead end. What the heck! I was sure it was this way! My brow furrowed. There had better be something amazing in the centre of this labyrinth! Okay, so it was an average garden maze. But at night, with this lighting. This maze had teeth, grizzly hedges, and sharpened thorns. I shuddered. Folding my arms.

A low rumbling sound from the side of me cut through my thoughts. I span around, catching my breath. What was that? Walking back down the path, I peered around the corner. Nothing. "Hello?" I said, uneasy in the darkness.

I walked a little further, taking a right, then a left. Stopping immediately as a low menacing growl echoed through the maze. It froze me to the spot, every hair standing on end. I've heard that before! Hell no! The wolf! My heart raced, chest searing from the pain. Hands clammy. Eyes wide. I took a deep breath and ran!

Back and forth, side to side. No matter which way I ran, the growling grew louder. I screamed as I turned the corner to see the huge grey wolf staring back at me. Its long sharp teeth bared, ready for attack. Turning around, I ran right and left, up and down. Completely lost and screaming for a way out. Then I saw it, the light of the garden path. A way out! The wolf pounded after me, leapt up and over. Blocking my exit.

I slowly moved backwards, but that seemed to anger it even

more. It padded forward, growling louder and louder. Sweat beaded on my brow. I tripped, landing outside the maze, flat on my back with the grey wolf towering above me.

Frantically, I scrambled backwards, my heart pounding harder. Tears streamed as the wolf stepped closer. Its snout touched my face, wet from the tears I'd cried.

It growled loud with its head held high and several other howls filled the night sky. Then it turned, it's hot breath coating my cheek, teeth bared, ready to bite.

This was it. The end of my existence. I screamed, pushing my arms out to move it away.

Suddenly, a loud howl echoed through the air. My heart skipped a beat and all the hairs on my body stood up at the power that radiated from the sound. Out of nowhere a huge jet-black wolf jumped in front of me, barrelling into the other wolf. I watched in horror as they both tackled each other.

What the hell was happening?

I sat scrambling backwards. My red velvet dress, muddied and torn. Nausea hit as dizziness took over. I watched them claw and bite at each other. The grey wolf yelped as the larger black wolf pounced, knocking it into submission. It was striking. An alluring jet-black pelt that shone under the light of the moon.

In the distance, several howls filled the night sky. The grey wolf pounced, only to be knocked flying by two more wolves that jumped to defend the larger black one. Shaking its muzzle, it got up, growled but backed away, snapping its teeth at the three. Clearly outnumbered, it ran back to the forest, the two new wolves chasing after it.

I sat on the sodden ground, shaking as raindrops fell. The black wolf stayed close; its head lowered as it walked towards me. Its ocean blue eyes were so familiar. My body relaxed as it padded closer. I didn't fear this wolf. That alone proved how insane I was; it was clearly larger, stronger, and more bloodthirsty than the others.

It watched me as it reached my body, rubbing its snout close, a low growl echoing in its throat. I reached out and touched his fur. Incredibly soft. It surprised me as I'd expected, coarse bristles.

I laughed as he nuzzled against my neck. "You like that, huh?"

It was official. I'd lost my mind.

He laid down, resting his head on my lap. I stroked him and smiled. Somehow, I knew he was my protector.

"Willa!" I heard Nic shout in the distance.

The wolf jumped up and had vanished.

Chapter Fifteen
Ethan

I teared through the brotherhood's house, anger screaming through my veins. How could she be in danger like this! That monster almost ripped her open! Hands clammy, fists pummelled, I lashed out, knocking a hole through the wooden door. Why was no-one protecting her? She was my wife, god dammit! It was their job to ensure her safety.

Alaric rushed through the broken doorway. "Alpha!" he said, warily.

I turned towards him, my mouth foaming with spittle. "Didn't you get the mind link?" I yelled. "The fucking Amber Rose brothers were here!" I slammed my fist on the table, sitting down. "Damn it! No-one will have her. She is MINE!" Alaric winced and kept quiet.

"You know Willa is under our protection! If she dies, we will never turn the humans! Never win the war!"

"Yes Alpha. I am sorry," he said, head lowered. "But with the party. The booze. The women…"

I narrowed my eyes. "You were more concerned about getting laid than the safety of this pack!" I shouted. "Alaric, damn you! You're my Beta. The pack comes first… AT ALL TIMES!"

Alaric nodded. The rest of the pack came in.

"What… so none of you cared about protecting us?"

The room remained silent.

"There was a rogue Council wolf in our bloody territory! AGAIN!" I screamed, "You call yourselves the strongest pack ever known." I shook my head and huffed, lowered my head, and sat down. "It could have killed her."

"I'm sorry," Alaric said. "It won't happen again."

I turned to the rest of my pack brothers, Aaden, Nicholas, Ricky, Gabriel, Michael, Wyatt, and Xander. They were as much at fault as Alaric was.

They all looked at me, bracing themselves for punishment.

"If anything like this ever happens again, I will not hold back. Do you hear me?" I demanded, raising my voice and standing up. "Now capture that mongrel and bring him to me!" I yelled.

Alaric nodded and ordered the rest of the pack out. He placed his hand on my shoulder. "I am sorry, brother." I nodded, and he left.

My inner wolf was still agitated. It made me uneasy. I could feel Willa's hand stroking my back. Smell her scent as I caressed her neck. I sighed. My body relaxes at the thought of her. Closing my eyes, I pictured her pale blossomed lips, her delicate body intermingled with my own. It was her I needed to calm my thoughts right now. No-one else but her.

Leaving the pack house, I walked up and over the bridge. Where was she? Last I heard, Nic had called to her, giving me the opportunity to hide my wolf away. She was human, after all.

My body tensed. What was I thinking? She'd never accept me. I was half man, half wolf. There was no way our undeniable bond could be sustained. It was unheard of. A werewolf with a human girl. But how could it be? Why did I feel the way I did about her? I closed my eyes as the sun rose. Imagining her body. Her slim, supple curves. Gripping at the thought of her touch. Her scent. Her kiss. Perhaps with a kiss we could be one. What if she could accept the darkness within me? The fire in my soul?

I sighed. But then, what about Danica? None of it made sense. She was my mate. My lover. How could a human girl take her place and be my one true destiny? It couldn't be true. My wolf lusted over something it could never have. I'd make Danica my mate and mark her like I should have all those years ago. She was mine, and I was hers. No-one else's.

When I entered the castle, it was silent, cold, and lonesome. Everyone was asleep. It must have been four, maybe five in the morning. I'd run through most of the night. A mess of illustrious thoughts. Possible beginnings and delicious destinies. I was exhausted. The guards were asleep at their post until I stomped my way through.

"Sorry, sir!" Henry said, as I nodded and smirked. It'd been quite the night, and I'd excuse their tardiness if they actually could stay awake for at least one night on duty. No wonder the rogue Council wolf got through our perimeter. The whole of our force was asleep, getting laid or lying in a ditch drunk somewhere. I shook my head. I pitied our next battle. This town needed shaping up. Or else we'd never survive another year with the Council on our backs.

Heading up the corridor and around the corner, I entered my bedroom. With closed curtains, the darkness greeted me. I squinted until my eyes adjusted. Wolf vision always helped ease any human shortcomings. As soon as I closed the door, I turned to see the Princess asleep in my bed. Wasn't she supposed to have her own bed by now? Surely sharing the same room was a recipe for disaster. And I knew for a damned fact that Danica would be pissed at this.

Standing at the edge of the bed, I could see her face. Following the curve of her chin, the line of her delicate neck, across to the sheet that blanketed her, caressing every curve as it captivated her body. What I wouldn't give to be that sheet right now. I shook my head. Fuck, man. Give it up. My wolf growled. It was damned hard keeping the urge to ravish every inch of her under control. She was mine. I had to make it so. Leaning forward, I moved in close, barely inches away. My heart pounded inside my chest. Hands clammy, body tense.

Lifting my shirt, I undressed. Stopping to look down at her frail figure. Rose red hair cascaded over her supple breasts as she groaned in her sleep, turning to face me. Her lips parted as I bent down beside her face. Warm, moist breath touched my body. The feeling of her next to me stirred the wolf inside. Hot sweat beaded above my upper lip. I could feel the wolf reaching out. Urging me to make her mine. I bent down as she opened her eyes. Eyes wide, sparkling in the morning sun. Mouth open, I leant forward. Her eyelids fluttered and then she screamed.

"What the fuck Willa!" I yelled as she pushed me backwards.

"Shit! Ethan?" she shouted, sitting up in bed, rubbing her eyes.

"Who the hell did you think it would be?" I asked, getting up from the floor.

The door burst open, and Alaric rushed in. "Are you okay

Princess….?" he asked, then saw me shirtless by her bedside. "Ah, sorry, Alpha!" he said, quickly closing the door as I growled.

"Alpha?" she asked, her brow furrowed. "And what's with all the growling? Do you have a condition?"

I frowned. "What growling? And no, I don't have a bloody condition. Why are you in my bed?"

"It's my bed too you know."

"Like hell it is. Now get out!" I shouted, stepping forward.

"No. You get out. I was fine asleep in here until you crept in like some psychotic killer."

My eyes narrowed. "What the hell are you on about?"

"Didn't you know there's been a murder on the property?" she quizzed, sitting upright.

"What murder?" How did I not know about this?

"The maid that helps me. They found her with her throat ripped out last night."

"WHAT?" Damn. Did I do that?

"You're a shit prince if you can't even keep control of your own castle," she said, eyes narrowed.

I growled and her brow furrowed. "What the fuck Willa. Get out of my damned bed." I yanked her arm and pulled her out.

"Get the hell off of me," she yelled, punching me.

"Seriously!" I growled. Fists pummelled. Body tense.

"You look tense, Ethan. Perhaps you need your beauty sleep," she snapped, flicking her hair as she stood up. Grabbing her dressing gown, she flipped me a birdie and left the room.

"God damned, that girl is infuriating." I huffed, frowning. Collapsing on the bed, and falling asleep to thoughts of Willa's hot, sweaty, naked body on top of mine.

Chapter Sixteen
Willa

Who the hell does he think he is!

I slammed the door shut as I stormed out of the room. He clearly needed sleep, as the asshole appeared to be dramatically more obnoxious than normal.

What the heck happened last night? First with the wolf, then the guard knocking on doors to check I was alright. That poor maid. Rose, I think… or at least I hoped that was her name. She was always nice to me. No-one deserved a fate like that. I shuddered, body tense. It was a horrible way to die… what if it was that wolf? The one that hunted me in the middle of the maze. If it weren't for that gorgeous black beast, I'd never have survived. But then, who were the other ones? The ones that chased the grey wolf away. I shook my head. Who knows? All I know is the Castle was infested with the damn things! At least it gave me time with the black wolf. I can't believe I wanted that, though. Time with a wolf? I'm clearly insane!

"Hi Willa," Cleo chirped. "Do you feel better?" Cleo asked as I entered the dining hall. Oswald and Bernadette turned and smiled. I smiled back and took a seat beside Cleo. I nodded. "Nicky told me about the wolf. He was a bad boy!" she said. The Grand Duke coughed, spluttering out a croissant.

"Cleo, dear, have you finished?" Oswald asked.

She nodded. "Yes Daddy," she jumped up from the chair, ran to give him a hug and skipped out of the room. Nic and two other men walked in, one I recognised from this morning. Nic was rubbing his head as they joined us for breakfast.

"How are you doing Willa?" Nic asked, as he beat the taller man to the last croissant. The taller guy punched him in the arm and grabbed another pastry instead.

"I'm good. I don't really know what happened."

"Well, you're certainly glowing… it looks like Ethan did his part as your husband last night," he said, winking.

I blushed, and Bernadette swatted him.

Oswald shook his head, sat upright, and leant forward. "It's awfully strange. There shouldn't even be any wolves in this area."

Bernadette nodded.

"Willa, I'd like to introduce you to Alaric and Tristan." She said, as both men looked up with mouthfuls of food.

The taller one held up a hand and spluttered, half a pastry sticking out of it. He removed it and coughed. "It is a pleasure to properly meet you, Princess," he said, winking. I narrowed my eyes, pouting. Okay, so he'd only seen me half naked in bed. Bloody Ethan trying to do God only knows what this morning! I huffed.

Tristan lent over the table and held out his hand to shake it. "That Buffon is Alaric, he's Ethan's Beta, err I mean… brother."

I frowned. "Okay," I said. What was with all these nicknames?

Tristan smiled. "I'm Tristan, the best friend."

"Oh, so you live here too?"

He nodded. "Yeah, Oswald and Bernadette raised me ever since I was eight years old." He smiled and nodded to Oswald.

They smiled. "It was our duty to protect him as our own," he said.

I smiled, gushing. That was really quite sweet of him.

"So where is young Ethan?" Oswald asked.

I blushed. Alaric coughed. "I, erm. He's in bed I believe."

Nicholas laughed, "way to go Willa!"

My cheeks reddened further. Tristan laughed.

Alaric sat forward smirking, "well tell him we may need his attention this afternoon."

"Okay, but why?"

Alaric stiffened. "The erm…"

"Oh, the maid, I'm so sorry to hear about her, she was lovely."

Alaric frowned. "Who told you that?"

"The guard who came in last night."

"What guard?"

"The one that was outside my door while I changed."

Alaric and Tristan looked at each other.

"What time was this?"

"Erm… a little after the wolf attacked. So, I'm guessing after midnight?"

"The guards were at the gate Willa."

I sat back. "But that makes little sense. Who was outside my room then?"

Nic sat forward. "Could it be the Council, father?" he asked, questioning Oswald. Oswald frowned.

"The Council?" I asked, brow furrowed.

"Oh, it's nothing, my dear," Bernadette said. "It's just the name of another family."

"Which one? I've never heard of them."

Oswald narrowed his eyes at Nicholas. Nicholas sat back and shrugged.

The door opened, and my maid Rose walked in. "Rose?" I blurted out, standing up and hugging her. She looked puzzled.

"Yes, mam?"

"I, I thought you were dead?"

"Pardon?" she said, looking over at Bernadette.

Bernadette shook her head.

"But the guard said you were. He told me I must leave at first light. He said there would be a car waiting."

Cleo frowned, pouting.

Alaric leant forward; his eyes narrowed. "So why didn't you?"

I shrugged, "I don't know… I guess I didn't want to run off with a stranger without talking to you first."

Alaric nodded. "Your instincts were right Princess."

Oswald stood up. "It is good that your instincts protected you, when I'm sure my men should have been." He looked over at Alaric and Tristan. Tristan lowered himself down into the chair as Oswald growled. "Willa, that was not a guard. We must have had an intruder." He looked over at Tristan and Alaric. "Boy's you know what you must do." They nodded, their chairs screeching as they stood up and raced out of the room.

"What's happening?" I asked, brow furrowed.

Bernadette stood up and walked over to me. "Willa, until we

find the person who entered your room last night, you must stay by Ethan's side."

I groaned and nodded. "Nic, take her back to her room please and inform Ethan." He nodded, walked around the table, and linking arms with me.

"Come on, Princess, we're going for a walk to find your husband," he said, grinning.

Nic gripped tight, grinning as he trotted down the corridor. He made me smile; always positive, always smiling. His humour made me howl and his curiosity… I could see him getting into trouble all the time. I smirked, listening to him telling me the story of Ethan, a bear, and a stick. The fact that Ethan ran scared at anything made me laugh out loud frequently.

Turning the corridor, we entered the bedroom. Ethan was nowhere to be seen. Damn, didn't that man ever sleep? I sighed, yearning to be close to him. Jeez, what was wrong with me, he was an obnoxious prick and there was no way I was letting my inner voice push me down that path again!

"Do I really have to stay with Ethan all day?" I asked, un-linking arms with Nic and walking over to make the bed.

He smiled. "You know we have servants for that."

I nodded. "Yes, but I'm quite capable of making my bed, aren't you?"

He smirked. "Yes, but seeing a lady bent over, straightening my sheets… it's the highlight of my day."

I groaned. "Really, you 're way too young for any lady, Nicky," I said, smirking.

He flushed. "It's Nic or Nicholas to you Willy,"

I laughed. "Do I look like I have a dick?"

He laughed. "I don't know, want me to check?"

I groaned, throwing a pillow at him.

"What's all that commotion outside?" Nic asked, walking to the window.

Commotion? I couldn't hear a thing. I walked over and looked down at the courtyard, there was a man standing by the gate, shouting something.

Nic grabbed my hand and pulled me out the door, down the corridor, and into the courtyard.

As I entered, I saw them through the castle gates. Five gorgeous men stood glaring at the guards, shouting and threatening them. They were striking. All tall, muscular, shirtless, and bloody sexy. It was clear they were from the same family; they shared similar features.

The Grand Duke stormed into the courtyard. "What is the meaning of this?"

The one with red shorts stepped forward. He was tanned, well-built, ginger haired and well over six foot 10. I shuddered, wrapping my arms around myself. Why were they shirtless? In this weather.

"Where is Princess Willa?" He asked in a low growl.

My eyes widened. Jaw dropped.

Why was he asking for me?

Chapter Seventeen
Danica

The sunrise streamed through the open window in my box room. I stretched out, yawning. My feet dangling over the end of my single bed. I'd had a few hours' sleep, enough to keep me sane for the rest of the day. But heck, I was tired. I sat up and stared out into the room. It was minimalistic, and I like to think I planned it that way. But really… you couldn't fit one person comfortably in here, let alone two. Ethan and I had tried it a few times. I grinned. Well, more than a few times. But those that say you can have sex anywhere they're lying. It's bloody impossible. Even for someone as flexible as me. Rough sex was my thing. A quick, easy release. But here, it felt claustrophobic. I much preferred being out running in the wild, up against a tree or a quick rumble in the undergrowth. Smiling, I rubbed my eyes, stretching out my toes. Opposite the bed a large picture of me and Ethan stared back, framed by white embossed wood and cyan painted walls. We'd never had much money here as a family, but the Council sent us enough to set up and start the business. The perfect cover story allowing us entry into Ethan's kingdom. What can I say, the Grand Duke and Duchess liked their jewels, and we were in the business to supply them.

I'd first met Ethan when the Grand Duke invited us to the castle to show our newest selection of rubies. The Duchess was a fan of this jewel, and we had acquired a platinum ruby and diamond necklace that the Grand Duke was interested in for his wife's birthday. As planned, I attended with my father, ensuring I bumped into Ethan as I entered his bedroom and saw him lying half naked on the bed. I apologised, of course, stating I was looking for the bathroom. Then as soon as he laid eyes on me, the magic of the spell encapsulated his body, triggering our supposed mate bond. It was hard to act out the mate bond as he threw his arms around me and kissed me hard. All I'd heard were stories of his arrogant attitude and his possessive nature. But over time I grew to like him. He wasn't the worst choice for a suitor, and I knew my efforts would be rewarded when I brought him home to Hela and the Council.

The phone rang. I reach out, fumbling for the hands free. "Hello?"

"Danica, is your father home?"

"Yes, who is it?"

"Tell him, Barnabus wants to speak to him." Shit. I knew who Barnabus was.

"Okay, give me a minute."

I eased out of bed; my body was still half asleep. "DAD!" I yelled, walking out into the hallway.

"What Danica?"

"Barnabus is on the phone."

Dad walked out of his bedroom in a dressing gown. His grey

hair sticking up as he hobbled across the landing. He took the phone and disappeared downstairs. I showered and applied make-up… not that it mattered. Ethan would love me, whatever I looked like. "What happened, Dad?" I asked as I walked downstairs. His brow furrowed. "None of your business Danica. Now go straighten yourself out. We have work to do."

I huffed, looked down at my carefully chosen outfit and huffed again, heading back upstairs to get changed.

After changing into a three-day-old short skirt and skimpy top, I went downstairs to get ready for opening up. Dad passed me on the stairs "much better!" he said.

It was my turn to open up the shop today. Dad had said we were expecting a new delivery of necklaces, it'd cost us a small fortune, but we needed new stock. Sales had been down in the last quarter, and if we were to stay here and do their bidding, then we had to stay afloat. There would be no more handouts.

I heard shouting coming from upstairs. Dad was cursing as something shattered against a wall. Shit. He was angry. I stayed in the shop, wondering whether to open early, so he had to put on a smile in front of the customers.

It was too late. The thud of his footsteps descended the stairs.

"DANICA!"

I cowered by the till. "Yes Dad," I said. My voice wavering.

"What the heck did I tell you!"

"What do you mean, Dad?" He entered the shop, pounding over to me, fists pummelled.

I held up my arms in front of me, backing into the wall. His face was red with anger, spittle foaming at his mouth. He grabbed my head, slamming it into the wall. I cried, falling to the ground, dazed. "I told you to keep Ethan on a leash Danica!"

The salty taste of tears cushioned my lips, and I cowered into a ball. "I am Dad. Ethan said he loves me. He still thinks of me as his mate."

"Then why hasn't he marked you, Danica!"

"He said he would."

"It's been four fucking years since Edwina cast the spell. You've had plenty of time!" His voice vibrated, echoing off the walls. He bent down, grabbing my hair, pulling me up to face him.

"I don't know what else to do, Dad!"

"You've killed us both, you stupid girl!"

"What?"

"He tried to kiss that stupid human today Danica. Not you. The fucking human!"

My eyes widened. Jaw dropped. I stood up, backed against the wall. "What!" How could he? Tears streamed down my face.

"He doesn't love you. He doesn't even care about you!"

"He does so!" I yelled, crying louder. "He thinks we're mated!"

"You stupid girl! He only thinks he is." He took a step back, shaking his head. "If he falls in love with her everything, we've achieved will be for nothing!"

"He won't Dad, I won't let him!"

He slumped down against the glass cabinet. "They'll come for us now Danica."

"What can I do Dad?"

"Get him to mark you. That's the only way."

I nodded, wiping my tears away. "I will Dad, I will."

Chapter Eighteen
Hela

The delicious delicacy of dark crimson blood slivered through my veins. His life force wavered as he gurgled and groaned.

"That was purely decadent!" I yelled, smacking my lips, and dropping the waiter to the floor. "Marcus, you must get me more."

The amber skinned man stepped forward. "Yes, my queen." Marcus bowed, looking down at the dead boy. "But few humans want to work here, my Queen."

I span on the spot, turning to face him, scowling. "Of course, they do. I'm their Queen."

Pippa stepped forward. "Technically, you're not their Queen, they're human!"

I flew across the room, slamming her body against the black stone wall, gripping her neck. She whimpered. "What have I told you about your smart mouth?" I spat.

Pippa shuddered, attempting to talk. I lessened my grip. "Never to talk, my Queen."

My expression darkened; lips curled upwards. "Then why did I hear your mouth moving?" I snarled.

"I was stupid. Please don't hurt me!" she begged.

Lips pursed, I burst into a symphonic song of callous cackles, dropping the girl to the floor.

"Be gone child!" I yelled, ushering her away. She ran over the slate tiles and escaped out of the tall black wooden doors, running as fast as her little legs could carry her.

I stood for a moment, sucking my tongue, tasting the fresh delicacy of my last meal. Lips twisted, I grinned, prancing around the onyx pillars as I danced to the music in my mind. I stopped spying myself, reflecting over from afar. Smirking, I jumped up. The reflection jumped with me. Star jumps came next, my reflection copied. I giggled, running over, hugging my mirrored self. Damn, I looked good!

The large ebony framed mirror reflected at me. My body a delight of curiosity in a world of colourless creatures. I felt disheartened by the world around me. Despairing at how nature developed such putrid creatures. It would be wrong to let them roam free and live their lives, destroying the very nature that birthed them.

I had to keep them from killing themselves. Someone had to handle them, someone had to lead. I'd always known I was made of something special. A hybrid Vampire, Werewolf, the first of my kind. That wasn't an accident. Daddy demanded it. I was the purest form of any supernatural in all the realms. I lifted my head and looked in the mirror. Jet black hair framed my porcelain face as bright red eyes stared back at me. I looked weak and featureless, but I was anything but.

I turned, looked over to see two servants moving the dead waiter's body. "Doesn't he look beautiful?" I asked. They both looked up, faces pale, nodding and bowing as they quickly heaved him out of the throne room.

As they left, Barnabus stormed through the open door. "Hela!" He yelled, shifting back into his normal pot belly body. His hair was a mess of ruffled blond curls, his body suffocated by a dark grey suit, with a black shirt and shiny black shoes. For saving him was over three hundred, this forty something lookalike was one of his usual choices. I pursed my lips, frowning. I simply could not tell if this was his actual human figure or a picked-up shift from years gone by.

I sat down on my throne, as head of the table. All seven chairs are situated around. We'd only filled a few. Barnabus was one... the most powerful shifter out there. Another was Alpha Henrick, the Hitler of our werewolf family. Another was Edwina, an almighty witch with a twisted mind... sometimes I wondered if her lunacy could beat my own. I smirked, watching Barnabus as he waited for me to invite him to the table.

I tapped my fingers on the black glass throne. Long nails scratching and screeching as I watched him squirm, jumping from foot to foot. He always hated the music of madness. The intensity of a high-pitched squeal affecting his weak spot. Hell, if he wasn't so weak, I might even consider him competition. A shrieking burst of irrational giggles escaped me. I creased over, absorbing my manic side. It was simply too spectacular. As the laughter shook my body, it broke free, until I gasped for air, holding my chest, pushing away the cackles and taking in the air surrounding me.

"Oh, Barnabus dear... sit down," I said, grinning.

He nodded and took his seat. He sat further down at the table beside Edwina and Ralph. Ralph looked up; his carrot topped head of hair gleaming. His demonic features made me crease with laughter.

He was the 'oh so typical demon', the cute little red critter with a pointy tail, deep red skin, and black lips. I smirked. Edwina, on the other hand, was regal in her setting, stylised by the glamour spells she conjured to corrupt herself. Her endless beauty always gave me a run for my money.

"What requires my attention?" I asked, turning to face him.

He coughed, clearing his throat. "Jolee is no longer contacting me."

My brow furrowed. I slammed my fists on the glass table. "What!"

He shuddered. "She's missing, Hela."

I growled. "She's dead then. She would never defy me."

He nodded. "It appears that way!"

"So where is Lucius? Why hasn't he come to me with this news?"

"He should have my Queen, but he's somewhat un-contactable at present."

I stood up with my hands on my hips, and teeth gritted. Growling, I stepped towards him. "Then go there and drag him out by his hair if you have to. Send two of the colourless, they'll soon bring him home," I said, remembering how adorable my tiny little ninjas were. I squealed, clapping. Barnabus nodded and grinned.

The Colourless were by far one of my most favourite creations. An army of shadow warriors trained in the art of ninjutsu, my group of murderous little ninjas. I grinned from head to toe. I only ever sent them on the most delicate of missions. Those that required the skill set of tiny men in tights hidden amongst the shadow realms. I smirked. Hell, I didn't know where they went when I wasn't around, but I imagined it to be a place of darkened delight, glorious, gruesome gatherings, and spectacular sadistic scream fests. I mean… one look at them and any puny mortal would go running. I smirked, twirling my body around an onyx statue standing tall in the corner. His face was sculpted with fear, his body cold, hard and delicious! I groaned, aroused, my body tingling from head to toe.

Shaking myself away from the blackened death of my previous suitor, I attended to Barnabus, my beloved shifter, and one of my trusted Council members.

"So, what do you know?" I asked, taking a seat at the head of the table.

"Jolee last reported that, the prince," he stopped and looked over at me, gulping. I waved my hand, ushering him on. "The prince is marrying a human."

Heat rose through my body. My teeth gritted. Fists pummelled, anger rising. I stood up, shoving the table forwards. Barnabus jumped off his chair just in time, landing on the slate floor. Edwina and Ralph turned, eyes narrowed, picking up their drinks as Marcus ran in to mop up the spillages.

I snarled, baring my teeth, "he disgusts me," I exclaimed, my body shaking in anger. If my eyes could pop from pressure, or my head explode, now would be the time. I waited. No, not yet. I highly expected my rage to be the end of my hybrid existence. After all, how many centuries and how many temper tantrums can one girl have? I smirked, sighing, as I eased my body back into the chair.

"So, the most powerful Alpha on this side of the Atlantic is marrying a mere mortal?"

Barnabus picked up his chair, sitting back at the table. I admired his obnoxious muscles as he did so. Then he sat down. I could crush him, I thought, staring at his biceps.

"Yes Hela. He is indeed marrying a human."

"What about Danica? Why isn't he marrying her?"

"I don't know… perhaps the spell didn't work after all?"

My head snapped to question Edwina. She held up her hands as

I narrowed my eyes. "It had better work," I growled. Edwina nodded, stood up and left the room. I could only guess she was off to check how magical her magic actually was. I sighed, staring at the door, then back to Ralph, my teeny tiny red demon with the pointed tail. Bubbles rose through me as an explosion of laughter burst from my body. What can I say…? I like things in small packages. Ralph stared at me, frowning.

"Oh, Ralph, my adorable little red demon, what do you have to tell me?"

He huffed. "Nothing, Hela. What can I say, Hell isn't missing you yet."

I snarled. "Of course they are, I'm their Queen damn it."

He smirked. "Yes, your majesty," he snarled, jumping off the chair and bowing tiny little bows as he left the room; his forked tail swaying after him. My forehead hit the table; arms outstretched. "Burgh," I groaned. Life was too hard.

"Hela?" Barnabus asked, his fingertips reaching for my own.

"Burgh," I groaned again. A bloody human! My inner wolf sulked. How could he marry a stupid little human! He was with Danica. She was going to bring him here, to my palace, to me. We could have had so many hybrid babies, so, so many! "Burgh."

I sat upright. Barnabas's hands darted back to his lap. "Hell… he married a girl, didn't he?" He nodded. "Well, there's something."

I clapped my hands up high. "MARCUS!" I yelled; the door flung open.

"Bring me a toy." Marcus nodded and left, closing the door behind him.

Barnabus rolled his eyes.

"What!"

"Do you really have to torment them in front of me?"

I giggled furiously "oh Barnabus, my boy, are you feeling a little queasy in your old age?"

His brow furrowed. Lips pursed.

"I can let you join in if you'd like to?" I smirked.

"No, thank you!" He huffed. "So, what would you like me to do about the situation?"

I stood up, swirling and twirling around the room. My rhythmic body gliding and sliding down the black onyx pillars. I tiptoed over to him, giggling as I lay my hands on the back of his chair. It was marvellously magnificent. What a keeper she must be. A puny human girl with nothing to give gets to take the hand of the most powerful Alpha out there. A burst of giggles erupted from me. My eyes rolled as I gripped his chair, coughing up phlegm.

"Oh Barnabus, silly old you!" I said, laying my hands on his shoulders. He tensed. "We're going to host a spectacular celebration for the newlyweds. Send word. Invite them, and it'll be the last dance of their devastating lives." I cackled, swirling and twirling, as he nodded. No-one would survive the blast my celebratory ball would give them. It would be magnificent! "There must be fire dancers, girls on silks, strip tease artists for the boys in the club… oh, and what are those enchantress creatures called?"

Marcus looked up. "Succubus?"

"Yes, we need those, plenty of those!"

"But didn't you wipe out their race?"

I laughed, patting him on the shoulder, gripping his neck between my cold, callous hands. "There's always a few escapees, Barnabus… FIND THEM!"

Barnabus shook as I tensed my grip, pulling away and bowing as he left the room.

Marcus entered, threw in a young girl, and slammed the door

behind him.

"There there my pretty," I said, wiping her fallen tears. "This won't last long." And with that I raised my head back, my fangs protruding and sank them down, slamming into her carotid artery, watching the sparkle dissipate from her eyes, silvered eyes, as she withered and died in my arms.

Chapter Nineteen
Ethan

Tristan caught up with me in the corridor. "Ethan, your father is asking for you."

I nodded and followed him into his office.

The Grand Duke looked up from his papers, sitting at his old mahogany desk. "Ethan. What happened to your shirt?"

Tristan chuckled under his breath.

I huffed. "What did you want, father?"

"Sit down, son."

My eyes narrowed; brow furrowed. "Why?" I asked. Taking a seat.

"You won't like this," he said. Shoving a letter in front of me.

It was from the Council. Tristan took it and read through. His smile lessened with each sentence he read.

The Council was a hierarchy of every known supernatural creature. Built by Werewolves, Witches, Shifters and Vampires. I shuddered. The bloody dead things always gave me the creeps. It had existed for centuries, governed by the one and only Queen of Hell, Hela, the hybrid.

Hela used her power and influence to build a reformed supernatural race. One where only the elite survived. There used to be many more creatures alive and kicking, but the Council wiped them out. Hela saw them as impure, insignificant, and powerless.

The Council stood as the single most deadly force this godforsaken planet had ever seen. Well, until FALCON came along. We'd stayed off both their radars for years now, but ever since Alpha Henrick from the Amber Rose pack joined the Council, they were quite interested in our pack. The Amber Rose pack made sure of that.

They gained their numbers by feeding off the weak. Building them up to survive. Bigger. Better. Brighter. Their training was bloodthirsty. Their ideals barbaric. If you joined them, they would protect you and yours. But if you betrayed them, it meant death to every soul you ever loved. I'd heard cases of entire packs being wiped out when they no longer wanted to serve the Council. Lucky for us, father had never signed up. But it seemed something new had piqued their interest.

"What do they want?" I asked. Tristan groaned, shaking his head. "FALCON won't allow them Grand Duke! She's human!" I leant forward, snatching the letter from him.

They were demanding an audience with Willa!

"FALCON won't know until it's too late!" Oswald said, leaning across the table, taking the letter from me.

I sat frozen. Eyes wide. Why did they want her? She was already married. To me! Why did they want a human? Did they know about our plan?

"Alpha Henrick has secured a seat by Helas side. He now stands for werewolves everywhere," he said, snapping me back to reality.

I growled; eyes narrowed. "He will NEVER stand for us!"

Oswald stood up and paced the room. "No son. He won't!" he paused, looking at me. "Son, he won't take Princess Willa. She's family now."

I nodded. Unsure if I was angry, sad, afraid, or shocked. He stopped to face me, his expression stern. Shoulders raised. "But, they could try to take her from us."

I gripped the edge of the seat. "OVER MY DEAD BODY!" I roared, standing up and kicking the chair across the room.

"Shit Ethan!" Tristan said. "Calm the heck down!" He picked up the chair and placed it back in front of the desk.

"Son," the Grand Duke said, walking over and placing a hand on my shoulder. "We have the strongest pack. But the Council is dangerous. They have more members than we do. If the witches alone targeted us. It would be a bloodbath. You know how powerful Edwina can be."

Tristan walked over. "It would be safer for Willa and for the packs if we handed her over."

My wolf was furious. Hand Willa over to the enemy. I wanted to rip Tristan apart for even suggesting it.

The Grand Duke sat at his desk and sighed. "We may have to bring our plan forward."

I sat down, slumping in the chair, feeling defeated. "She doesn't know yet."

"Then we have to tell her."

I nodded. Shit. That wouldn't go down too well!

Oswald tapped his fingers on the desk. "If we go to war with the Council. FALCON will step in."

"But wouldn't they join us? We are after all on the same side."

Tristan stepped forward. "You know that's not true. Since Nathaniel left, FALCON has been at war with all wolves. They'd rather see the Council kill us. Then they'd clean up the Council after we'd been defeated."

I sighed. He was right. We could have really done with the London wolves on our side right now. But Nathaniel was nowhere to be seen. "What if I sent one of my pack to London… to locate Nathaniel?"

Oswald's eyes widened. "You could. But then that's one fewer wolf to turn the humans."

Tristan perched on the edge of the desk. "We've got to do something, sir."

I sat back, an uncomfortable silence filling the room. "What about Nic?"

The Grand Duke sat forward. "No, it's too dangerous!"

"It'd be more dangerous if a war broke out here and we weren't ready!"

He sighed, lowering his head. Oswald looked up; his expression filled with sadness. "Okay. But he takes Alaric!"

"What! I need Alaric, you know he's my beta."

"He's also your brother. You know Nicholas would get into no end of trouble in London."

Fuck. He's right. I was forever cleaning up Nic's messes in New Haven. I huffed. "Fine."

"Speak with them. They will leave by the end of the week."

Oswald stated. I nodded, stood up, sighed, and followed Tristan out.

They had put me in a terrible position. We were going to lose one of our best fighters, Alaric. But if Nic and Alaric could find Nathaniel, they might gain FALCON's help. Nathaniel would know how to contact them, set up a meeting with their founder, explain our need to destroy the Council before it destroyed us. I know they have many supernatural races on their side. I'd heard rumours of an underground lair, hiding among many of the Councils' targets. Perhaps together we could end the war once and for all.

But then, how would they take us turning a city of humans into vicious werewolves? I think they'd be pretty pissed at that. My brow furrowed as I lowered my head. We're fucked either way! I sighed, wandering through the castle grounds.

Chapter Twenty
Willa

Nic let go of my hand and stormed forward, balling his fists. "What the fuck do you want?"

"Get back, child. We're here to speak to Princess Willa." My brow furrowed. Who were they?

Nic growled, his body shaking with anger. "CHILD! I'm sixteen!"

The older boy gritted his teeth, clenching his fists, ready for a fight. The guards tensed up, pushing the seven brothers back. Muscles and testosterone battled at the gates. The red head roared, while the blond one growled furiously. The younger one to the left, though, he looked familiar. Was that the intruder from last night?

"Get back son!" The Grand Duke demanded, pulling Nic back.

"Where is she?" Another asked. "We know you have her here!" the younger one shouted.

I stepped forward, somewhat unafraid of them. His gaze met

mine, and he smiled, his body relaxing.

In a moment, every one of them turned to face me. "Willa," they whispered.

Who were they? Why did I feel like I should know them?

Nic stood next to me, angered.

"Willa come here. We won't hurt you."

"That's what murderers say," Nic said.

The older brother growled.

They stepped closer in unison. The guards tried to hold the line as the taller one with ginger hair reached out to touch me. Who were these men? Mesmerised, I lifted my hand, reaching forward, fingertips an inch apart from his. Then my body flung backwards, captured in the arms of a muscular, growling man. That woody scent engulfed me. I knew who it was… Ethan.

He stepped in front of me, slapping my hand down. The brothers growled.

What is with all the growling?

He clenched his fists, puffed out his chest and stood firm, ready to fight. "Get back!" he yelled. Growls erupting within him.

"Or what?" the taller one asked, push harder against the guards

The Grand Duke stepped forward and pulled Ethan back. "Does your Duke Henrick know you're here?" he enquired.

Henrick… I know that name… Isn't he the Duke of the Amber Rose brothers, the ones that Ethan and his family, my family, hated?

Oswald stood tall. "Perhaps I should call him. I am sure he would enjoy knowing that his sons broke the peace treaty we put in place."

"Peace treaty?" the taller one spat. "More like a bloody cage!"

Ethan laughed. "You don't know what a cage is, mongrel, but I can show you one if you like?"

The taller one's expression darkened. His eyes narrowed as he stood tall, baring his teeth. His second in command whispered something in his ear, and he tensed up. Fists pummelled. "FUCK!" he yelled. "This is far from over!" he ushered the group away. "You'd best treat her well!" he shouted as his second in command pulled him away.

My jaw dropped. Why did they care how I was treated?

"I'll treat her just like you treated Layla!" Ethan boomed. Tristan winced, grabbing Ethan's arm as he charged forward.

"Not here man!" he said, "Think of Willa!"

"FUCK!"

The brothers turned back, ran at the gate growling, pushing to get in. Ethan huffed, stepped back, and let Oswald handle it.

"Back away" Oswald boomed. Bernadette stood beside me, shielding me. Cleo giggled. "Not here!" Oswald yelled, nodding in my direction.

The brothers huffed, their chests dropped, bodies relaxed as they pulled each other away.

Ethan growled as he watched them leave. What the hell just happened? Why would a perfect, and I mean perfect stranger demand Ethan treat me well? What did he know that I didn't? From what I heard at breakfast. These were the villainous traitors that royally stabbed my new family in the back. My brow furrowed; eyes narrowed. So why did I feel like they were actually good people?

Bernadette stepped forward and placed her arm around Oswald, soothing him. "Why would the Council send the Rose brothers?" she asked.

He shook his head. "They were checking our defences," he said.

Ethan's shoulders drooped. "Why did they want Willa? They best not bloody touch her!"

Tristan pulled Ethan over. "Man, you need to calm down. They used her as an excuse. You know the Councils behind this."

"Fuck the Council!"

"Maybe one of them was the intruder in Willa's room last night," Nic said.

Ethan roared, paced over to me so we were face to face. His expression filled with pure disgust. "THEY WERE IN MY FUCKING ROOM?"

I stepped back as he deafened me. "Technically, it's our room," I huffed, biting my bottom lip. Tingles swept over me. Heat gushed as a wave of arousal flooded throughout my body. He stepped forward. Fists pummelled. Sweat beading on his brow.

Shit. What was wrong with me! I thought, fanning myself as I sat down. I should fear him. He's clearly a man on a ledge right now. But damn, he looked hot when he was angry.

Ethan's body shook, pouring with sweat, a deep growl echoing from his throat. "DID THEY TOUCH YOU?"

He grabbed my arms, pulling me up, shaking me. "Get off me!" I yelled, pushing him away. He growled again, pulling me closer. "Like I'd let any of you touch me!" I spat, angry and losing control.

His brow furrowed; eyes narrowed.

Tristan stepped toward Ethan. "Damn, man, back off of her! Don't lose control."

What the hell did that mean?

Ethan blinked, dropped my arms, and stepped back. He growled, deep, throaty, and pained. He took a deep breath, watching me as I bit my lip, the tension arousing each of us. Shaking my head, I took a deep breath, inhaling his woody scent before stepping closer. Grabbing his arms and pulling his body into mine. He allowed me. We stood nose to nose. His breath was hot, moist, and delicious. My lips parted. Heart pounded. God, I wanted him right there and then.

Mate

The courtyard was silent. All I could hear was the pounding of my heartbeat. The urge of his rugged breath. The temptation of his wet lips as his tongue caressed his lower one. I groaned.

"Inside now!" he demanded, pulling back and dragging me to our bedroom.

He slammed the door shut behind us, pushed me down on the bed, and sat on top of me. Wow, I was all kinds of hot right now. He glared as he held my hands above my head.

"How do you know them?" he snapped. The vein on his neck pulsating hard and fast.

"I don't know them!" I yelled, narrowing my eyes. Hot, bothered, and angry that he was holding me like this.

"Don't lie to me Willa!" He growled. "The Rose brothers knew you; I saw it on their faces." He held on tighter. Lent into my neck. His hot breath blanketed my skin as he growled, deep and hard.

I took a deep breath. My body urging me to wrap my legs around him and hold him tight. "They've got the wrong girl. I've never met them before." Technically, I hadn't, but heck, I felt like I had.

His mouth moved up to my ear. "Did you sleep with them last night?" he whispered through hot, rugged breaths.

"No, I bloody didn't." I yelled, kicking my leg up to hurt him. "What the hell Ethan, I don't even know them." I screamed as I kicked and flailed about.

"Stop fucking kicking me," he yelled, sitting upright.

"Let go of me then!"

"No!"

"Why the hell not!"

"I can't!" he said, his eyes wide, freeing my hands. He pulled me up to him, stroked the hair from my face, and placed his hot lips on mine. The kiss was intense, ravishing, and needy. Tongues collided as he pushed in deeper, stronger. My body ignited; electrical impulses rushed through my nervous system. I couldn't think. Couldn't breathe. I was completely lost in the moment, in awe of him, as he kissed me harder.

His hands groped my body as I pulled at his shirt. His touch made me gasp for more. He groaned, pulled back, and ripped my top open. Gripping my hands above my head, his kisses embraced my neck, breasts, and body. He suckled my nipple hard, working his way back up to my mouth. "Hot damn, you taste so sweet!"

My body weakened when he gripped me tight. His lips tender as suckled my neck, delicately biting and arching his body into mine. I groaned and gasped. Then he stopped. Why did he stop? I opened my eyes, looked at him hovering over my neck; at the love bite he'd surely caused.

"What's wrong?" I asked. My nails gripped him, urging for more. "Is it Danica?" I winced when I said her name. He narrowed his eyes, let go of me, and I slumped on the bed. Shit. Me and my big mouth!

With wild eyes, he stood up, lips pursed. The vein in his neck throbbing. "Never forget you're mine!" he said. His darkened expression returning. He looked into my eyes. They'd lost their sparkle as he stared at me. "Fucking mine!" he roared as he lent down, kissed me hard, then left the room.

What the actual fuck?

Chapter Twenty-one
Ethan

How could I forget Danica? I'd betrayed her, my mate. She'd never forgive me. But I couldn't. I couldn't help myself. Willa was so damned hot, tasted so sweet. She was mine, too. They both were. They had to be.

Tristan ran over to me. "Well, aren't you a sight for sore eyes, is she dead?" he asked.

I snarled, glaring at him. "No, she's not fucking dead, she's, she's… just leave it alright!"

Tristan held up his hands. "Do you really think that Alpha Henrick would risk crossing into our territory?" he asked as we observed the town from atop the hillside. So far, nothing looked suspicious.

I shrugged. "He's the closest Council member to our border, and after what happened with Layla, we've never seen eye to eye."

Tristan nodded. "Did they find her body?"

I grimaced. "No, after they took her to the Council, they executed her."

Tristan frowned. "But that's the Council saying that. She could still be alive?"

I sighed. "I wish she were. Cleo misses her dearly."

"As you do I presume?"

I nodded. My heart never healed after they took her from me.

"Did you two ever…?"

I smiled. "No, she wasn't my mate and even though I cared deeply for her, I could not take advantage of her like that."

Tristan nodded. "I understand. It's tough when you haven't found your mate."

I frowned; brow furrowed. "I have Tristan, in Danica. You know that."

His eyes widened. "Seriously? I thought she was only a plaything until you settled down."

My eyes widened, and I pushed him off the ledge. He landed on his feet, ten feet down. "Dick!" he yelled.

I jumped down next to him and smirked. "There's nothing here, let's head back."

Tristan brushed himself off and caught up with me. "What makes little sense, Ethan, is that Henrick never feared a battle. But he also never started one." I nodded. "The Amber Rose pack hasn't stepped over the border since they betrayed us."

I wracked my mind. It's true. After all these years, why now? Why would they risk an all-out war? "It's got to be the Councils doing."

Tristan nodded. "It makes sense. The Grand Duke said they've been ramping up their army lately. We may need to call on Princess Willa's family after all," he said.

"Not unless we have to. I don't believe Willa is fond of her family," I said, raising my eyebrows.

"Well, she won't mind them being eaten then," he said, smirking.

I laughed and pushed him sideways as we continued walking through the streets of the town below the castle. They'd get quite the shock when a pack of werewolves showed up to fight. Smirking, we made a stop on the way, entering the Crescent bar.

"Two pints of your finest, Dale," I said, slamming my change on the counter.

"No money necessary, Prince Ethan," he said. "I owe you for saving my chickens last week. That wolf sure looked hungry!"

I nodded, smiling. If only he knew.

Tristan smirked as we took a seat in the corner. "Wasn't that Nicholas?" I nodded. Smirking. He laughed.

Taking a sip of beer, he smiled, staring at me. "Your wolf likes her, doesn't he?"

"Huh?"

"The Princess. I've seen you around her."

"What. No, he doesn't. She's just fresh meat, that's all."

"Did you really call your wife fresh meat?"

"Well, no… yes, shit. Well, she is human."

He nodded. Smirking.

"And humans and wolves shouldn't mix, remember," I said, almost asking him. He nodded, and I frowned.

"Plus, I'm sure FALCON would be pretty pissed if you changed her."

"I'm sure they're going to be when we change her entire family's army."

"Shit. Is that the plan?"

"Yeah, well, that's what father wants."

"But what do you want? You're the Alpha now."

I shrugged. "I don't know. But I don't think Willa would like me changing all her family into werewolves, would she?"

He laughed. "Maybe ask them first?"

I nodded. "It's better to be a werewolf in a fight with another werewolf, than a tiny human against a big bad wolf," I said, taking a sip of beer.

"Red Riding Hood didn't have a problem."

I laughed, spitting out my beer. He patted my back as I coughed, shaking my head. "You're a dick Tristan!"

He smirked. "So, what are you going to do about your girl crush, then?"

"Fuck off Tristan, I do NOT have a girl crush!"

"Jeez, it's like fifth grade with Tracey Campton again," he laughed.

"Well, she was kinda hot."

"It was the height of summer, you dick. Of course she was hot," he said, laughing. "How was hosing her down going to help at all."

I laughed. "Worked though, didn't it."

He laughed, nodding, then frowned. "God, I miss being a kid, it was so much easier."

I nodded and chugged down the last of my beer.

"Being an Alpha is damn hard work," he said.

"You don't have to tell me! Since you took over your dads' old pack you've been as boring as Hell," I said, laughing.

"Yeah, says you, you're an angry asshole most of the time." He laughed, pushing me off the stool.

I laughed. What an idiot! Damn, I missed this!

Tristan continued laughing as he pulled me up. His expression darkened at the same time as I received a message through our pack's mind link. We both look at each other.

"Willa!" I said. He nodded.

"They're back!"

We ran out of the bar, down the old cobble streets of New Haven centre and back towards the Castle.

"Why would they dare come back?" Tristan asked, as we ran as quickly as we could.

"They've got a death wish!" I yelled, running past the hedge maze, down the path, and stopping dead by Darkwater Lake.

Tristan almost banged into me.

There lay Willa, reading aloud to Cleo. She must not have seen me until Cleo giggled. As she turned around, her expression changed. She smiled with a look of fresh hope. One dashed with a hint of anger. Her scent intermingled with my own. Two bodies yearning out to touch one another.

Tristan grinned as he stepped forward and knelt beside Cleo. "What's this you're reading," he said, bending down and looking at the cover.

"Get off Tristan," Cleo squealed. "It's one of my big books."

He stood up, holding up his hands. "Please accept my sincere apologies, Cleo," he said, then smirked.

Willa continued to stare at me. Cleo giggled again.

"Err, Ethan," Tristan said, patting me on the back. "We've got business to attend to?"

I blinked, my eyes widening. "Yes, of course!" Cleo giggled louder, and I frowned, patted her on the head and nodded to Willa."

Willa smiled, a smile that softened my gaze, warmed my heart. Damn, I had it bad!

Tristan grabbed my arm, laughed, and pulled me away. I sighed, heading to the pack house for the latest intel.

"Man, she's got you wrapped around her little finger!" Tristan said as we entered the pack house.

"Who has?" Nic asked, taking a seat.

I frowned. "No-one, mind your business."

"Willa, of course!" Tristan said, beaming.

Nic laughed. "Saw that coming!"

I growled, sitting at the head of the table. "I've already found my mate, Nic, you know that!"

His lips curved. "You think you have."

I growled. "I HAVE!"

He smirked. "Then explain to me why you're attracted to Willa?"

A low, deep groan sounded out from within me. I don't know. "It's nothing to do with you!"

"Well, if Willa's up for the taking?" he said, shrugging his shoulders.

I stood up and roared. Nic held up his hands. "Okay brother, I get the point!"

Tristan laughed. "You two are a bloody nightmare!"

Lips pursed; I narrowed my eyes at him. "Shut it, Tristan, and pour me a damned drink!"

Tristan laughed, handed me a whisky, and we all sat around plotting the downfall of the Hela, the Council, and the Amber Rose pack.

Chapter Twenty-two
Darius

The iridescent black palace stood before us. An icon of darkness to all supernatural kinds. Corridors of glass shimmered under the warmth of the sun. Radiant rays tried to push through the barrier, but Hela, being half vampire, had an aversion to sunlight, so she kept the light out as much as possible.

Don't get me wrong though, if sunlight could actually end her very existence, I'd be first in line to push her outside. Sadly, though, it just burned. We found that out when one guard attempted mutiny back when we were barely teenagers. We quickly learned from his mistake!

I looked over at Adam, my beta, as we marched up the gravel path, stones crunching under my boots. He nodded and smiled. This would not be easy but with my brothers by my side it would be manageable.

Our family has lived here for the last seventeen years. Taken in by the only hope we had. Father had thought it was a good deal at first. He'd made sure the humans cared for Willa. Then instructed us to take what little we had and plead forgiveness. We arrived at the palace gates with nothing left to lose. Hela saw that. Took hold of us and shaped us into the warriors we were today. It was a last-minute decision, but it meant a lifetime of misery. I huffed as we entered their glass corridor. Well, not quite misery. We had all the freedom we needed. As long as we brought in the abysmal creatures that didn't meet the charter the Council had formed.

They killed the lesser beings on sight. No trial. No chance for justice. It didn't matter who you were or what you liked. If you were born to a lesser being, you were born with a target on your back.

We'd been lucky we'd survived so far. The training grounds were horrendous. Making us men, they said. Bollocks to that. It was a bloodbath and if it weren't for my brothers, not one of us would be still standing now. We always had each other's backs, had to. My father didn't exactly step in and save us.

"Do you think father knows?" Harper asked as we walked towards our father's office.

"Hmm, I'd say so." I said, a smile glinting in my eye. After all this time, what did he expect? He couldn't keep her from us. Not anymore. She had a right to know where she belonged, and she had little time left. She needed to know!

"Won't he punish us?"

I smiled. "No. He's been wanting to know about her for years now." Okay, he hadn't. But it made my brothers feel better to think about that.

"But he told us to leave her alone."

"Yes. Yes, he did." My eyes narrowed. "Okay, so he might be

angry." He would be!

Harper nodded.

"He might not know," Stefan cut in. "We were careful. He could think the Council sent us on a job, we might pull this off."

Harper laughed. "Father isn't stupid. We've never taken this long to finish a job."

My brow furrowed. Harper had a point. We'd been on endless jobs before, and we've never taken this long. Bollocks. He knew.

"Uh guys." Stylan whispered. "I think he knows," he said as we entered father's office. I followed his gaze and froze. Shit. It was a poor plan!

He stood a few feet away, his eyes narrowed, fists pummelled.

"Where were you?" He roared. We stepped back.

When every one of us refused to answer, his eyes narrowed, and he stepped forward, lifting my chin with his hand. "I asked, WHERE WERE YOU?"

I felt Stylan flinch besides me; he was not used to this side of father.

"Father." I began. "We saw Willa," I confessed. It was pointless trying to lie. He already knew.

He let go, shook his head, and sat at his desk. His head in his hands. His silence was worse than the frenzy. I could feel the hairs on my body standing on end. My brothers fidgeted behind me.

"Why?" he asked, raising his head. "We've spoken about this before, several times. You should have left her alone! Why would you do this?"

"We missed her father. She has nearly reached the age of the prophecy!"

His eyes flashed with anger. "I told you, Hela will kill her. She will not stand for a human with the werewolf gene."

"But why? She's still as much a wolf as we are!"

"No Darius, she isn't. Her human side is dominant. Her wolf gene was and will always be dormant." He shook his head. "If Hela finds out…"

I lowered my head. "I'm sorry father, I didn't think."

"You never do! I told you that when the time was right, you would see her again."

"When is that father?" Stefan demanded. "It's been over seventeen years!"

"She's beautiful father. She's grown into everything we thought she would be and more," I shouted. "Don't you care?"

Father remained still; his brow furrowed. "Of course, I care. But she's vulnerable as a human, you know that!"

"When will she change?" Harper asked, stepping forward.

Father shook his head. "I don't know that she ever will."

"But the prophecy?" I asked.

"It's pure nonsense Darius!"

"The witches didn't seem to think so." I huffed. "Edwina said a flaming red wolf would bring us peace."

"All the more reason to keep Willa in hiding. If Hela believes for one minute that Willa's a threat to her, she will have her, and everyone close to her executed!"

"But like you said," Harper said. "She's only a mere human."

Father looked up, his expression darkening. He nodded.

My lips pursed; eyes narrowed. "A mere human with a destiny to bring peace to the supernatural world."

"She has to be a wolf for that!" I argued.

"If it's meant to be, it will be Darius!" Harper said.

"Stop quoting mother!" I yelled; my heart was torn with grief. My brothers sighed.

"She even has flame red hair, like Edwina said." Stefan said.

Father snapped his head round, glaring at Stefan. "When did you talk to Edwina about Willa?"

Stefan stepped back. "I didn't. It's the stories Edwina told us when we were growing up."

He sighed. "Okay."

I took a deep breath. "She deserves our honesty, father," I added. It was the truth; Willa had been alone all these years. The family she had was awful to her, and now she was married to our strongest enemy. I sighed. Ethan and his family once meant so much to us. But when they sat by as our home burned to the ground, watched us starve and never offered help. That was an act that we could not forgive. If only the Grand Duke had cared enough. Could it have made a difference? Would we still have ended up in Helas claws, with her Council of sadistic cronies. But alas, they had their reasons. I believe the Grand Duke was quite fond of Layla. Father said he saw her as a daughter. So, I understood why they cut ties with us. I just didn't like it.

Whatever the past, Willa deserved to know what happened. She had a right to know who my brothers and I were to her. Who we all were to her, and we needed her in our lives. She could be the one that frees us, the one they wrote about. We needed to tell her the truth if it was the last thing we ever did.

Chapter Twenty-three
Willa

Ethan growled when he walked into the dining room for breakfast the next morning. I looked up from my cereal and glared. Where did he sleep last night? Hell, I bet he was with Danica! I shuddered at the thought of her name. He sat himself down opposite. So close, almost an arm's reach away. Whenever he was near, it became hard for me to think. He stared across the table at me, his gaze raw, his eyes undressing me. Locked in a battle of illustrious thoughts, he made me feel weak. But I liked it.

I finished my cereal and reached over for a pastry. At the same time, he did. Our hands touched. Skin warm, supple, and tender. My body tingled, I melted inside. Staring up into those ocean blue eyes, the tinge of green defiant against all nature. He was hot, sexy, and licking his lips. I parted mine and gasped, aware of the family chatting around the table. But there was nothing. No motion, no noise, except for me and him. Locked in desire, wanting to ravish each other right there and then.

He pulled away. Left the pastry and opted for another. I shook my head, his loss. I took it and sat, picking at it, my body tingling, melding into the chair. Heck, I wanted him badly! The more he pushed me away, the more I wanted him closer. I licked my lips, tasting the chocolaty centre of warm, gooey goodness. Mmm! I could get lost in this moment. Scrummy food and an appetising dessert sitting before me. Taking a deep breath, I took in his earthy scent. The aroma of the forest tingles through my senses. What was it about him? Why did his muscular body, his hot-tempered attitude, and his dreamy eyes affect me? Hell! What was I saying? They'd affect any hot-blooded female with a pulse! I smirked, chuckling under my breath.

Ethan watched me, clearly annoyed by my presence, as his eyes narrowed when I chuckled. I smiled in return.

Shit. What the hell is wrong with me? Granted, he's bloody sexy, but really, he's only a man. I don't need him in my life. Husband or no husband. I was a free woman and could do whatever I pleased.

Duchess Bernadette smiled, looking over at me. "Did you have a pleasant afternoon yesterday?" she asked.

Ethan's darkened expression flashed over his face as he glared at me. Clearly a warning to shut up.

I rolled my eyes. "Yes, thank you Bernadette. I spent some time in my room, then took a walk in the gardens again. Cleo joined me."

Cleo jumped into the seat next to me. "Sure did. We talked about the maze and the secret way out." She said in a high-pitched tone. "Then we talked about the roses that Willa liked, oh and then boys," she said, giggling.

I laughed. Heck, she was too cute. Ethan groaned, finished his pastry, and stood up.

"Ethan, wait," his mother said.

He groaned again. Jeez, he acts like a child!

"Yes, mother," he said as he took a seat.

"What did you get up to yesterday?"

He huffed, staring at me. "Just the usual with my brothers."

"So, no visiting the town last night?" I asked, knowing full well that was where Danica lived.

He shot me a look of pure anger. "No, I stayed up with my brothers last night," he spat.

"'Tis true," Nicholas said as he bounded into the room. "Old Ethan here had girl problems."

My cheeks flushed and Cleo giggled. Ethan glared at him.

Oswald chuckled. "Oh, son, we all have girl problems," he said, smirking. Bernadette nudged him, narrowing her eyes. He laughed.

"Well excuse me," I said. "It's time I got ready for the day."

"Where are you going?" Ethan demanded, glaring at me.

I raised my eyebrows. "Well Husband, the weather has forecast sun all day, so I'm heading to the vale to swim in the lake, would you care to join me?"

"No!" he said, gripping the table.

Oswald sat forward. "Ethan, you must go. She can't go to the vale alone. Not with the wolf sightings lately."

"Ah yes," Bernadette said, folding her arms.

"I'm sure I'll be fine," I said, smiling and leaving the table. Heck, I didn't think of that. What if the wolf comes back? I huffed, hurrying down the corridor. With narrowed eyes, I pouted. I couldn't let him tell me what to do. If I wanted to go to the vale, I bloody well would! It'd serve him right if a ferocious wolf ate his wife! I shuddered, jumping as Ethan caught up with me halfway down the corridor.

He growled under his breath. "You can't go there alone."

I stopped and spun around to face him. "Why on Earth not Ethan?"

"Because I said so."

"And I'm supposed to live off your every word, am I?"

"Yes, well, no... Fuck!" he said, kicking at the ground.

I smirked. "Well, I'm going with or without you."

"FINE!" He stormed off, his body tense, fists pummelled.

"Fine," I said, yelling after him.

What a complete ass. Wow, it was a nice ass at that. What the hell is wrong with me? My brow furrowed as I entered our bedroom, leaving the view of Ethan's ass walking away behind me.

I sighed, heading over to the bookshelves. Running my finger along them, I picked up a few, settling on Bag of Bones by Stephen King. It sounded like one of his lighter stories. I sure as hell didn't fancy IT or Pet Cemetery when heading into a forest alone.

Packing a small bag, I added the book, a towel, a change of clothes, and headed over to the kitchen for snacks. No daily picnic by the lake could go ahead without snacks, a good book and a few drinks to settle one's nerves. I smiled, thinking of Juliet. She'd usually be the one 'borrowing' the beers from the kitchen when the chef wasn't looking.

When I entered, it was quiet, not a person in sight. Easy pickings. Smiling, I opened the fridge, added two bottles of some local brew, a bottle of water, a slice of cake, an apple, and a punnet of grapes. Perfect, I grinned. Heading back to change.

After changing into my swimming costume, I covered myself with a dress for the journey.

Just as I was about to leave, there was a knock at the door.

Chapter Twenty-four
Ethan

Danica's eyes lit up as the bell dinged. I closed the door, and she ran over, planting a kiss hard on my lips. I smiled. Damn, I'd missed her. An older couple by the jewellery counter tutted. Danica smiled, held my hand, and pulled me into the back room.

"I've only got an hour," I said. Danica's eyes narrowed.

"Why?"

"Willa's going into the Vale. She needs protection."

She huffed, let go of my hand. I could feel the tension in the air. "Then get one of the packs to do it."

"I can't Danica. She's my responsibility."

"That whore is no one's responsibility. I'm your mate. Not her!" she yelled. The bell dinged as the old couple left the shop.

I sighed and lowered my head. My wolf growled angry at her words. Danica's brow furrowed. "What, so your wolf likes her but doesn't like me?" she asked. Tears welling in her eyes.

"No," I said. Pushing my inner wolf down. "You know I love you!"

"I love you too, but that doesn't explain why you've never marked me."

"I know… and I will. He will." I said, placing my hand on my heart.

"When?" she asked, her expression darkening.

"When he's ready." I stood tall, taking her hand. "Look Danica. I know you're my mate. That's what matters."

She nodded, wiping her tear-stained face. I hated seeing her like this; she was right; she was my mate, and I had to convince her she was it for me. My wolf groaned, settled down, and disappeared from my thoughts. I pulled her in close and kissed her.

"I won't be long," I said.

"What, you promised me you'd spend today with me."

She's right. I did. Shit. This is hard. "Get someone else to babysit her. It doesn't have to always be you!" she snapped. "It's not like she's even that important!"

My brow furrowed. I pulled back to look at her. "What do you mean?"

"Her own family hated her. I spoke to that sister of hers. She had some things to say."

I huffed. Willa's family hated her. My heart sank, and my head lowered. She must have suffered for so long with them.

"Didn't you know?" she spat, grinning. "Jenna said she was adopted. Found in the trash outside their mansion." She laughed.

"In the trash?" Shit. That's horrible!

"She said the duke adopted her with his dead wife. But when

Jenna came along. They wanted nothing to do with Willa. They only kept her to sell to the highest bidder."

"Shit!" I lifted my head. They were going to sell her. Is that what happened? They sold her to be my wife so they could pay off their debts. My hands clammed up. Body tense.

"Yeah. So, they conned you. She wasn't even a Princess to start with. Just some slave girl thrown out with the trash." Anger flashed through my eyes. No-one deserved to live like that! No-one deserved to be thrown out and bargained with. I wanted to rip that entire family apart. Starting with her dick of a father. I growled. I'd have my chance, bide my time. Then when it came to changing them, I'd rip every fucking one of them apart.

Danica's brow furrowed. She studied my face. "Why are you angry?" she said, puzzled. "I thought you hated her?" I panted heavily. My wolf raging from the inside. Growls escaped from my pursed lips, and I stepped back from Danica.

"Why did you contact her family?" I asked. Fists pummelled as the palms of my hands bled from the nails embedded in them.

"I didn't. Dad did."

Why would Lucius Daventry care about Willa? My brow furrowed. Danica stepped forward. Took my hands in her own and unclasped my fists. "He was worried about you," she said. Stepping closer still. "He knows you're my mate. He thinks of you like a son Ethan." I smiled and nodded. I was lucky to have him as part of the family.

I looked over at her. She seemed saddened at the thought of her father. "Speaking of which... wasn't he watching the shop today?"

She bit her lip and looked down at the floor.

My brow furrowed; eyes narrowed. "Where is he Danica?"

Her bottom lip wavered. I stepped forward, taking her body in mine. "Is everything okay, my love?"

"Yes," she sniffled.

"So, what's wrong?"

"I wish I could tell you Ethan, I really do."

I pulled back, resting my hands on her forearms. "You know you can tell me anything."

She took a deep breath and sighed. "He will be gone for some time."

"Why?"

"I can't say, Ethan, please don't push this!"

I sighed. "Okay."

"For now, let's put him to the back of our minds and make use of the time you have left with me."

I narrowed my eyes. "You make it sound like it's the end, Danica what's happening?"

"Nothing. Dad will fix it. It will all be fine."

I sighed, pulled her in for a tight embrace. "Okay, but if you need anything. If it's money you need, please ask!"

She sighed and wiped her eyes. "It's not money Ethan. Please don't worry. It'll all be fine," she said, clearly faking a smile.

Her hands moved up my arms, around my back, and she moved in for the kiss.

Hot. Sensual and longing. Damn, I needed this. I pulled her body close to mine and lost myself in the act of pure sexual gratification.

Chapter Twenty-five
Willa

"Where's Ethan?" I asked, opening the bedroom door to a man with spiked blond hair.

"Ethan apologises, but he is caught up with other business."

"Okay, so why are you here?" My head lowered. I hated to admit that I was hoping Ethan would join me.

He smiled. "I'm Aaden, the Alphas…" he coughed. "The prince's friend."

"What's with this Alpha thing? I've heard that several times now!" I asked, frowning.

He scratched his head, feigning a smile. "It's a nickname, Princess. Nothing to concern yourself with."

I nodded; brow furrowed. There was still something they weren't telling me. I stepped out of the door as Aaden stepped to the side. "It's Willa please! So why are you here?"

"Ethan would like me to accompany you to the Vale."

"Oh, he would, would he?" I huffed. He smiled and nodded.

"Fine. But I'll be fine on my own."

He grinned. "I know Prin… Willa, but it would make him feel better."

I laughed. He knew Ethan well! "Okay. But no cramping my style," I said, smirking.

I hunched my bag on my shoulder. He smiled and offered out his hand. "I'll carry it for you."

I smiled. "I can carry my bag you know."

"I'm sure you can. But it'll give me something to do."

I nodded and smiled, handing him the bag. "Thank you, Aaden."

We walked through the castle side by side. Aaden chatting about Ethan's glaring business deal was the reason he couldn't join me. I knew he was lying, and he was awful at it. His mouth twitched whenever another lie passed through his lips. I sighed. "Aaden… you can stop." He turned to face me, lowering his head.

"I'm sorry Willa, I know he'd be here if he could."

"That's just it Aaden, he can, but he's chosen not to be." I folded my arms, and we continued to walk in silence.

Coming up to the Darkwater lake, I recalled the evening not so long ago when I entered the dreaded hedge maze. Could it really be that I'd not been here that long? It felt like I'd lived here forever.

It was the night of the wolf. Actually, the two appearances of the same wolf. The grey one. Why did it attack me? My lips pursed. Perhaps it didn't. Somehow, after all the time I'd spent with it. It'd never once lunged at me. It'd come close. Strikingly close. But not one time did it finish me off, lunge at my throat, bleeding me out over the roses. I smirked. I'm not sure why I smirked, but I did. Somehow, this thing I'd been scared of, didn't seem that scary anymore.

But what about the others? Perhaps Duchess Bernadette was right. I shouldn't be going into the vale alone. I'd heard several more howls in the distance. This side of the vale seemed to crawl with them. I'd seen the grey monstrosity, the other two that chased it away, and then there was the black one. The soft, jet-black wolf that snuggled its head into me as it protected me from the beast before. I sighed. He'd felt familiar. Perhaps one wolf that my adopted father found me with as a baby? There'd been rumours he'd saved me from the wolves that day. But then that was over seventeen years ago. I couldn't have been over twelve, maybe thirteen months back then. I was toddling, apparently, sitting against the fur of a pack of wolves. They must have found me. Protected me as their own. But why?

I huffed as we entered the forest. The clearing so bright and beautiful in the midday sun. It was warm for this time of year. Summer had not long turned to Autumn as the leaves on the trees withered into their rainbow display before they withered and died. The sun shone high above, warming the lake as I undressed, ready to swim my worries away.

Aaden sat by a tree, checking out the surroundings. He didn't seem the least bit interested in the half naked woman before him. But then I didn't want him to be, did I? Perhaps only to make Ethan jealous. Not that it'd matter. He didn't seem the slightest bit bothered with me since our bedroom episode.

As I dipped my toes in the lake, I shuddered. It was a little cooler than I remembered. Nevertheless, I'd get used to the temperature, no doubt.

Aaden jumped up on high alert. "Get in the water," he yelled.

"What?" what did he think I was doing? It was too cold to run in and start swimming. "Give me a minute!" I said. His eyes were wide as he stared into the distance. What is wrong with him? The forest leaves shook as hundreds of birds took flight, flying over and away from us. Aaden ran over to the lakeside and stood in front of me. What the hell is going on?

I stepped back, grabbing the towel from the floor, covering myself up. "What's wrong?"

"It's the Council, Princess stand back!" His body stiffened as he stood, feet apart, ready for a fight.

"The who?" I took a step back in the water. Icy tendrils crept over my feet, up and above my knees.

"It's a group of them."

"Who Aaden?"

"Were… I mean men!"

I took a deep breath, unfolding my arms. "Men… really, is that all! The way you're carrying on it was some giant monster or something!" I don't know what's got his knickers in a twist. But he was seriously high on something absurd right now!

I listened out. It was silent. Even the birds had vacated this ludicrously dull plan of his. Was this Ethan putting him up to this to scare me into following his rule? Or perhaps Danica… she was surely angered at my arrival; let alone the fact I married her lover. Shit! I stared at the back of Aaden. This wasn't some kind of hit, was it? A murderer for hire. After all, how well did I know him? I tied the towel securely and balled my fists. There was no way he was taking me down today! No bloody way! I pushed him forwards, my eyes narrow, breathing slow and heavy.

"What!" Aaden asked as he darted forward, turning around. "Why'd you do that?"

"This is a shitty game you're playing, Aaden! Did Danica put you up to this?"

"What! No! Princess, get in the sodding water!" He righted himself and stood in front of me. Damn, was he being serious?

In the distance, the bushes rustled. My heart pounded as I heard voices slurring into one another as a group of men laughed and joked. Shit. Maybe he was right. But what's got him so on edge? It's only drunken tourists wandering too far from the town centre!

Aaden snapped his head round, a darkened expression on his face. "Get in the water," he whispered, urging me to swim into the lake.

"It's too cold," I said. Adamant I would stand my ground. Fuck. I was stupid.

"Please Princess. Get into the lake."

"Fine," I said, dropping my towel.

"Now what do we have here?" A butch man said with fists twice the size of my own delicate hands. A group of five men sauntered out of the bushes. I stepped backwards into the cool safety of the water.

"No, you don't missy," the black-haired, scrawny looking lad said as he ran forward and grabbed my arm. I put my hand to my mouth as he closed in. The stench of stale whisky and old sweat covered his body.

"Get the hell off me!" I yelled. My body tense, heart racing. Aaden pushed him off and two of the men grabbed his arms, pulling him like he was being stretched on a rack. Their medieval grins showed their true selves. They weren't here for a laugh. They were here to maim, kill, and slaughter. The third man with wild blond hair ran up and raised his fist, uppercutting Aaden right in the chin. Aaden's head slammed backwards, his eyes rolling back as he straightened up. The wild guy continued punching again and again in his stomach. Blood spurted from Aaden's mouth as I screamed for them to stop.

The butch leader laughed. "My, you are a pretty picture aren't you." He stepped toward me. "She said you would be." Shit. Danica! I stepped backwards. Synchronised movements as we danced around each other, with him enjoying the game far more than I. "Oh don't run darling. We haven't got to know one another yet." He licked his lips as he looked me up and down, reaching forward and pulling me into him. I resisted, pulling back, squirming in his giant arms. A grubby palm gripped my chin, turning my head from side to side. He lowered his head, his nose touching my neck. "Oh my, you smell so sweet!" he yelled, his hands gripping me tighter.

"Back off!" Aaden gurgled, blood still flowing freely from his mouth. He struggled with the two men that had his arms.

The butch leader grinned, held me back, and turned to look at him. "Or what?" he said. "You gonna shift in front of the human?" he enquired, with a knowing sparkle in his eye.

I saw Aaden tense up. A low growl stirring within him.

Human?

Wasn't everyone human?

Aaden growled. "You don't want to do this," he threatened.

"Oh, we really do," the butch leader said.

"If any harm comes to the Princess. Ethan will rip you apart."

The men looked at each other and laughed. "Oh, she's a Princess… even better," the leader said. "Don't you think if Prince Ethan actually cared, he would be here right now?" My heart sank. "It's not safe in these parts of the woods, you know," he said, laughing.

Aaden growled louder, baring his teeth. Bloody spittle coating the ground before him.

The butch leader gripped my hair and yanked me close again. I could smell the stench of days old whisky on his breath. His other hand grabbed my bottom as he pressed his vile lips against mine. The other men laughed. Aaden roared. I bit the leaders' lip and he let go, pushing me backwards. Angered as the blood trickled down his chin. He roared loud and deep, and before my eyes, his body groaned and creaked. I scampered backwards when he let go. His bones enlarging, skin turned to fur. His mouth grew out, sharp canines gnashed at the surrounding air.

He howled as he shifted, his body disappearing under the coat of a wolf. A huge dark brown wolf. My eyes widened; my jaw dropped.

WHAT THE ACTUAL FUCK?

Chapter Twenty-Six
Ethan

Wrapped in the arms of my mate, I pounded away. Her lush, voluptuous body lay beneath me. Sweat beaded on my brow as we continued to entangle in our deepest desire. She groaned, pulling me in for a deeper, stronger kiss. I carried on, thrusting faster. What was wrong with me? Why didn't it feel like it used to? No matter how much she groaned. How hard she wriggled beneath me. It wasn't getting me going at all. I sighed, pushing harder.

My mind kept roaming back to the Princess. To our kiss. Our hot, tangled kiss; made from illustrious thoughts and darkened desires. What was it with her? She'd been in my life only a short while, but fuck, she was turning it upside down.

I shook my head. Danica groaned below me. Something felt off with Willa. Something different. I urged to be next to her. Be with her. Inside her, not Danica. I panted harder. It wasn't right. Why did she affect me this way? My wolf growled deep within. I needed to get to her. Be with her. My inner wolf yelled at me to go. Find her. But why? Why was the need so intense right now? I was in the middle of what should be thrives of passion with my mate and all I could think about was my Princess, my Willa.

Where was she, anyway? She should be back by now. Perhaps Aaden was showing her the sights of the vale. I growled. That had better be all he was showing her! I sighed. Of course, he wouldn't. He was a member of my pack. The Sunset Banes pack. The strongest pack in the whole of the UK. There was no way he'd go against his Alpha.

Willa would be fine in his care. He was one of my most loyal members. Strongest too. I'd picked well, sending him with her today. I knew he could be trusted. Yet why did I have a powerful urge to go find and protect her?

I rolled off Danica. It wasn't happening today. Something felt wrong.

"What?" Danica asked, huffing as she sat up.

"I'm not feeling it right now," I said. Pulling on my trousers.

"It's her, isn't it?" she said, anger flashing in her eyes.

"I don't know. Something feels wrong." She was right, though. I didn't understand these feelings. But right now, I wanted to be next to Willa. Not Danica, and it wasn't even my wolf talking this time. I looked at Danica. Fuck. What was wrong with me?

"That bitch!" she screamed, standing up.

Alpha.

Alpha. The princess is in danger.

My mind link activated. It was Aaden. Shit. I knew it! I jumped up and ran out of the shop as quickly as I could.

"Ethan!" Danica yelled from the shop entrance. It was too late. I was already gone.

Fear engulfed me. Clutching my body as it shook, threatening to shift right here in the town. My heart pounded as I ran. Thumping through my chest like a train derailing. I sped down the street, past the Crescent Bar and Eatery, knocking a couple of tourists flying as I leapt through the crowds.

Willa was in danger. That's all I knew. I summoned the pack on the way and ran into the Vale as fast as I could. I had to get there. Had to save her. Something was wrong. Aaden wasn't answering me. It wasn't like him. There must be something wrong. Shit! If I've put her in danger because I wanted to spend time with my mate, I'd never forgive myself!

Running up the hill and through the entrance to the vale, I roared. Loud. Deep and hungry. Something was wrong, and I wanted to make damned sure they knew I was coming!

What was it with her, though? I had this feeling before my mind link activated. It's like I knew she was in trouble. Knew I needed to be by her side. I guess you could call it instincts. Why the hell didn't I listen to them?

Reaching the opening to the lake, I could hear the growls of hungry wolves, heavy breathing, and a potent scent of fear. Crimson blood had been spilled, and it wasn't only a wolf's blood, there was a mix of humans too. This would not be pretty!

Chapter Twenty-Seven
Willa

Reality shattered before me as the huge brown wolf bared its teeth. My body shook, face paled, hands clammy. I was a rabbit in the headlights, and it paralysed me beneath it.

I could see Aaden struggling against the men that held him. He mouthed the words 'I'm sorry', roared uncontrollably, shifting into an even bigger wolf. My heart pounded. Shit! This can't be happening. Aaden's wolf growled deep as he leapt through the air, landing on the enormous beast before me. I shielded my head, wrapping myself into a ball on the ground. The other men shifted, and a multitude of wolves danced within a bloody battle before me. Aaden's blood splattered across the ground. Autumn leaves became soaked in blood as Aaden snapped and bit back at the wolves that attacked him. But even though he was the largest, they still outnumbered him.

My mind numbed except for the howls of pain his wolf endured. He was protecting me, even at his own cost. I watched in horror as the five wolves' bit and battered at him. He yelped as one bit into his leg. Another took a chunk out of his shoulder, tossing him to the side like a rag doll.

My mind was awash with fear and sorrow. Aaden's wolf was limping, his body a mass of dirtied blood, broken limbs, and torn ligaments. I gripped at the muddy lakeside. My eyes wide, jaw dropped. He couldn't survive much longer!

Taking a harsh breath, I pushed myself backwards, my bottom muddied from the lake's edge. I had to help him. He would die if I didn't, and I knew that meant I'd be next. My heart pounded like a train speeding along the tracks. Teeth gritted, head screaming out in pain. It focused me, as my anger leapt to new levels, breaking through the brink of insanity. I frantically searched for something. Anything to take down at least one of the almighty beasts before me.

There was nothing except a heck of a lot of forest. Vivid Autumn leaves, charcoal grey rocks, the burnt umber of shredded tree trunks. It lost me in the blood splattered hell of nature. But what does nature do best? Survive! My eyes rested on a rock about the size of a football. Now, granted, I wasn't exactly the muscular type, but I was sure as hell going to take that adrenaline and channel it into strength right now. I leapt forward, ran, and almost tumbled over a thick branch. Bonus! I threw it beside the wolves. That's my Plan B. Grabbing the rock, I watched, waiting for my moment.

Aaden was still going. Still harnessing his inner wolf as he ripped one of his attackers to shreds. I shuddered from the sight of the carnage and from the shit I was about to cause.

Taking a sharp breath, I gripped the rock, not taking my eyes off the scene before me. Stepping closer, I was within arm's reach of the wolf that had its jaw round Aaden's neck. I took a deep breath and slammed the rock down as hard as I could. Crash. Crushing its skull as it whimpered. The impact forced the rock from my hands, and I jolted backwards. Its jaw releasing his neck. Aaden staggered back, then lunged for another wolf. I didn't waste a minute and picked up the rock again. The wolf was down on the floor, dazed. I raised it as high as I could, my arms shaking from the weight. Slamming it down, harder this time. Grunting, falling backwards as it hit. The wolf fell silent.

Aaden continued to take on the other three. But one stood tall. Whimpering at the loss of his friend. The huge brown wolf. The leader. He charged forward, leapt over Aaden, and landed before me. My blood drained. I stepped back once, then twice. Tripping over the large branch I'd placed as Plan B. Scrambling to get up, the wolf pounced, landing on top of me. I grabbed its snout, slicing my hand as it caught between its teeth. Blood fled down my arm. The angry wolf growled, gnashing its teeth together, aiming for my face. I pulled free. Screaming as it bit down on my arm, ravaging me like a chew toy.

Eyes darting to the side, I clambered out, fingers gripping the branch. Reaching out, I grabbed it, yanked it up and slammed it in front of me like a shield. The wolf snapped, biting, splintering the branch into nothing. My body was on fire, adrenaline depleting, pain taking over. Soon there would be no use. No matter how hard I kicked, or how much I flailed about, there was no way I could free myself from the inevitable.

Hot, moist breath smothered my face as the beast lunged at me, its teeth clamping down on my forehead. Pain screeched through my body. Nerves ignited, exploding in my head. Dizziness took over as shards of glass speckled before my eyes. Gripping the beast's face, I pushed it back, screaming louder and louder.

My body writhed as it bit down harder. Thick blood covered my face. Its canines threatening to break through my skull. Darkness enveloped my vision. There was no way I would make it through this if I passed out.

Kicking and pushing the wolf away, I sobbed. My hand still gripping its jaw like the last defence before the ultimate finale. But before its razor-sharp teeth could clamp down, a loud howl pierced the air. The ground vibrated with such a force that my body bounded up and down against the muddied landscape.

A jet-black wolf crashed into my captor, sending him flying off me. It was the same elaborate beauty as before. The same wolf that had saved me from the maze, I despaired. It didn't waste any time pouncing on the wolf above me, gripping his neck with its sharp teeth, pulling his throat out.

The brown wolf's body crushed me, drenching me in its blood. I'd scream, but I'd lost all ability to summon any strength as my body withered away, with my life force draining every second that passed by.

The black wolf gripped the limp body and tugged it off me. It turned, staring with those ocean blue eyes, then let out another powerful howl and charged at the other wolves.

I backed away, gripping my arm to stop my blood spurting all over the forest.

My saviour charged forward, flinging another wolf against a rock. I watched as he leapt on top of him, ripping him apart. Closing my eyes, I lay cold, my body relaxing as the pain eased and my soul fluttered away. Breathing slowly, my body paled. I hadn't much time left.

In the distance, several howls screeched through the air. It shook me. The familiarity of them forced me to open my eyes, look up. The black wolf stopped and growled, taking charge of the fight. Digging its teeth into his next victim. The ground vibrated. Trees shook and seven more wolves joined the fight. The scene before me was a mess of tanned browns, deep reds, and charcoal grey. A mix-match of wolves battling to the end. How could he win now? The black one? They severely outnumbered him.

Howls and whimpers broke out as the grey wolf I recognised from the maze broke free of the battle and walked up to me. He whimpered as he came closer, eyes solemn, wide, and saddened. The black wolf growled behind him. Howling loud before he pounced. The grey wolf whimpered as it flung him into the side of a tree trunk.

The black wolf stood above me, protecting my fallen body as blood dripped from his lips. Panting heavy he pulled Aaden's wolf close. Growling at the seven wolves as he stood between me and them. The grey wolf shook its head, walked over to stand in line with the others, and they all looked at one another.

Moments later they shifted, grunting and groaning as their fur disappeared, faces reformed and skin wrapped itself over their human forms. Seven muscular men stood naked before us. I recognised them. Knew them somehow. They were the men from before.

The one that was once the grey wolf stepped forward. My black wolf growled. I pulled myself onto my elbows, wiping the blood from my right eye.

"Willa," he said. His voice is soft and subtle.

My brow furrowed. Which hurt. The black wolf growled again.

"Willa, it's me," he said.

My lips pursed. Who? I didn't know him.

The man to his right stepped forward. "Willa, do you remember?" he asked. His wild blond curls blowing in the wind.

"Shit. Her head!" the redhead said.

I shook my head. "What?" I spoke. My voice was shaken and uncertain.

"Brothers," he said. "We're your brothers!"

The black wolf growled, stepped back, turned to face me, and lowered his head. His silky fur disappeared as he transformed into a man right before my eyes. Not just any man. But a very naked, hot, tanned, and muscular Prince Ethan James Bane.

He bent down before me. His eyes searching my own. "Willa," he said. His voice edged with worry. He gripped my arm and shouted something at the men behind him. My mind numbed as they all shouted at once. The world a blur of broken voices, unspoken words, and deadly secrets. His worried expression was the last thing I saw before I finally closed my eyes and fell into the unconscious dreams of another life and one more death.

Chapter Twenty-Eight
Hela

"Don't you think Rambo looks exquisite in this?" I asked, squealing at the fact Rambo, my pet gorilla, was wearing a made to measure tuxedo. Rambo roared, battering at his chest.

"Now now Rambo, be nice to the dressmaker!"

The young lady was shaking. Her face paled under the light of the moon. "I said, don't you think Rambo looks good?" I asked her again.

She nodded, "yes your majesty!" Her trembling hands gripped the ladder as she climbed up and placed the dickie bow around Rambo's neck. Rambo roared again, hitting her away. The ladder tumbled, as did she. Rambo roared, his canines clearly on display. He jumped up and bounded the ground, smashing his enormous fists onto the dressmaker's petite frame. She screamed, coughing up blood.

"Rambo!" I scolded. "That's naughty! Bad Rambo!"

He turned and looked at me, then groaned, sitting on the floor, nudging the dressmaker.

She lay there crying, choking on her own blood, gasping for breath. Walking over, I inspected her. Hmm. "Oh, Rambo, you've crushed her lungs! That's very naughty! Now how are we going to get this dickie bow finished!"

He groaned, pouted, then roared at the dressmaker, clearly angered at the continuous noises she made. A fist smashing later, and all was quiet in the palace.

"Oh well," I said, stroking Rambo's fur.

"MARCUS!" I yelled. The door flung open.

"Yes, my Queen."

"Fetch another dressmaker. This one had an accident."

Marcus walked over and sighed. "Yes, my Queen."

He ordered two servants to take her body and dispose of it. Leaving Rambo and I in peace.

"So, Rambo, what do you have planned for today?"

He battered his chest. I laughed. "Oh, you are so funny! Care to dance?"

I swirled and twirled around the room, taking Rambo's hand as he jumped up and down in excitement.

"I'll teach you Rambo, come on!"

An excitement of noises escaped him as he spun around to the music of our minds, just like me.

The door flew open. Barnabus walked in, pulling a blindfolded, handcuffed Lucius Daventry behind him.

"Weeeee!" I squealed. "You found him!"

"It wasn't difficult," Barnabus said, pushing Lucius to the floor. "He was still in his shop!"

"Excellent!" I rubbed my hands together. Lifting Barnabas's blindfold, Rambo stood beside me.

Lucius jumped, screeching, as Rambo roared in his face. I laughed.

"So, Lucius, I hear you've been a very naughty boy!"

Barnabus smirked. "Shall I request Edwina's presence?"

"No, please don't!" Lucius begged. "I'll tell you anything!"

"What!" I said. "That's no fun! Keep it to yourself. I'd much rather Edwina extract information!" I pouted.

Barnabus nodded and left the room.

Rambo stood tall next to Lucius. "So, Lucius… what do you think of my Rambo? He looks spiffing in his fantastic tuxedo, don't you think?"

Lucius nodded, whimpering. Rambo jumped up and down, battering his chest.

I grinned. He was right. Rambo looked dashing today.

The door opened, and Barnabus and Edwina walked in. Edwina nodded, walked over to Lucius, whose face paled at the sight of her. I smiled. "Let's begin!"

Edwina smiled, rested her hands on Lucius's head, and her eyes rolled back.

Lucius's body shook. The noise that protruded from his lips was one of pure anguish, a groaning wail as agony took over and he became one with the pain that betrayed him.

Edwina hummed as she held tighter. Lucius's eyes silvered, his nose and ears bled, and the wailing quietened as she took every memory from him.

Letting go, he fell to the floor. A lifeless, empty body with no memory of the life he once held. I grinned as his breathing faltered. Rambo roared, picked him up, and hugged him like a teddy bear. He looked at me, eyes wide. "Yes Rambo, you may keep him for your collection."

Rambo roared again, battered at his new teddy bear, and dragged him across the floor as they left. As they left, Lucius's arm trapped in the door, tearing free from his lifeless body.

"MARCUS!" I yelled. He entered, slipping on Lucius's blood.

"Yes, my Queen."

"Clean that up," I said, pointing to the dead arm.

"Yes, my Queen," he said, ordering a servant to do my bidding.

"So," I said, turning to Edwina. Her eyes were back to normal, and she had a darkened grin over her face. "What did he know?"

"Well Hela, he certainly had a story to tell."

"Go on…" I said, ushering her to sit at the table with me.

Barnabus joined us.

"He knew of a young girl that was adopted by her parents. Found by the rubbish, a slave girl with no home."

My brow furrowed. "So why did they take her in?"

"The previous Duchess could not have children, so the duke bought Willa home as a gift to her. They raised her as their own, well, until wolves killed the Duchess."

My eyes widened. "By wolves you say?"

"Yes, the very wolves that you sent after the Amber Rose pack."

"Oh… I remember that!" I squealed. "I sent them to cause a rift between the two families!" I clapped. "It worked too!" Edwina nodded.

I grinned, then sighed. "It's a small world, isn't it! Who would have thought the woman they killed was Willa's adopted mummy?"

Edwina laughed.

"So, what else did Lucius know?"

"He believes there is something wrong with Ethan."

"What?"

"He has noticed,"

"Had noticed"

"Sorry, your majesty, he had noticed." I grinned, nodding. "That Ethan was drawn to Willa, and Willa to Ethan."

"But it's unheard of for a human and a wolf to be mated," I wretched. "It's vile!"

"Indeed!" Barnabus said, listening in.

Edwina continued. "Ethan is suspecting that he has feelings for Willa."

I growled. "What does that mean for our Danica?"

"It means she must secure the mate bond immediately. If she doesn't, I don't know what will happen to our spell."

"Your spell Edwina!" I growled. "It had better bloody work!"

"It will be Hela. I will reinforce it immediately."

I nodded, scowling.

Edwina upped and left the room. Leaving Barnabus tapping his fingers on the table.

"So Barnabus, care to dance?" I asked, standing up and offering my hand.

"Of course, Hela." he smiled, taking my hand as we swirled and twirled around the room.

Chapter Twenty-Nine
Ethan

It was pure slaughter. The scene before me was a massacre. Every wolf who'd attacked Willa dead. My wolf had frenzied. I'd seen red when I saw how badly they'd hurt her. I couldn't stop even if I wanted to, not that I did. As soon as we'd seen the brutality he'd caused her. Witnessed him biting down on her head; my wolf and I, we'd both snapped. Their bodies in pieces before our eyes. Yet it wasn't enough. The rage still burned within me.

They'd hurt her, my Willa. Death was too easy for the pain they'd inflicted. In one swift motion I placed on the shorts I'd dropped nearby, gently picked her up, and held her close to my chest. She was out cold. Blood flowed freely from the nasty bite to her arm and hand. She was so pale, fragile, and motionless. Her chest rising, slow but steady. There was blood all over her face. Her hair matted covering the teeth marks. I felt bile pull up from my stomach. Anger retched from my throat. I growled in pain at what they'd done to her.

"I'm sorry, Alpha," Aaden said, lowering his head. "There were too many."

I nodded and placed my hand on his broken shoulder. He was a mess. He'd done everything he could to save her. The fact he'd even survived was a miracle. I knew whose fault this was, and it wasn't his. It was mine.

She was mine to protect and if I hadn't been so caught up with Danica, none of this would have happened. My wolf huffed in agreement. He was mad at me too. But he couldn't hate me more than I could hate myself right now.

I turned to see them. All seven of them stood there naked and pissed off.

"Ethan," Darius said. I hadn't seen him since he'd come for Willa at the gate that day.

"What?" I growled. Angry he was anywhere near her.

"Did you not hear what Harper said?"

Of course, I fucking heard it. The whole bloody world probably did too. They think they're her brothers. It's got to be another ruse, staged to take every last thing I cared for. Wasn't it enough that they'd destroyed Layla all those years ago? Now they wanted her. My Willa. My wife!

I scowled at them. My eyes narrowed, breath heavy. "I heard you," I said.

"It's true," Darius said.

"Like fuck it is, you've got two sisters, Darius, and Willa isn't one of them!"

Harper stepped forward, his red hair glinting in the light. "Don't you remember?" he said. "Our mother was pregnant when you betrayed us."

"WE BETRAYED YOU!" I roared.

Darius stepped forward and pulled Harper back. "Now isn't the time," he said, looking at Willa. Her injuries worsened by the minute.

Aaden placed his bloody hand on my arm. "Alpha, we need to get her back to the pack house."

Shit. He's right. And he didn't look too colourful, either. There was so much blood, it surprised me he had any left to give. He was wavering, too. Struggling to stand. He needed help as much as Willa did.

"This isn't finished," Darius yelled as they turned away. "You'd better protect her, Ethan!" He growled as his brothers pulled him away.

Fuck! Didn't he think I knew that. I'd screwed up. I'd never do it again. Holding Willa close, breathing in her scent. Lavender and roses. I swooned as I picked up the pace. Aaden hobbling behind. Alaric ran up.

"Take Aaden," I yelled, sprinting past with Willa.

Alaric nodded and provided himself as a crutch to Aaden.

We needed to get to the pack house, and we needed to get there now!

Running through the gardens, two ladies turned and gasped. Shit. She was a sight. She had lost way too much blood. There had to be some way of saving her! If I didn't replace it soon, she'd bleed out and there would be nothing I could do!

That's it! I'm O negative. I can give her mine!

Get the medical supplies out. I need to donate my blood to Willa; I yelled through the mind link.

Xander replied. Onnit Alpha!

As I stepped into the brotherhood house, a few surprised gazes flew my way. Xander ran in with the direct transfusion kit. It was dusty. We'd tried nothing like this before. I pulled it open. Two cannulas, some sterile gloves, clear tubing, micropore tape and a set of instructions. What the fuck! I stared over at Xander. He shrugged his shoulders.

Tristan walked in, talking to Wyatt. I laid Willa on the table. "Fuck man, what happened?" He said rushing over.

Alaric trudged in with Aaden. Wyatt grabbed his other arm, helping him to a chair. Wyatt turned to face me. "Alpha, why is the human here?" he asked, his tone edged with disapproval.

I snapped my head to glare at him. Teeth bared; fists pummelled. Aaden shot up, groaning, standing between us.

"That human is your Princess!" he said. His shoulders tensed as he gripped the table to steady himself. "She risked her life to save me. Took out a wolf by herself. I'd be dead if it weren't for her!"

My chest swelled with pride. Willa fought to protect one of my own, risking her own life knowing she was no match for a wolf.

"Shit!" Wyatt said, nodding in admiration. He took a deep breath. "Sit down Alpha. I've seen how to do this before."

I nodded, sat down, and rolled up my sleeve. Wyatt inserted one needle into me. I jolted, growling at him.

Tristan burst out laughing.

"Shut it!" I yelled; my fist now unclenched.

Wyatt inserted the other needle into Willa's vein. Attached the tube to me, then sucked on the other end of it. "What the fuck Wyatt! Where have you seen this before?"

Wyatt got the blood to flow, spat out the end, and quickly attached it to Willa's needle. "YouTube," he said, grinning a bloody grin.

"Damn it, man," I said, sitting back in the chair. I sat watching Willa's chest rise and fall. Her breathing is slow, yet stable. Colour rushed back to her cheeks. Her body heated as she soaked up my blood.

"She's accepting it Alpha," Alaric said, stepping forward and placing his hand on my shoulder. I nodded, smiling.

"Accepting what?" the Grand Duke said as the door flew open. There stood my father, mother, and Nic, my annoying younger brother.

Alaric stepped forward. "Father, he had no choice."

"What happened?" my mother asked, her voice shaking as she spoke.

Father walked in. Stood at the table, looking down on Willa. "Who did this?"

I shook my head. "I don't know. There were five of them."

Aaden stepped forward. "I'm sorry Grand Duke. It was my fault. I couldn't protect her!"

Father gripped the side of the table. "Are you telling me, Ethan, that you let your wife enter the vale with only one guard?"

Shit. He had me there. I nodded, lowering my head. "I fucked up!"

Mother growled. Fathers' eyes widened; teeth bared. "You sure did."

Nic walked over and lifted the tube of blood that flowed from my arm to Willa's. "Err, what's this for? Looks like a torture device." He grinned.

I glared at him. "She'd lost too much blood," I said, taking Willa's hand. It had warmed up some more. It's working. I smiled.

"What if she rejects it?" Mother asked, her face filled with worry. She walked over to Willa's side and placed her hand on her forehead.

"She won't mother. She's already so much better! Look!" I said, showing them the teeth marks on the side of Willa's forehead. They were already healing. I sighed with relief. Willa was getting better. I could never make this up to her. But for her to accept my blood. It meant there was a new future in store. One that somehow also involved my mate, Danica. I scratched my head. Was it possible to fall in love with two people at the same time? My eyes widened. Shit. Does that mean I love her? My wife. My Willa.

Willa groaned beside me. I stood up quickly. The room span as I grabbed the table. Willa opened her eyes. Forest green irises stared up at me.

My heart skipped a beat as my name escaped her delicate lips.

"Ethan?" she rubbed her eyes.

I nodded, pulling the needles from our arms. Xander placed a plaster on Willa's, and I shooed him away.

I looked down at her. Her beautiful body was lying before me. She was the perfect picture of health, as her body had healed rapidly.

"What happened to me?"

"Don't you remember?" I asked, staring down at her serene, porcelain face.

She shook her head, then winced.

"Rest now, we can talk later." I said, caressing her cheek. She closed her eyes, disappearing into the land of dreams. I picked her up, smiling as I carried her to our bed. Finally, all felt right with the world.

Entering the room, I gently laid her down, covered her over, and sat beside her. My mind replayed the events that took place. Were they in Council? Had Hela sent them to take Willa to the palace? No, they'd stunk of whisky. Just some rogue pack members wanting to play with their food.

Assholes! If I could kill them again, I would!

I sighed, thinking about her lifeless body. Then… my eyes widened; hands gripped the bedspread. Wait! The Amber Rose brotherhood was there. They're her brothers! What the actual fuck!

Chapter Thirty
Willa

The hammer drill continued as I woke from my dream, drilling down into my skull, searing pain shooting across and down over my body. Nerves ignited; electrical spasms connected my nervous system. Something was charging through. Pulling and shoving at my body, wrapping its claws into my skin. Deep inside I'd awoken, like never before. It felt as though this was meant to be, yet what it was I didn't know. All I knew was the face before me. My Husband. My Ethan.

I blinked twice as Duchess Bernadette turned off the bedroom light. "Is that better?" she asked. I nodded. "I'll tell Cleo you're awake, she's been worrying."

Ethan thanked his mother. She smiled, picked up the washcloth and bowl, and left the room.

"Is she okay?" I asked.

Ethan looked at me. His brow furrowed. "Who my mother?"

I nodded. He smiled. "Yes, she's fine. She was helping me clean your face. You still had blood in your hair."

"Oh!"

Ethan sat forward. "Do you remember what happened?"

I nodded and shook my head, then winced. I must have looked crazy. Heck, I was crazy. What do you call a wannabe Princess that visualises men turning to wolves?

"I think I need a doctor!" I said, as clear as day.

Ethan gripped my hand. "Why? What's wrong?"

"I think I need my head checking, Ethan!"

"Oh, no it's fine. The bite marks have healed," he said, smiling.

"No, not that… wait… did you say bite marks?" He nodded. "So, it was real?" I sat back in the bed, pulling the cover up to my neck. My arm was covered in old scars. Old… bite marks?

"Yes Willa. You saw wolves. It was all real."

I gulped. Nausea hit, purging my body of its sins. "Bowl!" I yelled.

Ethan grabbed me, placing the bin in front of me. I threw up.

"That's gross Willa!" He put the bin down.

I smirked, wiping my mouth. "In sickness and health Ethan."

He snarled. I grabbed his arm, running my hand up it. I knew what he was. What he could be. But it didn't scare me. It made me feel safe. "I don't remember werewolf being in the marriage contract?"

He smirked.

"So, did you really kill all those people?" I asked.

He nodded. "It was us or them. You've entered a new world now."

"A new world? What are you on about?" I asked, frowning.

He laughed, "humans live their lives thinking they're at the top of the food chain, when in real terms… they're far down at the bottom of it!"

"Well, that's a scary thought," I uttered. Ethan turned to me, stroked my arm, and sat back on the bed.

I huffed, "it must be a dream… you're being nice to me!"

He growled.

"So that's what all the growling's about, your inner wolf's been itching to get out."

His eyes narrowed. "Really Willa, you're hard work!"

"I aim to please!" I smirked. "So, what's this all about, a spooky new world," I said, sitting upright in bed, intrigued.

His brow furrowed. "I'm not telling you unless you take this seriously!"

I laughed. "You huff way too much for a man Ethan, is it a wolf thing?"

"Willa!" he growled.

"Fine. Go ahead. I'll be serious," I sighed. Jeez, he was grouchy today!

He nodded and relaxed on to the bed more. "Well, there are werewolves, us," he said, smiling. "But there's also other supernatural's. Witches, for example… They've been around since the birth of time. They keep to themselves. Except for Arwen, she has been allied with our family since we saved her daughter from the Pyres all those years ago."

"Pyres?"

"Witch trials."

"Shit! How old are you?"

He laughed, "not that old! It was my ancestors." He smiled. "But we can live for much longer than a mere human."

"Wait. Really?" He nodded. "So, I'm going to be an ancient, wrinkled oldie and you'll be this age?" I gagged. "That's so wrong Ethan!"

He laughed. "It's not like that, we can slow down our aging, but not stop it."

"Oh…" I pouted. "That's still as bad."

He laughed. "Anyway, that won't matter in a minute."

"What? Why?"

"Well, are you going to let me finish?"

I groaned. "Okay, but have I met Arwen?"

"Actually, you would have… she was at our announcement party."

"Oh." My head lowered.

He smiled, taking my hand in his. "It's fine. She actually quite liked you."

I frowned. "You say it like it's a hard thing to do."

He turned to face me. "No," he smirked. "But all witches are hard to please!"

I smiled, looking into his dreamy, oceanic eyes.

"Do you know others?"

"Yes, but they're Council members. Witches can be incredibly powerful; many have tried to control them. A guy called Crowley tried to weaponize them back in the fifties, but the Council soon saw to that. They're the only ones who've succeeded though."

I sat listening, gazing down at the sheets. Satin red flowed through my fingertips. I relaxed my grip, and the cover fell down, revealing my bloodied swimming costume. He stopped and stared at me. His body tensed as he breathed heavily, hunger in his eyes. Moving his hands to trace over my waistline, then to my back, he gripped me behind. I could feel the pull between us, an unearthly magnetism grasping at each of our bodies, and at that moment, I knew, somehow, we were meant to be.

I leaned into him, eliminating the last shred of space between us. He looked deep into my eyes, his stare hungry, begging for more. Putting my arms around him, our bodies merged. My bare skin kissing him as he growled, pushing me down on the bed, lifting off his shirt, wrapping his powerful arms around me.

Our lips touched, and his tongue explored every part of my mouth. Pulling back, he sucked my lower lip, placing kisses down my neck. His teeth nip at my skin, finding their way to the strap of my swimming costume, bringing it down off my shoulders. I groaned as my breasts were uncovered. His lips latch onto my nipple. I moaned, lips parted, a gasp escaping me. Arousal flows within as he licks and sucks my breasts, leaving a love bite here and there. Wriggling below him, my hips raise, eager for more.

He grabs my waist, positioning me under him. With one hand gripping his back and the other lower down, I felt for his erection, finding it pushing hard against his trousers. Pulling at his belt and unhooking his button, I stroked it. He groaned, kissing me faster. Pulling his trousers over his hard buttocks. He looked up, his expression softening as he searched my eyes. "Are you sure?" I nodded. Biting my bottom lip.

He grinned, kicking off his trousers, grabbing my legs, and pulling me down to the bottom of the bed. I laughed, unhooking my arms from my swimming costume. Kneeling on the floor, he rips the material down and off, tossing it over his shoulder before sliding his tongue across my thigh, kissing and suckling, one inch at a time. I tense as his fingers find themselves inside me, moving up and around. Urgent moans escape me when he slides two fingers up and down, causing an intense friction inside. Whimpering, I buck my hips up, crying out for more. Ethan nipped at my thighs, teeth grazing the skin as he moved over me, his tongue sliding down, tracing around my clit, sucking it in his mouth.

Growling, he slides his fingers out, "Fuck you're so wet!" his blue eyes meet my own and he licks his lips, climbing on top, kissing me hard and fast. His hand moves to my breast. His mouth delicately kisses down my neck, hovering for a moment, teeth bared as he playfully nips my skin. Groaning, I arch up, urging him inside.

Growling, his torso vibrates, his erection pushing against my thigh. Biting my bottom lip, I grip harder. Nails digging in. Wanting, no, needing more. Grabbing my neck, he holds me in place. "Do you want more?"

Oh God, I want more! I raise my legs, roll my hips, and he positions himself, thrusting deep inside. I gasp as a sharp pain tinged inside. My stomach tightens, and I arch up, curling my chest into his. This was it. The moment I'd been waiting for. The moment I'd saved myself for. He was mine, and I was his.

He pounded up and down, thrusting quicker, harder, deeper, as I screamed in ecstasy. The eternal bliss I felt when he was inside me was everything I ever hoped it could be. My legs trembled, and I gripped his buttocks, pushing him deeper inside. The only sounds around us were the bed as it banged against the wall, my moans and the wet sounds of our bodies connecting. Ethan pulled at my hair, tugging my head back, lips trailing down my neck. I moved my hips in time and he thrust in faster, deeper still. Gripping him harder, I feel myself reaching my peak. My stomach tightens, and I tense, weightless, in the moment.

The intensity of pleasure rippled through my body. Sweet moans escaped my lips. A flood of ecstasy blasted through me, every cell igniting. I climaxed seconds later, tensing inside, pushing his body to the brink. Gripping hard with my nails, I scream out, biting down into his arm. He continues to thrust deeper, even more aroused by the screams that escaped me. The orgasm lasted longer, his body moving faster. A breathy moan leaves my lips as my legs' grip harder.

"Ethan!" I cry out, as it becomes too intense. Every part of me exploding in a display bigger than any you'd seen on Bonfire night.

I tensed, then released as he came. His body arching upwards, stiffening, as he let out a powerful roar, loud enough to wake any and every person in the castle.

I laughed as he pulled himself out and off me. Stars floating across the ceiling. My vision an epic fantastical symphony of colours and blurred images.

"Wow!" I said, still laughing.

"Fuck me!" he said, collapsing next to me.

"That was better than I ever expected!" I exclaimed. My cheeks still flushed from our rampant activities.

He sat up on his arm, his brow furrowed. "Was that your first time?"

I nodded, still smiling.

He smiled a smile that even the Cheshire Cat would envy. He kissed me on the lips, pulled me into his arms and we fell softly, safely and satisfyingly to sleep.

Chapter Thirty-one
Willa

As I awoke, night had turned to day. Rays of sunlight cast down, sharp lines cutting through the gap in the curtains. A gust of wind blasted through the open window, wrapping itself around every inch of the room, tendrils of light trickling over my bare body. I shivered as I rubbed my eyes, blinking a few times, focusing on the naked body next to me. Ethan. He snored, his growls erupting in his throat. My body relaxed as I buried my head into his chest. Wrapping his arm around me, he woke, pulling me in closer.

Stretching, he planted a kiss on my forehead. "Morning, beautiful," he said, smiling.

I looked up, losing myself in his dreamy, oceanic blue eyes. I smiled. This moment right here… it was perfect.

"Are you hungry?" he asked.

"Famished," I said, grinning.

"Ah, so you've worked up quite the appetite?" he smirked.

I laughed, sitting myself upright. "And who is to blame for that?"

He looked side to side and held his hands up, smirking. I frowned, laughing. A grin ravished his face as he sat up and pulled me in close, kissing me deeply. As we came up for air, I sat back, staring at him.

"What?" he asked, puzzled.

"I'm just thinking," I said, smiling at him.

He sat forward and took my hand, tracing his fingertips around my palm. I squealed, pulling my hand away. "Ah, ticklish then?" He winked, then launched at me, tickling me.

Squealing, I hit out at him, playfully pushing him away. "Back off," I squealed, hiding beneath the sheets.

Ethan laughed. "So, what do you want to do today, Princess?" he asked as he sat upright, gazing at me.

I smiled, "well there's a few things I'd like to know first…"

His brow furrowed. "What's that?"

"Well," I said sitting forward, "Can you carry on telling me about the supernatural?"

"Oh, so you're intrigued, are you?"

I smiled, nodding.

"Well, besides werewolves and witches, there are also shifters. Now shifters can appear as innocent as they come, but they can be nasty sons of bitches. You never can see their true face. Shifters live their life however they see fit and with whomever's skin fits best." I shuddered.

"Shit!"

"Exactly!" he sighed. "There are also demons, not like the ones on TV, with a human appearance. No, they screwed these demons over at birth. They literally come out like in the first story books, with red skin, point tails and forked tongues." He laughed as my eyes widened. Smiling he continued, "they're mardy creatures too, and you'd never want to cross one. They hold a grudge for all time."

My eyes widened. "Jeez, so they're like really red, with horns and tails?" I smirked.

"Ah, but don't forget the evilest of all the supernatural's. The ice-cold vampires. They run the Council with Hela. Some call them the Dark Ones, which suits, as they're as creepy as fuck!"

"Vampires are real?" I said, intrigued.

He laughed. "What, so you're not intrigued by werewolves, but vampires…"

I smirked. "Well, all those films and books… are they like the books?"

"Ha, no! They definitely don't sparkle!" he laughed. "They're also nasty assholes. I'm yet to meet a nice one!"

I laughed. "Fair enough, so are all your family part of this Council I've heard mentioned?"

He sat back. "Damn, no! They're the route of all evil. Hela is a hybrid. As nasty as they come. She's the only ever hybrid that's been born. She's part wolf, part vampire, and therefore immortal. I mean us wolves, we can slow our ageing down. But not like vampires, they live until they're killed." He shrugged, "and the killing part, is the part I like best!"

"So, what's the Council do then?"

"Hela wants to purify the races. I don't know why, considering she's far from pure. But she orders the mutilation of all lesser beings."

I shuddered. "What like humans?"

"Yes, and everything else."

My brows raised, "so am I in danger?"

"You were. The Council had demanded an audience with you. But you're not now?"

"Why not?"

His eyes narrowed, and he stared at me. "Err… the only way I could save you was to give you my blood."

"Okay, gross… but thank you, I think."

"That means you've changed."

"What do you mean, changed?" I asked, looking down at my body.

He smiled. "You're a werewolf now, Willa, you're one of us!"

I froze. Breathing halted. Movement stopped. Everything ended. "Well Shit…"

Ethan laughed and sat back.

"A werewolf… really?" He nodded.

"Crap… like fangs and fur and four paws?" He grinned, nodding.

"Shit." I said, looking down at my hands. "And claws?" He nodded again, chuckling.

I paused, staring down at my body. "So, what does that mean?"

He smiled, closing the space between us. Holding my neck, he pulled me in and kissed me. My heart drummed harder, breathing fast and shallow. I wanted him. Wolf or no wolf. I wanted him. He pulled away.

I huffed, crossing my arms. He smirked. "So, I'm a werewolf?" He nodded. "Can you tell me more about your kind?"

He smiled. "My kind… and now yours." I frowned, pouting.

"So, what does it mean, Ethan?"

He grinned. "How about I show you, not tell you?"

I smiled, nodding in encouragement.

He jumped off the bed, his naked body highlighted by the summer sun streaming through the open window. He stretched, jumped up and down, his cock flapping in the wind. I laughed, he smirked. It looked like he was warming up for a triathlon or something!

"Well, get on with it then!" I shouted, smirking.

He turned, narrowing his eyes. "It's not like I usually shift on demand, you know."

"Aww, do you have stage fright?" I asked, laughing.

He turned to face me, growled, and shifted into a huge jet-black wolf. Growling, he padded his way over to the floor. I should be scared… right? But how could I be? This gorgeous furry beast had saved my life and made me his. I'd never felt safer!

I swung my legs off the bed and my feet hit the cold wooden floor, only to be warmed by his silky fur as he brushed up against me. His body towered over my own as I sat there on the bed, his stature one of power, dominance, and greatness. Hot breath tinged my face, and he nuzzled into my neck, fangs brimming with my collarbone. I shuddered as the scent of arousal caressed my body.

I gripped his fur, pulled him into my neck, urging him closer.

Mate!

The voice caressed through my mind. He was indeed my mate, my one and only and from what I can gather we were in this together, forever, now, and always, and with that he growled, deep, heartfelt, and lovingly as he sank his canines into my neck marking me as his forever more.

Chapter Thirty-two
Ethan

The seduction of my mates' warm blood flowed freely in my mouth. My wolf had chosen, and he'd chosen well. With Willa it came naturally. My inner wolf purred, pulling away as my mate groaned in pleasure. My body pulsated, nerves ignited, muscles stretched and shaped into the form of my human body. But with this change came the realisation of the fantasy world I'd lived in. Staring into those emerald green eyes, I knew. Willa was always mine. Her body was made only for me. Her scent caressed my nostrils, breathed into my lungs as I absorbed her very essence. I needed her touch again so badly, her body corrupting my nature like a drug to a junky.

She smiled, lent forward, and kissed me. I was besotted by her, it was physically impossible to pull myself away, so she did it for me.

"Ethan?" she said, her porcelain face lit up as I greeted her with a nod and a smile.

"Are you okay Princess?" I asked, sitting my naked ass down on the bed beside her.

She nodded, grinning, looking down at my manhood.

"Oi, eyes up here," I said, smirking.

"Or what?" she asked.

I grinned, turned, and jumped on top of her, my manhood standing to attention. She grinned, pushing me backwards. "Back off, Mr!" she yelled, laughing as I tickled her.

In a mere second, my world collapsed. The fantastical view I had of mate-hood diminished as the bedroom door flung open. Willa screamed, gripping the red satin sheet, covering herself as she backed into the headboard. Right there, silhouetted by the beaming stream of sunlight from the corridor, stood my voluptuous brown-haired beauty with anger in her eyes.

"ETHAN!" she yelled, running forward.

"What the hell Danica!" I said.

The room became hazy, spinning in circles. She ran and ran. Two, then three Danica's blurred before my eyes. What was happening?

Darkness bled through my vision, spotted images streamed through my mind. Four years of history came crashing down. None of it real, the life I'd lived a misshapen memory, manipulated by Danica herself.

Willa screamed as their two bodies clashed together, blood splattering across the bedspread. "Wait!" I yelled. "Stop!" My body still frozen to the spot, eyesight dwindling as the fog of my past distorted my present.

Willa cried out, gripping my arm. I could tell it was her from her gentle touch. She grounded me, and the room slowed the merry-go-round I was riding. Life before me sharpened as I could finally focus on her naked form. Her pale porcelain face had darkened, eyes wide, jaw dropped as she fell to the bed, the side of her face caved in.

Before me stood Danica, a very vile, evil, and twisted Danica. Her body repulsed me, and no matter how hard I tried, I could not understand how I'd ever seen her as an equal. She was beautiful, but her beauty disgusted me. She was simply severe to look at. Her tone of voice screeched inside my head. Even her odour sent shivers down my furious form.

I stood up, gripped her wrist, taking the bloodied candlestick from her thick brutish hand.

"ALARIC!" I yelled, demanding an audience with my Beta. Danica screamed and spat at me. Alaric ran in, panting.

"What the fuck?" he yelled, grabbing the demonic Danica off of me.

"Take her and get help!" I yelled, rushing to Willa's unconscious side.

He nodded and pulled her from the room. Tristan ran in. His face paled, jaw dropped. "What happened, man... did you murder your bride?" he asked, puzzled.

My eyes narrowed. "Course I fucking didn't! Tristan, help me with her!"

"You need the doctor, man."

"Go get him!"

Tristan nodded and ran from the room. I slid over the bed and held Willa's bloodied body in my arms, resting her head on my lap. Her beautiful face was broken, eye socket set back, cheekbone cracked, lip bloodied and swollen. Her red hair appeared to soak up her vibrancy as her life force bled out of the wound to her forehead.

Danica had tricked me. Somehow over the last four years she had taken over my mind and moulded it to her will. I'd followed her freely, without remorse, and with not knowing even my own true self. No wonder my wolf had always hidden away. He'd hated her. He'd seen the truth, but my stubborn human side could not see it. Whatever magic she had cast on me had taken my soul and entwined it to hers. It would have carried on too. I would have continued on the soulless journey of this fantastical life. Living a lie for so many years and to say I was hot damn angry was a fucking understatement. I sighed, taking a deep breath. But now wasn't the time. I looked down at my bloodied mate. My Willa.

My mate had freed me from the claws of she-devil Danica Daventry. Her being here had made my heart open. I felt for the first time. Really felt. Danica had corrupted me, taken over my life, and beat me down. Fuck! I sighed, staring down at Willa, already healing. Damn, that's fast! I can't wait to meet her wolf, my Luna.

My brow furrowed as I watched her.

Her eyes graduated forward. Cheekbone reshaped and blossomed. Lips uncut and rose red. Forehead stitched up, knitted together and fresh. There she lay, within my grasp, the most beautiful person I had ever seen, Willa Rose.

Fluttering eyelids opened. Vibrant emerald green eyes shone. Rose-red lips curled upwards and the exquisite creature before me smiled. I took a deep breath, stroked the side of her face, and lent down to kiss her.

"How?" I asked. She shrugged and smiled, sitting up.

The doctor ran in, stopped, and looked around for a body. I waved him off as he tutted and walked out. Tristan ran in after him.

"What the heck, man!" he said, skidding to a stop.

"I know!" I said, staring at Willa.

Willa's brow furrowed. "What's wrong?"

Tristan stepped towards her. "Err, what's right, love. Your body was out cold a minute ago. Face smashed in, blood everywhere. No wolf can heal that fast!"

"Don't you mean Luna?" Ethan said.

"Shit really!" Tristan said.

"What?" Willa asked.

Tristan smirked. "you're his Luna, he marked you."

"Oh, right that… okay!"

She looked at me, brow furrowed. I nodded, then snapped my head to Tristan. "Tristan leave us." He shrugged, nodded, and left the room muttering, closing the door.

"Ethan?"

"Yes Willa…"

"Did I die?"

"I'm not sure Willa," I said, frowning.

"So, what happened? Is Danica dead?"

"I wish!"

"Wait! What! I thought you loved her," she said.

I smiled, sighed, and moved closer to her. "No Willa. You broke the spell. Danica was a traitor; she had manipulated my mind for over four years!" I shook my head, seething as my inner wolf growled."

"Wow Ethan! How the hell did that happen?"

"I don't know, but when I find out I will cut down every single person who aided that treacherous bitch!"

Willa sat back, took a moment, then scooted up next to me. She cupped my chin, drew my face to hers, and kissed me hard. The taste of her flowed into my mouth, exciting my senses and arousing my body to epic proportions.

Drawing back, she smiled. "I'm glad you're free now!" she said.

"Me too."

Willa stood up and took my hand, pulling me over to the en-suite. She turned on the hot water. We stepped in, cleaning away our past lives, and stepped into our new life together, mated and in love.

Chapter Thirty-three
Willa

Another day passed. A day of both pleasure and pain. The sexual gratification of my lover turned into my senses, and the pain of the betrayal he had lived through for all those years. He didn't seem hurt by it, more angered at the injustice he had suffered by the hands of the Council itself. He had thought he was living his best life, when really, he had lost four years to fake emotions and manipulated memories. It wasn't living; it was surviving.

Living meant more than being alive. There were many people I'd known throughout life that ate, drank, breathed, and went through the steps of life, but never actually lived. Not for themselves anyway. I sighed, looking down at the snoring Alpha by my side. I hadn't truly known what living meant until I'd stepped foot in this Castle.

Marrying Ethan was the best thing I could have ever done, even with it being punishment or payback from my adopted family.

Smiling, I sat upright, staring down at his tanned torso, chiselled jawline, deep, scrumptious lips. Hmm, the very sight of him had me tingling for more.

The morning light touched his body in every place I wanted to. Wild hair wrapped around his neck, teetering on the edge of his ears. His shoulders were built like a gladiator, solid, yet cushioned enough for me to curl myself into. My fingertips tickled over his arm, tip toed over his shoulders, and pinged him on the nose. He woke up sniffling. "What the?" he asked, his expression softening as he saw my amused face.

"Did you just flick my nose?"

"I might have," I said, chuckling.

"Well, that's that then!" he boomed, sitting upright and pouncing on top of me, holding my hands above my head, kissing me.

"Burgh, morning breath!" I said as I wriggled out from under him.

"Oh, don't you like it?" he asked, breathing out over my face.

I gagged, jumping up from the bed, grabbing his arm and pulling his heavy body towards me. "Go brush your teeth you dirty hound!" I laughed, pushing him towards the bathroom.

"Hound!" he laughed. "I'm a wolf!" He pulled me in after him, handed me a toothbrush and demanded I also brush my own teeth. To be fair, he had a point. My breath wasn't exactly rosy this morning!

After washing and dressing, we adjourned to the banquet hall. Meeting Bernadette and Oswald for breakfast. They were both deep in a heated conversation and when we entered Bernadette's expression saddened.

"How could we have not known?" she asked as we sat down beside them.

With a sullen expression, I placed my hand on her shoulder.

"From what Ethan tells me, no-one could have known!"

She took my hand in hers. "I am so sorry this has affected you, Willa." Tears escaped her vibrant blue eyes.

Shaking my head, I closed the space between us and held onto her. "It was no-one's fault Bernadette, and it has all worked out in the end." I said, pulling away. She nodded, noticing the mark. Oswald placed his hand in hers.

"Today we will find out what that traitor knows," Oswald stated, taking a sip of black coffee. "For now, though, we build our strength and eat." He ushered for us to take a helping of cereal and pastries from the table. I nodded, smiling, and stood up to fill my coffee from the machine behind.

Ethan laughed, beating me to it. "You know we have waiters to serve us?" he smirked.

I gave him a sarcastic smile. "You know I'm quite capable of fetching my own coffee!" I poured myself and Ethan a cup. "See, that wasn't so hard, was it?" I snarled, smirking afterwards. Ethan slapped me on the bottom as we walked back, laughing.

Nic walked in. "Morning," he said in a chirpy voice.

"Morning Nic," I said, sitting down and taking a pain au chocolat.

"French today, I see?" he asked, nodding at the pastry.

"Indeed, would you care for one?"

"Oh, no." He shook his head. "Have you seen the French ladies, they're not to my liking."

"Nic! Don't be so vile," Bernadette scolded. Ethan sat down and slapped him on the back of his head. Nic choked on his coffee.

"What mother!"

"That was one girl from camp, Nic," Ethan said, laughing. "Just because she didn't kiss you under the maple grove you've hated them ever since."

"Have not!"

"Have so!" Ethan replied, smirking.

I sat forward. "Oh boys, you are both as bad as each other," I said. Everyone laughed.

"See, she fits right in," Nic said, winking at me.

Alaric came in chasing a very loud giggling, Cleo. "HELP!" she squealed, running up to me and hiding in my arms.

Alaric stopped dead. "Fine," he smirked. "But I'll get you back later you little squirt."

I smirked. "Why don't you sit next to me, Cleo?"

"Thanks! Ooo Ethan bit you! Was it nice?" she asked. Alaric and Nic looked over. Alaric nodded to me and smiled. Nic grinned.

I smirked. "I'll tell you when you're older."

She huffed. "Can I have a coffee?"

I laughed as Bernadette choked on hers. Oswald growled as he read the newspaper. "I think that's a no," I said, smirking.

Cleo stuck her bottom lip out and pouted. The waiter smiled and poured her an orange juice, filling her bowl with cereal and milk. "Thanks, Mr," she said with the biggest smile.

"So," Oswald said, looking over the table. "Where's Tristan?"

Ethan scowled. "He's with her."

Oswald nodded. "And what has he found out?"

Ethan went silent, eyes narrowed. "He said she wants to talk to me."

My eyes widened. "Huh? How do you know that?"

Nic laughed. "Mind link, baby wolf. You've got a lot to learn"

I snarled at him. He laughed more.

"Are you going?" I asked Ethan. He sighed, placing his head in his hands. I reached across the table to him. He looked up. "How about I go with you?"

Bernadette shook her head. "No Willa, you've been through enough at the hands of that girl."

I nodded. "Yes, but I'd like to know why she tried to have me killed."

Ethan glared. "Do you think Danica sent the wolves that attacked you?"

"Of course, she did, who else would?"

Ethan's brow furrowed. "It doesn't sound like something she would do." He paused. "But then again…"

"Did you really just vouch for her?"

Ethan laughed and shrugged his shoulders. "Bad habits die hard Princess." I narrowed my eyes and thumped his shoulder.

Cleo scoffed, chewing her cereal while talking. "Danica's a horrible person." I smiled, lifting her chin up, so she ate more quietly. Ethan laughed.

"Fine. We'll go together. But you stand behind me at all times," he demanded.

My brow furrowed; lips pursed. "Err no. I'm more than capable of looking after myself."

"That's what I'm afraid of!" he said, frowning.

"Okay, I'll stand beside you, but we both stand back… agreed?"

He nodded, growling.

"It's nice to see someone putting the Alpha in his place," Tristan said, walking in. Ethan stood up and punched him in the shoulder. He laughed.

"Your turn, brother," he said.

He nodded at me. We both stood up, said our goodbyes, and headed to the dungeon below the Castle.

Chapter Thirty-four
Hela

The day had turned severely sinister as Marcus entered the room. One might say, the glorious sunshine shining through the glass corridor would warm the hearts of any hardened soul, but for me it only gave light to my cruel nature. I smirked; my eyes narrowed as I watched Marcus await instruction. It was clearly callous to call oneself cruel. But no doubt that the minds of others agreed with my diagnosis.

Marcus stood in the glass corridor. A frail amber skinned creature with his ruffled blond hair, wrinkled eyeliner and longer than usual forearms. He stepped forward. Blond streaks cascaded under the sunlight, shining through the glass ceiling.

We entered the throne room; Black Onyx pillars framed my view. At my request, they had decorated the room ready for the ball. The celebration of the most powerful Alpha, this side of the Atlantic. Marrying a mere mortal, and not even a princess of that. Her name was Willa, Willa rose, to be exact, where she had come from, no one knew, but where she'll end up. Well, I'd make damn sure everyone would know that! I cackled. My eyes widened with glee.

"Marcus, I said come here."

"Yes, my Queen," he said as he entered the room.

"Now is everything ready."

He nodded. "Everything is, as you asked it to be."

"Good, good," I said, clapping frantically. The evening was going to be simply spectacular, an enchantment of marvellous magnificence. An array of ferocious fire eaters, seductive silk symphonies, and devastatingly deadly dancing. I not only looked forward to the spectacular stage of events, because I cherished the fact that I planned it. I was delighted more in the display of the mortal buffet they would serve later that evening.

It was so simple, so easy. I knew my plan would play out just as I wanted it to. I'd even invited the stupid human population, if only to make Willa feel at home in my palace.

Well, I grinned, licking my lips. I wonder what Prince Ethan would look like. It had been a while since I'd seen him, many years in fact only glimpsing him through the siege of battle when we overthrew the White Kingdom to the South. I'd always kept my eye on him. He was the Alpha to the pack that I'd never been able to turn. The one true kingdom that never faulted or ceased to exist. I tried to turn them to my ways, but no matter what I did, or where I came from, they always had another way out; always one step ahead, whereas I was simply two steps behind. I didn't like to admit it. Weakness was not something I felt any human or supernatural creatures should have. But it was something I gained from my mother, the delight of normality that she was. My father was a monster.

They'd called him The Langer Man back then. But he was Loki, God of all mischief. He enjoyed playing and toying with me all throughout my childhood, only ever present to encourage murder and mayhem. It was his doing that caused my vampiric nature. I sighed. Half smiling, half frowning.

I became a vessel of ultimate power. The first hybrid, the one and only. I tried time and time again to create more hybrids, but they either died or became one or the other, a wolf or a vampire.

No one seemed to be powerful enough, no one seemed to take the venom as well as I had. I always thought that the Alpha Prince Ethan would be my strongest contender. His body was powerful, mind infinite. If anyone could do it, he could. It was only a matter of time though, I'd sent Danica over there many years ago, four in fact. She had won his heart with Edwina's help. But now this mere human was in the way it was simply catastrophic! I had to ensure she didn't destroy my plans and make a fool out of me! I growled, rubbing my hands together.

By the end of the night, Willa rose would no longer exist, and Danica would be his one and only there to pick up the pieces and comfort his highness. I grinned profusely.

"So, Marcus, tell me about the plans for this evening's celebrations."

Marcus nodded and stepped forward. His amber skin illuminated against the Black Onyx pillar he lent against. If it weren't for his frail figure and boring supernatural nature, he might actually have been standing in my court. It was only the fact that I enjoyed watching his withering, amber skin glow that I kept him around. I wasn't even sure what race he actually came from. But there was no doubt I had erased the rest of his race many years ago as I had with all the other impure ones. Marcus grinned. "Well, the festivities will go ahead as planned, with the fire dancers to begin with. Whilst they busy the minds of the crowds, our very own seductresses will siphon the life from every mortal, absorbing their energy, and sashaying them through to the kitchen, seduced by Abaddon's song."

I squealed eagerly as I sat on my throne. My feet tapping on the floor. Bouncing fingers entwined. I leant forward, eager to hear more.

"Well, my queen. After the entertainment has passed and the chef has prepared your meals, it will be time to take your seats and dine."

"Oh, I like the sound of that, Marcus."

"Well, as you know, my Queen, the meal will be exactly as you deemed it to be. With each mortal being served on a plate, ready for our supernatural guests to take their fair share." He smiled, and I nodded, clapping my hands.

"Oh Marcus, you do tease me!"

He grinned. "Princess Willa will most likely disagree with our plans. But I feel it will give her an adequate welcome into our supernatural world."

I howled in joy. Marcus stepped back.

"It's spectacular. Yes. It's simply sinister, scandalous and severe!"

Marcus smiled. "Well, I couldn't have done it without your amazing ideas, my queen."

"Of course, Marcus, of course," I kept smiling at him. "What ever would I do without you."

"I'm sure you would more than thrive, my queen. After all, you are the most powerful person in the whole of the supernatural world."

"Indeed, indeed. I am indeed." I smiled, fidgeting on my throne. "So, do you think she will like my celebration? It's such a beautiful way to bring a daughter of light into the darkness, don't you think?"

"I believe she will be ecstatic, my queen. Completely overjoyed… at least at the start of it." He smiled, leaning on the onyx pillar again. "Have you had a thought about what you're going to do with her?"

I sat there, silent for a moment. Lips pursed, fingers tapping. "Well, I'm not sure which would be more significant… the rack, or Prince Ethan, to see her flesh ripped from her precious little body?" I squealed again, jumping up. "Ooo then, we could serve her limbs to every supernatural creature as dessert? Leaving her simple little head to prince Ethan himself. I think that will go down fantastically. Don't you think Marcus?"

Marcus grinning like a Cheshire Cat. "I'm sure it will, my Queen."

I clapped, "So go Marcus. I have many plans to put in place. It's going to take quite a few hours to even get ready for this celebration!"

"Of course, my Queen," he said as he bowed and walked out, closing the door behind him.

It was simply spectacular. I was going to be the one to end the stupid princess's life. Then my little prodigy Danica will be the one to pick up the pieces of our broken prince, weaving everything into place. He would have no choice but to join me, as after he'd marked Danica. I would threaten her life, which of course she knew about and would play along. And then he'd only have one choice to save her, and that would be to join me. I squealed again, swirling and twirling around the room.

Chapter Thirty-five
Willa

I'd never been to the Dungeon before, and I was quite thankful for that fact. Walking down the spiral staircase, we entered a dank, dark lair that looked like it had been built centuries ago. I hated to think of the people that were held here through the years.

Straw covered the muddied floor as we walked past two empty stone cells, rusted bars shaped the gates in place, as both stood wide open. Torches were lit against every wall. I stopped and peered inside. Ethan stood beside me, watching as I examined the area before us. The light of the midday sun penetrated the cell from a small, barred window. Every cobweb shimmered and sparkled. In the corner a rack stood against the wall, dusted and semi-covered with a ragged brown sheet. My eyes widened; jaw dropped. Did they torture people here?

"Bloody hell, Ethan, tell me you don't use that thing?"

Ethan frowned. "No… although, it may come in useful for Danica."

"You can't be serious!"

He huffed. "Fine. No, but she needs to pay for what she's done."

"I agree, but there's the police for that, Ethan!"

His expression lightened as he placed his hand on my shoulder and smiled. "Princess, that's for humans. Things are different now you're a wolf."

I stepped back. "So, who governs the supernatural?"

He sighed. "Well, Hela tried to, but her reign is brutal. The Council hunts and kills every supernatural deemed below their perfection." I shuddered. "So, we follow our own system here. We will hear Danica out, find out what she knows, then send her to FALCON for questioning."

"FALCON?"

"It's a long story, but the short end of it is that they are an elite force of supernaturals and humans that have joined to bring peace between the races."

"Okay, so surely we should ask them to question her?" I asked, shuddering while looking over the rack again.

Ethan growled.

"Quit growling at me," I snapped.

His eyes widened, and he took a step back. I frowned at him, annoyed.

Holding up his hands, he nodded. "Okay, but it's kind of an automatic response Willa,"

I smirked. "Well, get it under control Ethan."

His expression softened, and the corner of his lips curled upwards. I stepped forward and kissed him gently on the lips. Wrapping his arms around my waist, he pulled me in tighter.

"Hot damn, you get me going so easily," he growled.

I smirked, pulling back. "Right, let's get this over with."

Nodding, he took my hand, and we walked hand in hand to the cell at the far end of the dungeon.

Danica was sitting on a dank mattress on the floor. Her tear-stained face flickered in and out of shadow as a chilly breeze played with the torchlight. Wind swirled through the cell, swarming up a tornado of dust and dirt. I coughed, stepping back. Ethan let go of my hand and ran forward, grabbing Danica by her neck and lifting her up and off the floor. Her legs dangled, feet kicking as her weakened body fought his strength.

"ETHAN!" I yelled, rushing forward, grabbing at his arm.

He turned to me with anger in his eyes. Tears welled, and he softened to my touch, dropping Danica to the ground.

Lighting a couple more torches, the light remained more stable. Ethan stood with his back to the wall, watching my every move. I left the cell and came back with two chairs, one for both of us. Placing them down, I nodded to Ethan. "No, I'll stand," he said, growling past me at Danica.

Danica remained in a heap on the floor. I stepped forward and placed a chair down opposite my own. A good couple of metres between us.

I sat down, motioning for Danica to follow. She growled; her expression filled with hatred. "NOW!" Ethan boomed behind me, making me jump. Turning to him, I frowned. "What?" he said, shrugging. He stepped forward and placed his hands on the back of my chair, fingertips caressing my shoulders. Danica growled, stood up, and sat herself down in the chair.

I looked up at Ethan, motioning to ask what he wanted to know. He sighed, taking his hands from the chair, fists pummelled.

I smiled, "it's okay," I said. He stepped back, his body clearly fighting a change.

"Keep him away from me!" Danica yelled, her chair legs screeching against the concrete floor.

I turned to face her. Her expression was one of distraught. But even though I felt a twinge of sadness for her, I had to remind myself that she had stolen the life of my beloved for the past four years. She had taken him. Toiled with him. Tormented his body and coiled it into her own. Bile wretched in my throat at the thought of it. No wonder Ethan felt so angry with her so nearby. The stench of her scent was putrefying, she reeked of betrayal.

I coughed, swallowing my sick. "Danica." I said. She glared at me. "Why did you do this?"

Her lips curled. "Which bit?"

"To Ethan… why did you cast a spell on him?"

She laughed, her chair wobbling below her force. "I didn't, baby wolf, Hela did."

"Hela's a hybrid wolf and vampire, she's nothing like a witch, you heathen!" Ethan spat.

Danica laughed again. "Hela has an army at her fingertips Ethan, she could crush you and your stupid little family like insects." Ethan growled. "Instead, she wanted to save your souls, bring you into her bosom, just as she did me all those years ago. Without her we would be nothing."

"You stupid girl! What makes you think she would have spared any of us?" Ethan took a step towards her.

"Because she promised me," she spat.

My brow furrowed. "And does she always keep her promises?" I asked.

Danica sat back, her body relaxing into the chair. "Most of the time," she said.

I turned to Ethan and motioned for him to step back from her. "What do you mean?" I asked.

Danica's bottom lip quivered as she looked to the floor. She wiped the tears from her eyes. "She promised me, and my father would be safe."

I leant forward. "You are... aren't you?"

She laughed, wiped her eyes, and sat up straight. "I wouldn't call this safe, would you?"

My eyes narrowed. Lips pursed. "But you are safe. We just want answers then you'll answer to FALCON."

She laughed, looking up at Ethan. "You haven't told her, have you?"

Ethan scowled at her, growling.

"Told me what?" I asked, brow furrowed.

"I'll never make it to FALCON deary. They'll kill me way before them?"

"Huh?" I said, shocked. "Of course, we won't!"

"No! Not you, you stupid whore. The colourless!"

"What now?"

Ethan shook his head and sighed, stepping to my side, looking down to face me. "The Colourless are one of Helas creations." He paused, scratching his head. "Simply put, she created an army of midgets."

I coughed back my laughter.

"Don't laugh at me, bitch! They're coming!"

Swallowing back my laughter, turning to her. "I'm sure Ethan's pack is more than a match for a group of midgets Danica."

"You're so bloody stupid!" she yelled, shaking her head.

Ethan cupped my chin and crouched down beside me. "It's your pack too now."

Danica gagged.

Ethan snarled, kissed me and said, "The Colourless are the toughest form of warriors there are. Their small stature means they can infiltrate even the smallest of spaces. We'd never see them coming."

"Plus, she has hundreds of them!" Danica said.

Ethan nodded.

"But surely we can take on mini humans?"

He smiled, his expression softening at my innocence. "They're not human Willa. They're shadow warriors. Murderous little bastards that can step through the realms and enter any place unseen."

"And don't forget they're highly trained! They're her pet ninjas!" she exclaimed.

"Oh!" I said. "So why hasn't she sent them before?"

"Because she wants him." She pointed at Ethan. "That's why!"

"But what for?"

"Ethan has the most powerful pack this side of the Atlantic. Hela wants power, and she wants her own hybrids. She believes Ethan will help her birth them."

Ethan growled. I shuddered. "So, she wants a mate?"

"She will never have one, Willa!" he said to me.

"She doesn't care that you've mated yourself to that," Danica spat, pointing at me. "She wants hybrid children and will take you and your sperm dead or alive."

"Jeez, this is turning into some wild messed up stalker movie right here!" I said, sitting back, frowning.

Danica laughed. "There's no point fighting it, Willa. She will laugh and bathe in your blood as she takes Ethan for her own."

"Like fuck she will!" I yelled, standing up.

Ethan growled, stepped forward, and pummelled his fists.

"Leave her Ethan. Let the Colourless come for her. She's no use to any of us now!" I yelled, kicking my chair over and storming out of the room to Danica's cruel laughter.

Ethan joined me, wrapping his muscular arms around my body.

"Did you know?" I asked.

"I knew she wanted our pack to join her… but not the reason." How did he not know she wanted him to be her baby daddy? I shuddered. I messed the whole thing up. I couldn't contend with that. She was an all-powerful queen, ruler of the supernatural kind, and a hybrid; and by the sounds of it, completely insane. How could I protect Ethan? Keep him safe? Keep him mine. What's saying she won't have another spell cast on him, destroying everything we know and love?

I sighed. If we sat around doing nothing, we were screwed. "Well, it's no good playing defence, Ethan. It sounds like those nasty little midgets can get in anywhere. We need to play offence."

Ethan's lips curled upwards, and he kissed my forehead.

"Princess… you're a genius!" he said, picking me up into his arms and running out of the room. "Offence it is," he smiled. Kissing me hard.

Chapter Thirty-six
Ethan

So that didn't go down as bad as I thought it would. But being in a cell with Danica fucking Daventry! It was bloody hard! Ripples of shivers rose through my body. I had given up everything for that woman! It makes me sick to the stomach!

"Are you okay?" Willa asked, turning towards me as we walked towards the library.

"Yes." I smiled, taking her hand and spinning her around. Catching her fragile body in my arms, kissing her hard.

She laughed, a sound I welcomed the most amongst all the darkness. Willa was my window of light in the shadowed world we lived in. Without her, everything would have crashed down into the abyss. I sighed, continuing to walk hand in hand. Cleo skipped down the corridor with a wild smile plastered over her face.

"Cleo," I said, capturing her as she skipped by, tickling her sides while she squirmed to get away. She grabbed on to Willa for protection.

"Ethan, Noooo!" she shrieked. Willa laughed, and she laughed hard.

Picking Cleo up, I tossed her over my shoulder and spun her around. She was as light as a feather. "Put me down! Put me down!"

Willa pulled her off and helped her shimmy down my body. "No fair, Ethan!" she said, stomping her right foot down.

"Oh Cleo," I said, laughing. "What are you doing in this dark, dank corridor?"

"I wanted to see if a wolf had eaten Danica yet," she exclaimed, her eyes wide, smiling.

Willa shuddered. "Cleo, we won't murder anyone!"

"But why? She was mean!"

"Because it's not the right thing to do. You should only ever attack to protect yourself or your loved ones."

"Yes, that's why you should make her dead."

Willa smiled. "We've caught her now, there's no reason to hurt her."

I narrowed my eyes. Things were going to be different now Willa was by my side. She'd show me the humanity I much needed to see. Perhaps death wasn't always the answer. I shrugged; brow furrowed. Perhaps death was too easy for the likes of my vicious ex-girlfriend. The Colourless would surely saviour every moment they had with her. It's lucky Willa doesn't know the pain they'd inflict. Or she may choose Danica's death as a mercy.

Cleo huffed. "Okay, so can I go now?" she asked, tugging at my arm.

Smiling, I nodded. "But stay away from the dungeon Cleo, there are monsters down there," I yelled. Cleo shrieked and ran out of sight.

Willa punched me in the arm. "Don't be mean, you scared her!" she said, frowning.

I laughed. "It was meant to; it's better she fear the dungeons then be down there when the Colourless come."

"Are we safe if they come here?"

"No," I said too quickly. Her eyes widened. "Perhaps you should stay by my side every second of the day… just in case."

She smirked. "Is that an invitation?"

I grinned, faced her, and pulled her in close. Roses and lavender engulfed my senses. "Oh, it definitely is!" Closing the space between us, she gripped my back, digging her nails in. Our lips touched, softly at first, then harder as we delved into the depths of each other's mouths, delighting in the taste, growling, holding her tighter.

Willa pulled back. "Weren't you going to show me the library?" she said, smirking.

"Oh, I can think of several things we can do behind the bookshelves." Pulling her vibrant red hair back, planting butterfly kisses all over her neckline.

"Like read books?" she said, her breath hot and rapid.

"Oh, much more than that!" Picking her up, I threw her over my shoulder, running to the library. Willa squealed as we flew down the corridors, passing Nicholas on the way. He laughed, stepping out of the way.

"ETHAN!" she shrieked.

I laughed wholeheartedly. Placing her down beside the grand entrance to our library. Willa punched me on the arm. It tickled somewhat. I smirked, holding the thick oak door open so she could see inside. Willa gasped and walked in, her breath escaping her as she became mesmerised by the library surrounding us.

"This is magnificent!" she said, her feet tip tapping over the tiled floor. Spinning around, she could see rows upon rows of books, old oak shelves spiralling around the tower as far as the eye can see. Each level had a spiral staircase, walking the beholder up further into the delight of knowledge. I wasn't much of a reader myself, but I knew Willa was. Why I hadn't shown her sooner, I don't know! I sighed; head lowered to the floor. I knew why. Danica!

"This is now my most favourite space!" she exclaimed.

I smiled, nodding. "You're welcome here anytime you wish, Princess." Walking over to the windows over the other side of the tower, I drew back the curtains and let light flood the room. It was a dusty old place, hardly used bar from Cleo's hide and seek games. Nicholas sometimes ventured in here to escape reality. But besides that, even my mother didn't venture into the stories untold here. I think she was more of a learn on the job type… much like me.

Willa turned and hugged me tight. "It's fantastic Ethan! So, what would you recommend?"

"Erm…"

"You've no clue, have you?" she said, smirking.

"Well…"

"Please tell me you can read," she taunted, laughing.

"Cheeky!" I laughed. "Of course, I can, but I'm no nerd."

She winced, laughing. "Oh Ethan, you're missing out on so much!"

"How about you give me the cliff notes version?"

Laughing we went up a few levels, and I watched as Willa ran her hands over the dusty spines, stopping at an old book labelled "Hela, daughter of Loki." She picked it up.

"Is this the same Hela… from the Council?"

I shrugged. "Must be. I don't know any others."

"Who's Loki?"

"Some Norse God I think, well from what mother used to tell me."

"I think I've heard of him."

"Mother would always blame Loki's influence if any of us played tricks on her when we were pups."

"Pups?"

"Yes," I laughed, forgetting she knew little about our kind. "Baby wolves."

She nodded. Opening the book, flicking through the pages. "Look," she said. Pointing at a hand-painted drawing, rich in colour. Hela's jet-black hair stood out against the cream pages. Her face was twisted. Half wolf, half vampire… and as bloodthirsty as they come.

"Is this her?" she asked.

"It must be. I've never actually met her."

"Wait, there's a passage about how she became a hybrid." She read aloud. "From the torturous depths of a treacherous journey, the Langer man came. Hidden beneath an array of decadence, his foiled eyes and sullen breath took hold of the audience before him. In dance or rhyme, he swirled his sorcery around the bodies of every mortal in play. Neither man nor woman denied his touch, pressuring for more as he merged them into his own, a playroom of spectators applauding his display."

Blackened hearts breathed their last breath as his ashen touch encapsulated their hearts. Delving into the minds of men through fear, mistrust, and paranoia. The Langer man sat back and watched as the musings of humanity took over. Their bodies were taken by the master puppeteer himself.

Over the hours that came, a sadistic show of massacre and mayhem uncoiled. Mortal men tasted the blood of mortal women, and mortal women avenged their fallen by savaging the bodies of dismembered men. The Langer man sat there in agreement, applauding the musings of many until only one survived that torturous dance of disaster that day.

That one was our very own, our sole survivor, our Hela as she's known too many. Hela bathed in the blood of her tribe, suckled down the life from those she took, and in her victory, she became the first of her kind, a Hybrid birthed through the flame of fire, destruction, and death. The Langer man overjoyed at his creation, but his victorious celebration became that of his barbarous death. Age didn't take him, Hela did. For the God Loki could only visit our realm in the frame of another, and on this occasion, he had chosen a mere mortal to embrace his magnificence. But as any wise one would know, as a new baby vampire, Hela was starved of blood. She lay wild and rampant, draining every living creature in sight. But with her new hybrid abilities, she became downright evil, and her fathers' musings no longer affected her. A brief battle later and the God-like creature named Loki was no more. His soul was sent to the afterlife to battle for freedom once again. But never to this day has he resurfaced, and no one knows what became of him." I sighed. Damn!

"Bloody hell. She's had quite the journey," I said.

Willa's face was sullen. "I feel bad for her."

"Don't. She has made up for what happened to her by torturing thousands of innocent supernatural's over the years."

"What about humans?"

"Oh, she happily feeds on them," I said. Willa shuddered. "That's why FALCON wants her reign to end."

"There's got to be something we can do to stop all the bloodshed."

"There is." I grinned. Willa placed the book back on the shelf and we walked down the spiral stairs, sitting on the old couch in the centre of the room. Sunlight bled through the window, lighting up my beautiful mate's face. Every serene part sparkled a little more.

"So?" she asked, sitting down beside me.

"She invited us to the Palace."

"What… why?"

"She wants to meet you. But she believes you're still a human."

"Well, technically I've not changed yet."

"Shifted you mean."

"Whatever," she said, holding her hands up, smirking.

"So how about we take her up on that offer, bring our pack and Tristan's pack as back up then take her down once and for all."

"Isn't that risky, she will be in her own home, she'd have the advantage?"

He nodded. "Yes, but we'd have the element of surprise."

"What do you mean?"

"She won't expect us to actually attend her celebration. Let alone with two packs in tow."

"Okay, what about any guards?"

"We take them out first."

"Not kill them, I hope!"

I smiled, taking her hand. "Only if we have to." She bit her bottom lip and nodded.

"Will they be there?"

"Who?"

"The ones who think they're my brothers?"

I sat back, eyes wide. Taking a deep breath I said, "so you heard that then?"

She nodded, sighing. "They feel familiar to me Ethan."

"But if they were your brothers Willa, you'd have already been a werewolf."

"Oh,"

"So, they can't be. It must have been one of Helas ploys to get you to her Palace."

"But isn't that what we are doing, anyway?"

"True, but with this, we'll be ready."

"So, what can I do?"

"We will keep Hela occupied, then when the time is right, I'll need you to make your excuses and leave the room, joining the pack; while I take her out once and for all."

"I'm not leaving you!"

"You must Willa. If she captures you, all will be lost. I couldn't live with myself if anything happened to you."

Willa sighed, biting her bottom lip. "I understand, I will."

I nodded, lent forward and gently kissed her forehead.

A moment of silence passed as we both mulled over the gigantic mess we were about to get ourselves into. Surely Willa should stay here, where it's safe? I sighed. But then… is it safe? If the Colourless are really on their way, then I was more worried about them than one hybrid Queen. Either way, both packs will be there. My pack will guard Willa with their lives. She will be safest amongst us all.

"So, when is the ball?"

"Three nights from now…"

"Shit!" she said, gulping.

"Shit indeed."

Chapter Thirty-seven
Ethan

Fathers' office was chilly today, maybe because of the icy winds of winter, as they set sail. I yawned, waiting for him to finish on the phone. From what I could tell, he was discussing the spell with our one and only witch, Arwen. Apparently, she hadn't even realised I'd been living a lie for the past four years. If she didn't know, then it must have been Edwina.

Oswald sat forward in his chair. "Son, have you given thought to what the Amber Rose brothers spoke of?"

I huffed, "that bunch of degenerates aren't worth even considering!"

"I understand your apprehension, Ethan. But if they are a danger to our Luna, Princess Willa, we must know about it."

Slamming my fist down, the desk rattled. "They'll never step a foot near her ever again."

He nodded, scratching his head. "But it makes little sense. Why would they risk encroaching on our land?"

"Because Hela knows Willa's adopted! She put them up to this!" I stood up, pacing the room. "She already took four years of my life and now she wants to take my mate too!"

"Ethan, sit down, you're making me giddy!"

Growling, I sat down. Nic walked in.

"What's going on now?" He asked, his wild hair unkempt and in need of styling.

I shook my head. "How about you sort yourself out before sticking your nose in my business!"

He blew a stray feather from his face. "What? Don't you like the fresh look?" He smirked.

"You had better not have killed any more chickens on the Jenkins farm." I growled.

"Me?" he exclaimed, his hands on his heart. "I would never do such a thing!"

My inner wolf growled, wanting to bring this pup down before me. "It's a good job you're my brother!"

He grinned. "So, what's this about the Amber Rose macho men being Willa's brothers?"

I sighed. There was no point in keeping anything from him.

Father shook his head, sat back in the chair, and nodded.

"They can't be her brothers' father," I said. She wasn't born with the wolf gene.

"How do you know?" Nic asked, taking a seat next to me.

Narrowing my eyes, I frowned. "Because she wasn't a wolf before I gave her my blood, idiot!"

Nic laughed. "You'll never learn, will you," he said with a sly grin. "Not all wolves can shift."

Father shifted in his seat. "That's a good point!"

"No. I've never heard of a wolf that couldn't shift!" I paused, thinking. It's impossible! Every wolf I've ever known could change at will. "Don't mess us around, Nic! If she were a wolf before... and even if she couldn't shift... then surely she'd have heard her inner wolf crying out to her?"

"Yes, and have you asked her?"

"What asked my new wife if she heard voices throughout her life... err... no!"

"Want me to?" He smirked.

I frowned, taking in his bemused expression. "You're actually enjoying this, aren't you?"

"Well, we need to know if she had any wolf-like abilities when she was a child, don't we!"

"Fine." I huffed. "But she's my mate. I'll ask her."

Nic smirked, stood up, and stepped back. "There's no time like the present. Report back when you're done." He laughed.

I stood up and groaned. "You realise I'm the Alpha right?"

"Yes, of course Alpha. But now Willa's whipping you into shape, you might actually show some compassion around here!" He laughed and ran out the room just as I swatted him on the back of the head.

"Boys! Boys!" Father said as we left. Nic ran down the corridor as I entered the courtyard to find my gorgeous mate sitting on an old wooden bench by the apple tree. She looked peaceful. She had a book in her hand. The book we'd seen in the library. The one about Hela and her history. I shuddered. The thought of that vile leech made me cold to the core.

"A little light reading I see?" I asked, planting a kiss on her forehead and sitting beside her. She smiled.

"It says here that Hela was born a wolf and when The Langer Man bit her, she changed and became a hybrid."

"That's what I was told, yes."

"So, do you think she was always this evil?"

"Most likely."

"But wouldn't she have been part of a pack? She would have surely had friends, family?"

"Yes, but The Langer Man made them turn on one another."

She frowned, "how?"

I smiled. "You're quite the inquisitive one today, aren't you! Vampires have certain abilities, and one of them is their ability to coerce humanity to do their bidding."

"But they weren't human?"

"True, perhaps they were weak-willed." I smiled as she closed the book.

"Well, she sounds like a force to be reckoned with… are you sure this is the right plan?"

"Yes, it has to be. The only other option is to wait until she sends her troops over here and outnumbers us ten to one."

She sighed.

"My father spoke of changing humans to wolves, creating an army that way."

Willa's eyes widened. "I'm not sure I like that idea!"

"Me neither, as it would mean, many baby wolves running around town. It would cause chaos, but if this doesn't work, it may be the only plan we have left."

She nodded. "So, when do we leave?"

"I have a few things I need to put in place. The celebration is this Friday."

"How far away is it?"

"It'll only take the morning to get there. We can leave Friday morning, hold up in a local hotel until it's time."

"Okay, and what should I bring?"

"Ah, mother has already sorted that, just bring your beautiful body and I'll be more than happy." I grinned, my hand resting on her upper thigh.

"Mmm, so we get a few nights together first," she asked, smirking.

I grinned, my hand trailing up her thigh. She gasped.

Standing up, I lifted her into my arms, cradling her perfect body, and kissed her hard. She giggled, placing her arms around my neck.

"Where to, husband?" she asked coyly as I bounded down the corridor.

"Can't you guess Princess?" I smirked, turning the corner and opening the door to our bedroom.

"Oh Ethan, you know how to romance a girl!" She giggled as I placed her on the bed, jumped on top and ripped her clothes off, stripping my own off at the same time.

Moments later, we were naked, hot and grinding back and forth into an orgasmic crescendo, both erupting at the same time.

Breathless and exhausted, I held her. "How about after all this madness, I take you on an actual date?"

She smiled, curling my hair behind my ears. "I would love that!"

"Then it's a date!" I smiled, kissing her, suckling her bottom lip.

Smiling, she kissed me back, pulled away, and caressed my face. "I'm glad I married you."

I laughed; she was so sincere. "I'm glad I married you too." Sitting up and taking her hand, I knew that now was the time I needed to delve into her past. We all needed answers to these questions and if there was even the slightest chance, she was a Rose by blood I needed to know. I sighed. What could it mean, though? A human born from a wolf's body. Such a thing should never exist. But if it did, then she already carried the wolf gene, even if it was dormant. Well, until now.

"What's wrong?" She asked, her brow furrowed.

"Nothing is wrong, my love," I said. She must have heard me sigh. "I was thinking back to your life before we met."

She shuddered. "It wasn't what they made it out to be. When Nora married my father, he changed. I guess the Duchess's death affected him more than I realised. Nora took advantage of his loneliness, his vulnerability. Then after Jenna was born, she'd cemented their union and weaselled her way into the manor, kicking me out."

"What do you mean?"

"It doesn't matter. It's in the past and I want to stay here, with you, in the present."

My expression softened. "I understand." Looking down, I watched as she experimented with her necklace. "Your necklace. I've seen you playing with it before. Where's it from?"

"My birth family, this is all I have of them."

Leaning in closer, I inspected the intricate loops of the necklace, the amber crystals adorning the delicate rose. A rose I knew only too well. The brothers had one just like it tattooed on their shoulders.

I growled, tensing up. "The Amber Rose pack."

"Who?"

"The men you saw at the gate that day."

"The ones who think I'm their sister?"

I nodded, growling.

"Could it be true Ethan?"

"It makes little sense, Princess. If you were their kin, then you'd share the wolf gene and would have shifted as a child."

"I knew nothing about them though."

"Maybe that's why... maybe because you mortals bought you up, so you never embraced your true nature." I scratched my head as she sat up. "But still... that wouldn't have stopped your inner wolf releasing itself." I paused, taking a deep breath. "Did you ever have any abilities as a child?"

"Like what?"

"Enhanced senses, the ability to heal really quick... or even a voice in your head?"

She shook her head, narrowed her eyes, lips pursed. "Then again, I heard a voice screeching at me when I first came here." My eyes widened. "Oh, and I've never really needed to heal quickly. I don't think I was ever sick."

"Hmm, you must have been ill at least one time?"

She shook her head.

"Well damn, maybe you did always have the latent wolf gene after all." She shrugged. "So... what did the voice say?"

She smiled, "Mate."

Chapter Thirty-eight
Darius

"Haven't we waited long enough?" Harper asked as he slammed his pint down on the table.

I sighed. Bollocks! He was right. We should have heard by now. The other punters turned and glared. They didn't appear to like newcomers in the dingy Grey Pheasant Inn. It surprised me they even served us after Harper went off at a local last night. The barkeep had thought about it, though. Not serving us, I mean. And I wouldn't blame him. I looked down at the mahogany round table covered in yesterday's beer. Burgh! Why did we come back here? "Darius!" Harper yelled, pushing my elbow, snapping me out of my wandering mind.

"What?"

"Willa... don't you care?"

My eyes widened. "Of course I bloody care. Why do you think

I'm still here waiting for her!"

"What if she doesn't remember," Stylan asked, narrowing his eyes, hiding behind his long brown hair.

"Then we try again!" Stefan nodded, signalling the barkeep for another round of beers.

He sighed. "Ethan won't let her anywhere near us."

"Maybe he would. But maybe she doesn't like us!" Stylan said, accepting the pint from the barkeeper. "Mate, it's got a lipstick mark on it!" he complained. The barkeeper huffed, took the pint, and went back to fetch a new one.

"Make sure he doesn't spit in it," Stefan said, smirking. Stylan glared at him. He laughed. "Anyway Stylan, she doesn't even know us, how can she not love your caring smile!" He said, grinning as he pinched his cheek.

"Get off!" Stylan demanded, batting his hand away. The barkeeper brought back another pint, sploshing it over the table and down Stylan's leg. "Err yeah, thanks mate!" he said with a sarcastic undertone.

I smirked. Then phased out, watching the commotion at the pool table as a couple of locals smashed a pool cue over another guy's head. I sighed. Next time we find another bar! Hopefully, we won't be here that long. Maybe she'll remember and welcome us with open arms. Heck, who am I kidding! With Ethan as a husband, there's no chance of that! Lips pursed, I watched as they threw another guy out for assaulting a waitress. But then, we're her family. He's got to accept that… hasn't he? Smiling, I watched as my brothers scuffled, knocking the table, and beer sloshing everywhere. She's got to love us, right? Sighing, my heart sank. She didn't even know us. As far as she knew, we abandoned her all those years ago. Of course, she wouldn't accept us. Who would? But surely she'd feel it? The pull.

The familiarity?

Adam came back from the bathroom, taking a seat next to me. His expression puzzled over. "What's wrong, Darius?" he asked, edging his chair closer to me as I watched my other brothers laugh and joke together.

"What if she wants nothing to do with us?" I asked him.

"Then that's her choice and we must respect it." I nodded, smiling. Adam was the second born. He came out barely eight months after me. Father had said it was the longest Mum had carried a pup for. I smiled, remembering her cuddles. She had the longest arms that used to wrap me up safe against her bosom. Every day I miss her. Father said I'd only needed five months in the womb. Clearly ready to take on the world like a natural born leader. It wasn't the same without my mother, though. She was always the one person I could go to who would understand the pressures I was under. After all, keeping six brothers and three sisters safe wasn't a straightforward job. But then, after Hela had my mother murdered, my father joined her. He said he didn't have a choice. So, I stepped up and became their Alpha, their protector. My brothers and sisters needed one. I sighed, looking over at Adam. Without him, I'd have lost it years ago. He kept me sane. Adam had my mother's kind nature. Her ability to listen to and teach at the same time. He even called me out when I needed it. He was my Beta and didn't exactly have it easy.

"Everything okay?" he asked.

I nodded. "I was thinking about Mother."

He smiled. "I miss her too."

"She would have loved to have seen Willa one last time."

"Yes," he smiled, placing his hand on my back. "She would have… and do you remember what she would have said to ease your fears?"

I smiled, remembering back to her favourite saying. It was literally the answer to everything.

"If you had asked her if she thought Willa would accept us, what would she have said?"

My five other brothers stopped, turned, and smiled, speaking as one, "what's meant to be, will be!"

Laughter reigned between us. She was right, always was. Our mother believed in fate and destiny, she had hope when we didn't. She saw Willa as the one that would lead us to victory, believing her to be the prophetic red wolf. We vowed to protect her, our Willa. We promised our mother we would. After Mother died, Father continued to watch over her, ensuring she remained safe in the manor house she grew up in.

But one thing that made me smile is the fact that when we saw Willa last, she still wore my mother's amber rose necklace. A design we all shared in some form or another.

"Come on, lads," I said, finishing my pint. "Let's head up to the Castle and demand an audience with our sister."

"Yeah!" They all cheered. Adam patted me on the back and slammed his empty glass down.

"She needs to know the truth, brother. You're doing the right thing."

I nodded, slapping him on the back as we left the Grey Pheasant Inn.

We had camped out North of the Castle, at the edge of their territory. We've been here a few weeks now. Ever since our almost civilised conversation with our father. I sighed. He didn't understand. Edwina had said the flaming red wolf would appear as our saviour days before her eighteenth birthday… and if my calculations were right, that would be soon!

I had to see her. Had to see for myself. Then when I laid eyes on Willa, I knew. Her pale beauty, tender nature. She was everything the prophecy had said she would be, and more. She was our saviour, and it was our duty to protect her.

The sunlight waned as the sun began to set, casting its shadow over the forest beyond the townscape. A cool breeze rustled fallen leaves as we crunched up the path that led to the edge of the Elder Vale. It was a good job we had camped there; we'd heard the commotion as those thugs attacked our sister. If we hadn't had made it in time, would Ethan have been able to control his frenzy, or would he have turned on Willa, like he turned on us, all those years ago?

Granted, he'd been pretty pissed about Layla. Understandably so. I shrugged. We'd made a mistake. But we'd seen what we thought had happened and did what any worthy wolf would have done. We reported her. The problem was, we believed the Council to be genuine leaders, worthy and righteous. We never thought Hela to be a vicious, manipulative hybrid.

As we entered the vale, we made our way to our camp, collecting wood for the fire on the way. The night sky took precedence when we reached the camp. Something felt wrong. The birds took flight. Nature screamed, and Ethan and Tristan growled before us. Adam stood tall, ready to shift. My brothers held back, awaiting my orders. I stepped forward in human form. A bloody stupid idea really, but I had to show I was of no threat, or we'd end up in a mighty battle and I'm sure Willa wouldn't take kindly to her kin slaughtering her new husband.

"Where is Willa?" I asked, stepping forward, hands held out in front of me.

Ethan's black wolf growled. I'm sure it has grown since I saw it last. But then I doubt it, considering we wolves stop maturing after we reach a certain age. Unless he isn't mature yet? The thought made me smile.

Ethan shifted back to his human form. Tristan followed. Both grabbing clothing they'd left in the bushes behind them.

"Willa is at home where I can keep her safe," he said, his expression darkening as moonlight touched his features.

"We must see her and explain everything." I demanded.

"No!" he yelled, stepping forward.

Adam stepped to my side. My brothers followed.

"Back off!" Tristan growled.

"What do you want with my wife?" Ethan asked.

I shuddered when he said wife. It was hard enough knowing she was living there. Let alone sharing a bed with the very monster that drove us from our homes. "She is OUR sister Ethan! We demand to see her!"

He laughed. "You will demand no such thing. What do you want with her?"

"Only to tell her the truth," I said, taking a step towards him.

Tristan growled, and Ethan placed his hand across him, preventing him from charging towards me.

"Has Hela sent you?"

My brothers growled. They hated that woman. "No, we came of our own freewill and against our father's wishes."

"So, the old duke still lives then?" Tristan spat.

I narrowed my eyes. "He does."

Ethan stepped forward, there now only being a metre of space between us. "I would have thought Hela would have killed you all by now. Isn't that what she does to lesser creatures?"

I took a deep breath. He was baiting me. "No Ethan. None of us are here because of my father or Hela. We have information Willa needs to know."

"About the prophecy, by any chance?" Ethan asked, his eyes narrowed.

My eyes widened. "How did you know?"

"A good guess," he said, smirking. "So do you have proof?"

"Of what?"

"That my wife is your sister?"

"Yes." I turned to Adam, who pulled a photograph out of his wallet and handed it to me.

"Do you remember the last time you saw us all?" Ethan nodded. "When our two families were together that summer's evening. You and I were the eldest, playing in the Elder Vale I believe." He sighed, and I continued. "My brothers were in the lake and my mother was resting on the stone by the Oak tree. Do you remember?"

"Yes, what does that prove?"

"Do you remember anything about my mother?"

Ethan shrugged. "Can't you remember her heavily pregnant and false labouring when we were there? You and I had to run to help her." Ethan's expression changed. A puzzled look crept over his face.

"Go on…"

"The baby my mother was pregnant with who you never met until you married her. That was our baby sister Willa Rose." I handed Ethan the photograph I had taken of him standing with his mother by the lake. My mother resting in the background heavily pregnant.

Ethan paused, studying it. "That's a delightful story, but it doesn't prove that this baby is my Willa."

"It does if you test this…" I said, pulling the chain my mother had given me when she died.

"What is it?" he asked, looking at the vial of red liquid hanging from the chain.

"There are a few droplets of Willa's blood." Ethan looked disgusted.

"You bled a baby?"

I smirked. "Only a few drops, so when the day came, we could prove we were her family."

Tristan stepped forward and looked at the photograph. "Haven't you guys heard of DNA tests?"

Ethan nodded.

I smiled. "They weren't exactly easy to come by when Willa was born."

"Fair enough."

"So, will you let us see our sister?"

Ethan took a deep breath, looked at the photograph again, and smiled. "Yes, once I've had this tested." My brothers cheered. "But only if she agrees to it."

I nodded, offering my hand out to shake his.

He took another deep breath, gripped my hand hard, and said, "but if you hurt her, I will cut off your heads and feed them to that damned hybrid you all bloody worship." I pulled my hand away, stretching it.

"I understand… but just so you know. We loathe Hela and her Council and would like nothing more than to see it burned to the ground."

Tristan smirked. "I'm liking this one," he said, slamming his hand on my back. "So, tell me more about burning the Council down." I laughed, and we sat and talked out our differences, with a few beers by the campfire throughout the night.

Chapter Thirty-nine
Willa

Another day had passed with my head buried in books. It was quite comforting, considering the fact Ethan didn't want me to venture out alone. I could understand that, especially after what happened last time. But I missed the fresh air. I sighed, smiling. But it still wasn't as much as I missed him!

Ethan had ventured into the town late yesterday afternoon. He hadn't returned but sent word that he was investigating my brothers… if they were that. It was too much of a risk for me to be out in the open. All Hela would need is a sniper with an excellent shot. She didn't even need one of the supernatural kind. Frowning, I turned the page. The supernatural world was shaped between fantasy and reality. A world unseen to the human eye, yet one that lived right under their noses. Lips pursed; brow furrowed. I say 'their' as I'm not sure if I was ever part of the mortal realm. If the brothers are right in what they're saying, then I was always a wolf, just one that never shifted. In fact, through my life before Ethan, I can't recall ever hearing things or even seeing things. If I had, they would have locked me up. I smirked. Nora would have loved that. The crazy adopted daughter locked up in some mental institute somewhere.

Closing the book, I stretched, watching the waning light dwindle through the thick velvet curtains. The library was old, dusty and in need of a good clean, but it felt like home. A place I could escape to.

The old oak door squeaked open, grinding on its hinges. Ethan entered, looking flustered.

"Ethan!" I smiled, jumping up to greet him. Running into his arms I buried myself in his scent, woody yet hot with a dash of man sweat and cologne.

"Willa!" he said. Kissing my forehead. "I've missed you!"

"Me too! You were gone too long!" I said, snuggling him.

He smiled, his face warming as I kissed him hard.

"What did you find out?"

"Honestly, Willa," he said, taking my hand and walking over to the sofa with me, sitting down. "What Darius said resonates with me."

"Darius? Is he the older one?"

"Yes, the giant ginger-haired monster…. Sorry," he looked down at the floor, "brother."

"So, they're my brothers?"

"They have a vial of your blood Willa."

My eyes widened. "What?"

"Darius said it was so that when the day came, they could prove who they were to you."

"But couldn't they have got that from anywhere?"

Ethan nodded. "That's what I thought, but then they showed me this." He pulled out an old photograph of a family, seven brothers, two sisters, and a heavily pregnant mother.

My brow furrowed. Lips pursed. "Please explain."

"I remember the day this was taken. My family was visiting the Amber Rose pack. It was the last day I ever saw Layla. I remember Gwendoline being pregnant. They say she was pregnant with you."

"Okay, but it's still not proof, surely?"

"Yes, but then he told me they were resting in the woods, hungry and homeless, when a man found them. He picked you up, took you with him. The family had nothing left to give you. But he did. He had a loving wife, a safe and happy home. He gave you the life they couldn't."

Tears welled in my eyes. "But why did they end up homeless and as near to death as you speak of?"

"The Council had taken everything from them. Their father." He stopped; eyes narrowed, then smiled. "Your father… he knew that if Hela found you, they would have killed you. He knew of the prophecy, of the human child that bore the werewolf gene." I nodded, blinking back the tears. Ethan rubbed his hand down my cheek and smiled. "He knew Hela would see you as a threat, so he ordered his sons to let you go."

Tears rolled down my cheeks, cushioning my lips. "So, he just left me?"

"No, he kept watch on you for years. He forbade the brothers to search for you. But he kept watch just in case Hela found you."

"So is the blood mine?"

He nodded. "I had Tristan rush it to the lab in town this morning."

I took a deep breath, wiped my tears, and sat up straight. Biting my lip, I nodded. "Okay, but what about this prophecy?"

"It may be better that I show you." He stood up, took my hand, lifting me up to meet him and guided us over to the far end of the library.

Past the spiral staircase there lay a selection of scrolls. Rummaging through, he opened several. "Ah, here!"

"What is it?"

"It's something my grandmother showed me when I was a mere pup." He smiled and looked at me. "She would have liked you."

Smiling, I placed my hand on his. He stretched open the scroll and opened my eyes to the wonders of the supernatural world. Every creature I could think of was drawn and hand painted on this scroll. It was a depiction of good versus evil. Many creatures bloodied in battle, dead or dying. But many had survived, and at the forefront of the survivors was a vibrant red wolf.

"She is the saviour of supernatural kind."

I traced my finger over her fiery red pelt. "She's beautiful!"

"She's you!" He nodded.

I took a step back. "But how? I've not even shifted yet. You don't know that I'll be a red wolf."

He ran his hand through my hair, smiling. "I do, look at your hair!"

"You're the human that will one day stand as a wolf. You will inspire the many and we will embrace this fight, removing all obstacles, destroying Hela once and for all."

"You really think I'm capable of all that?"

"I don't think you are, Princess… I know you are!" He stepped in, closing the space between us, kissing me on the lips. Tongues entwined. Tastes mingled. We were one and if Ethan thought I could be this wolf… well, I really hoped I could be. If not for his sake, then for the rest of the supernatural realms.

My body sparkled inside; sensations of bubbles fizzed through my skin. Was it true? Was I really this person? I took a deep breath. Did I really have an actual family? Brothers? Sisters? God, I hope they're not anything like Jenna! I shuddered. Ethan smiled, watching me.

"So can I meet them?"

"If you want to."

"Yes." I took a deep breath. "I'd like to meet them now, Ethan."

"Are you sure?"

I nodded. "But can you have the pack nearby, just in case."

Ethan smiled. "Of course."

"Okay, where are they?"

"They're camped on the edge of the vale."

My eyes widened. Memories closed back of the last time they ventured to our gates. What if they are here to hurt me? What if they're here to take Ethan away for her needs? I shuddered again, and with shaky hands; I sat down.

"What's wrong?"

"I don't know… well, I do. But I think I'm looking too hard at this."

"Follow your instincts, Willa."

"What instincts?"

"You have them. We all do." He took a deep breath and sat beside me. "When you saw them, how did you feel?"

How did I feel? At the gate they felt familiar. I wanted to touch that man's hand. I wanted to be beside them, but I never knew why. "They felt familiar to me."

"Then trust those instincts. If nothing else, they will always protect you and keep you safe from danger."

I nodded, biting my bottom lip.

"So, are you ready?"

"Yes… I think."

He chuckled. "I'll take that as a yes. I'll be with you and if you want to turn away at any time, let me know."

I smiled. "Okay."

He kissed my forehead, took my hand and we left the castle, ready to meet my brothers.

Chapter Forty
Willa

"Are you okay Princess?" Ethan asked, his face full of concern.

I nodded, biting my bottom lip. His eyes narrowed, and he gripped my hand tighter.

"Nothing will happen to you, I promise," he said. The packs roared behind me, keeping their distance but ready to jump in if we needed them to.

I took a deep breath and continued along the gravel path, my boots crunching over the left-over leaves. Autumn had come and gone as Winter took form. Jack Frost had blown his way over the lands, creating a blanket of icy frost that caressed every breath I took. It didn't help that I was panting. Breathing shallow and rapidly. My nerves kicked in as panic broke through me. I stopped, let go of Ethan's hand and lent against a tree, focusing on my breathing.

"Willa, you really don't have to do this!" he said, his face filled with concern.

I nodded, my bottom lip red raw from biting too hard.

He smiled sweetly, pulled me forwards and held me in his arms. Heat cushioned itself against me as his muscular arms held me tight, protecting me and calming my nerves. I snuggled into his chest. His heart was beating heavy and strong. I sighed, smiling. I could stay here. Like forever.

Mimicking his breathing, I calmed down to a steady pace. "There we go," he said. Smiling.

"I'm okay, nervous, I think. What do I even say to them?"

"What do you want to know?"

"Why didn't they fight for me? How could they have left me with Nora? If my father was watching me, he should have seen that they made me work as a slave every day." Tears welled in my eyes. "I don't even know when my birthday is!" I sobbed harder.

Ethan growled, pulled me in close, and held me tight. "Let it out Princess. Nora and your old family will pay for what they did to you."

Fists pummelled. I sobbed, my fists breaking against Ethan's skin. He held me tighter. My head buried in his chest. I took a few deep breaths, counted to ten in my mind, and regained control of myself once again. Wiping my eyes, I saw the slick, snotty trails I'd left on his top. Rubbing them away, I half laughed, and half cried. "Sorry," I said, wiping my nose. He frowned, stroked my cheek, and kissed my forehead.

Taking a deep breath, he looked straight at me. There was a kindness there. "You have every right to know the answers… and we will find them for you!"

I nodded, drying my tears. "When it's your real eighteenth birthday, we will hold a huge celebration. It will be the best damn birthday you've ever experienced!" He grinned. "You'll love it!" I smiled.

"Can my friends from the old Manor House come?"

"Of course they can! My home is your home, Willa. They are welcome anytime you want!"

I smiled. Eager to see Juliet, Valentino, and Angelo again. I missed them. They were all I had from my old life and now I was about to meet my biological family; I hadn't realised how much I needed them here with me.

"How about we contact them later today?"

"But the signals awful in the Castle Ethan."

"We have a home phone, you know." He smirked.

I laughed. I'd never thought to ask. "You're so old-fashioned!"

He laughed. "Why… don't people use house phones nowadays?"

"Not ones with wires, Ethan! We've all gone mobile now, you know." I smirked as he nudged my shoulder, took my hand, and kissed me hard.

"Damn you're too hard to resist!" He said, growling.

I smiled. "There's that growling again… did you know I thought you were ill when you kept growling at me when I first got here?"

He growled again. This time on purpose. Picking me up and running down the trail.

"Ethan! No!" I laughed. He carried me up the hill and laid me down on a patch of mossy grass. Kissing my neck, ravaging my body as his feverish hands traced a line from my neck to my perky breasts, all the way down to my knicker line. I squirmed. "But what if we're seen?" I panted, breathing hot and heavy for all the right reasons.

He grinned, kissing me harder. "Then let's give them something to remember us by!"

I giggled as he pulled down my underwear, wriggled out of his jeans and thrust himself inside of me.

Quick, hot, and heavy, we moved back and forth, deeper then deeper still. He lifted me up, backing against a tree as I wrapped my legs around his waist. Groaning, I dug my nails in, scratching his back, drawing blood. My hips curled forward, moving with his rhythm. Grabbing me tighter, he pushed faster, deeper. Moments later, he arched. The friction caused my stomach to tighten, toes to curl and my body to tense. I screamed out, gripping him tighter. He groaned, burying his head in my neck, nipping my mark as he came. I laughed when he released himself from inside of me, my legs jellified as I tumbled on to the floor. He chuckled as sweat beaded on his forehead and upper lip. Leaning forward, I kissed it off. The salty taste swirled around my tongue. In moments like these, I forgot the reality of what I was here for. I was happy. In love and with my husband, my mate. No matter what happened next, I knew I could handle it, as I'd have him by my side every step of the way.

Straightening our clothes, we stood up, kissed, and held hands. I took a deep breath; he watched me; brow furrowed. I nodded, heading down the hill towards the edge of the Elder Vale.

It was a journey I'd hesitated to take. But now I was almost here, it was one I was glad I was completing. Ethan was right. I needed answers. Needed to put the past behind me, and if this meant I could do that, then it was worth every heart-breaking moment I would endure.

Over the brow of the hill, I saw smoke from a campfire. Ethan pointed, "they're there." I nodded, tightening my grip and walking faster.

He smiled, kept up the pace, and we arrived in little to no time at all.

The first thing I saw when I entered the clearing was a campfire with seven men surrounding it. Each brother, unique in their own way, but they all shared the same tanned skin, the same muscular build, and the same smile when they saw me. A smile I was happy to see, and one I saw in the mirror every single day.

"She's here," one of them said.

The ginger haired man stood up. I remembered him as the leader of the group back when they arrived at our gates.

"Willa," he said. "I'm Darius." I nodded, taking in his features. He took a step forward, and Ethan growled as my hand tightened in his. "It's okay. We're not here to hurt you."

Biting my bottom lip, I nodded again. How could I trust them? Any of them? What if they were Helas puppets, like Danica was? He took another step forward, slowly. I could breathe in his scent. It reminded me of the apple blossom trees, back in the orchard where I grew up. Yet there weren't any at the manor house. This scent. This memory was from before.

I remembered batting at the boy in front of me, giggling as he pulled funny faces while eating a vivid red apple. Ginger hair curtained his face. His smile was infectious as I mimicked my own. He held my hand and helped me walk barefoot through the orchard, looking up in awe of the boy beneath the blossom. His face was young, his hand warm to the touch. I'd felt nothing but love for him, my brother back there beneath the apple trees. It was him. All those years ago, it was him.

My jaw dropped; face paled with recognition. They were all so familiar to me, every one of them. I dropped Ethan's hand, stepped forward and closed the gap between Darius and I, wrapping my arms against his thick muscular body.

Darius held me tight. "Willa," he said. Tears rolling down his cheeks.

Every brother stood up in unison, crowding around, holding

me as their own. How had I not remembered this? How did I not remember them? Even in the darkness and times of utter dismay, they were the light that bought me home. The family I'd loved and missed throughout my life. I remembered their scent, their laughter, their love of life. My home with the apple orchard, and the wooden tree swing beside the fishpond. I remembered my mother, her thick blond curls, her warm embrace on a cold winter's eve. I remembered my sister's smiles, twins who were closer than any two children could ever be, and then I remembered the changes. The wolves protecting my infant body. I remembered the hunter, my adopted father, as he took me away. The sadness of each wolf as it howled in anguish.

We'd been lost that day. No home. No food and rags left for clothing. I remembered the heartache as my mother died protecting us from the Council's guards. I'd never have survived if it weren't for my family. They put me before everything else, fed me before themselves, protected me from the pain of the life we had to endure. I was the human child to a pack of werewolves, and that meant I was both a blessing and a curse.

I'd heard whispers of the prophecy back when I was a mere babe, and that meant the ultimate sacrifice. I had to be hidden until the day came. They gave me up to save me, not hurt me, and no matter how hard a life I'd lived, it was nothing compared to the nightmare they must have endured.

Ethan stood speechless as my brothers let go. Jaw dropped, eyes wide.

I smiled. "It's okay Ethan. I remember them."

He nodded, his face still full of astonishment.

Darius spoke. "You remember us?" he said, wiping his eyes. I nodded and smiled. To see a fully grown man, built like a bodybuilder on steroids, crying his eyes out, was a sight you seldom get to see.

I smirked. His eyes narrowed. "What?" he said. Puzzled.

"It's rare that I get to see a grown man cry."

My brothers laughed. "Ha, she has a point, Darius. You look like a pussy right now."

Ethan smirked, standing beside me. Darius groaned, "Well, what do you expect, we've missed you baby sis!"

I smiled and took a deep breath. "So why now? Why not sooner?"

Darius tapped the ground next to him as he sat down. Ethan and I sat together beside him.

"The prophecy," the dark-haired one with the cheeky grin said.

With narrowed eyes and pursed lips, I thought about that. "Stefan?" I asked, uncertain.

"Yes! He said, flinging his arms up, fist bumping the air.

I laughed. "Tell me more about the prophecy please."

Stefan nodded as Ethan, and Darius sat discussing the Council and Helas plans for the future.

He sat down next to me. "So, there's an all-powerful witch…"

"Edwina?"

He nodded. "She told us what we kinda already knew. You see mum had said you were special, and we had to keep you safe." I smiled, remembering her embrace. "Anyhoo, Edwina said that a human child born to wolves would be the saviour of the supernatural world. We already knew it was you. After all, how many families birth a human instead of a pup?" I nodded. "So, Edwina told us that the human would change to her pure form before her eighteenth birthday."

"Oh, I think that's ages away," I said, smiling.

Stefan grinned as my other brothers smiled. Darius and Ethan stopped talking.

Darius smiled. "No Willa. Your Eighteenth birthday is during the cold moon, on the eve of the Winter solstice." I shrugged; I had no clue when that was. He smiled. "It's the 21st of December."

Ethan smiled as my eyes widened. "That's next month!" He nodded. "But I thought I was born in the summer? I've only just turned 17!"

Adam sighed. "That's what the humans told you, baby sister. That is when they took you from us."

"Oh!" My expression darkened. "So, all this time I've been celebrating my birthday, it's actually been the day they took me from my actual family?"

Adam nodded. Tears welled in my eyes.

Ethan brushed his thumb over my cheekbone, wiping a tear that escaped me.

Darius sat forward. "It doesn't matter now Willa. You're back with your family."

I took a deep breath, my heart breaking that I'd missed so much time with them all. Instead, I had to deal with Nora and her devilish daughter Jenna to contend with.

"I wish you'd have found me sooner," I said, my head lowered.

"We knew where you were. Father kept watch on you, but he forbade us to contact you."

"But why?"

"He wanted to keep you safe from Helas grasp."

"I understand that. But did he know how they treated me there?" I asked, feeling sick to the stomach.

Darius looked puzzled. Ethan growled, taking my hand as tears blurred my eyesight.

"I made the best of it. I had friends there, and they kept me going."

"What happened to you?" Darius asked, his face filled with concern.

Ethan growled. "It is a story for another time, Darius," he said, holding me and wiping my tears away.

Darius nodded. My brothers all looked angered, fists pummelled, teeth bared. "Look," I said. "I'm fine now. They just weren't very loving people." I said, feigning a smile. "It's in the past and we have bigger problems right now, don't we?"

Darius took a deep breath, and Adam rested his hand on my shoulder. "Okay Willa, how can we help?" Adam said.

Ethan told them of Danica and the spies that roamed our castle grounds. He told them of the threat of the Colourless. At which point Darius's face paled. We filled them in on Helas insane desire to have Ethan birth her children. Stefan gagged. Then about our plan to go on the offensive, attending the celebration she demanded we attend.

Ethan stopped, gripped the log we sat on, and looked at me with concern, then back at Darius. "Promise me one thing, Darius."

"What's that Ethan?"

"Promise me that no matter what, you get Willa out of there safely." Darius nodded.

My brow furrowed. "What? Wait! No, not without you!"

Ethan turned to me. "Remember your promise, Willa. I need to keep you safe!"

I sighed, biting my bottom lip. "Okay, but you had better come out of this unscathed Ethan James Bane!"

He smiled. "I will Princess, don't you worry!"

We spent the rest of the evening remembering old times. Laughing at my brothers' antics and feeling like I was part of something, something bigger and better, and somehow, somewhere,

I would be the one to turn this world around and shape it for a brighter future for all supernatural kinds.

Chapter Forty-one
Willa

The sun rose as I walked hand in hand with Ethan. His grip is strong and protective. His expression is calm.

"Deep in thought?" I asked.

He smiled. "Yes. I was thinking about your sisters."

"Who the twins, Myra and Lorena?"

"Yes. Do you think they're safe there?" he asked.

"Honestly, no. But I plan to find out."

He smiled and nodded. "I remember them too. I used to play with Myra back when we were mere pups."

"It's good you knew them back then." I smiled. "Did you ever miss them? It sounded like you were all very close."

"Honestly, no. I was consumed with anger about Layla. I never wanted to see them again."

"What about now?"

"Now I know they made a mistake. But it cost Layla her life."

He sighed. "I hate them a little less. But I still cannot forgive them."

I sighed. "I understand. It'll take time. She was like a sister to you."

He nodded. "It was a long time ago. But from what they told me; it sounds as though she was trying to save your adopted mother that day."

I nodded, biting my bottom lip.

"What was she like? Your adopted mother?"

"The Duchess was kind. I knew she wasn't my proper mother. She never hid that from me, but she cared for me. She couldn't have any children of her own. So, when Wilbert bought me back from the Vale that day, her eyes lit up." I smiled. "I was a grubby child with no home, no food, and my only comfort was a pack of wolves to keep me company. It was the height of summer back then, and Wilbert had been out hunting. I think he thought he saved me and that my brothers were going to hurt me. In some respects, he did save me though, as from then on, I was well cared for and fed and clothed… well, at least until the Duchess passed away." My heart sank when I remembered her screams.

"I'm sorry that happened to you," Ethan said, gripping my hand a little tighter. I nodded as we left the Elder Vale and entered the Castle grounds. The red stone castle stood in all its glory, saturated by sunlight, its vibrancy enchanting to every soul in New Haven. I was lucky to call this Gothic build my home and even more lucky to have this handsome man by my side. Somehow everything had come together. I sighed and smiled. All seemed right with the world.

Moments later, three guards rushed out, chased by midgets in ninja outfits. Shit! I didn't know whether to laugh or cry! The mini ninjas disappeared into thin air, reappearing before the guards slicing and dicing before we even had a chance to save them.

"Willa! It's the Colourless! Hide!" Ethan said, shifting into his giant black wolf before me. Ripped clothes scattered into the air like confetti. He roared, jumping forward, and grabbing one of the Colourless, tearing its tiny head from its tiny little body.

The gardens were swarming with the things. I stood there in shock, unsure of where to turn. Should I run and hide or stand and fight? My heart screamed fight, yet my head yelled inexplicably for me to hide, cower, and watch as my husband tried to take on the army. There must have been at least twenty of those things charging at Ethan. He had two on his back, one in his mouth, and a group crowding around him. Looking around the pebbled path, I searched for a weapon, but there were none. All there was were pretty pansies, delicate roses, and a tranquil lake beside us.

One of the colourless splashes in the lake, thrown off by Ethan's wolf. Its tiny body splashed about as it struggled to keep its head above water. I watched, puzzled. Couldn't it swim?

Ethan shook his pelt and another of the colourless was thrown into the lake. Splash! Head bobbing, his little body went under as he gasped for air. Why didn't they disappear, reappearing elsewhere? Are they afraid? Their soulless eyes widened as they swallowed hard, choking on their own surroundings. It must be the water! They must not be able to teleport when they're panicking in the water. My brow furrowed. Didn't Hela ever teach them to swim?

I turned to see Ethan panting hard, his body bloodied and broken. In the distance, wolves roared. The pack! They were on their way! I turned to see the two in the water lying motionless, face down. "Ethan! The water" I yelled. "They can't swim!"

Ethan looked up, growled as he saw me still stood there and nodded when he realised what I was trying to tell him. The problem with that, though, was that ten pairs of eyes were now trained on me. Little ninjas leapt in the air. Disappearing and reappearing next to me. "Shit!" I yelled, running towards Ethan. Ethan growled, shaking more of them off him. Whimpering as he tried to reach me. It was too late. One of the little shits had jumped on my back, blade to my neck digging in. I screamed, grabbing the blade. My hand is bleeding profusely. A baby roar interrupted the midget on my back as I recognised the little wolf charging forward. It was my new little sister, Cleo. Her eyes are kind and caring. She jumped on the midget, biting into its torso, maiming it as it teleported back to its gang. I fell to the floor, my neck pouring with blood, hand bloody and painful. Cleo roared at the other midgets as they battled her down to the ground, surrounding her little body as she shifted back to human form. Tiny little grins enveloped their mouths, blackened faces tore through the sunrise as four of them grabbed Cleo and disappeared with her into the nothingness.

"CLEO! NO!"

Ethan ran over, standing over my bloodied body, growling at any of the colourless that came near it. His wolf's eyes filled with sadness at his little sister being taken from us.

Three wolves joined in the fight and the colourless disappeared into thin air.

Ethan shifted back. His body was bruised and bloody. Hundreds of tiny blades had penetrated his skin, yet somehow, he had lived to see us through it.

I lay on the floor sobbing. It was my fault. Cleo was gone. They'd taken her all because she had tried to save me. It wasn't Danica they were after. It was me. I'd been the target all along and no matter how hard I'd tried. I was useless in a battle with those things. Why hadn't I changed into a wolf? Why hadn't I become this ultimate saviour everyone had spoken about? I was a failure, and that was the end of it.

Chapter Forty-two
Ethan

Cleo was gone.

Nicholas pounded over in wolf form, lay down beside me, and whimpered, scenting the floor. Willa crawled over, laid on Nicholas, and sobbed. Tears grimaced my face as their salty taste cushioned my lips. It was my fault she had gone. How had I not known they would go after Willa? I sniffled, wiping my tears away. Those little shits had better not touch a damned hair on her head! I stood up, picked Willa up in my arms and carried her back to the Castle. She sobbed the entire way there. Her body shook full force as she gripped at my chest hair. Nicholas, Alaric, and Xander walked behind us, staying in their wolf forms, in case any of those bastards were still around.

Mother came running out. "What happened? ETHAN WHAT HAPPENED?" I looked down, my body broken, bloodied and bruised. I looked a state, no wonder she was worried. Willa had already started healing. Her neck a mere inch of a cut and her hand sewing up nicely.

"Are there any in the Castle?" I asked.

"Any what, Ethan? Tell me what's happened!" she demanded.

"The Colourless Mother. They came for Willa!" Mother gasped. I placed Willa down and she ran up and hugged her.

Father walked out, followed by four guards. "That's not all they came for. Danica's gone."

"I'm so sorry. I'm so so sorry." Willa kept repeating. Her guilt was stifling.

"Willa, you did nothing wrong!" I said. "I failed you."

"Sorry for what?" Mother asked. Her face was full of concern.

My head lowered. "It's Cleo Mother… she's gone."

"WHAT!"

Willa stepped back to face her. "She saved me, Bernadette," she said, wiping her tears.

"Where is she?" Father asked.

I took a deep breath. "The Colourless took her father. I expect they've taken her to the Palace."

"Oh my God Oswald! Hela will kill her!"

"No! No she won't. We are going there right now. We will demand Cleo is returned to us."

Nicholas changed back to human form, tears in his eyes. "And do you really think that Devil woman is going to give us our sister back? Not a chance!"

Alaric and Xander turned back. Alaric stepped forward. "We must continue with the plan, Ethan. But while you're taking care of Hela. We will find Cleo."

I nodded. It was a good plan.

"But what if she's not there?" Mother asked.

"She will be Mother. It's the morning of the celebration. She is using Cleo to lure us there."

"We were bloody going anyway!" Willa yelled, her emotions

wild and rampant. Anger flashed through her eyes. Eyes that now glimmered red around the edges. I could see her inner wolf pushing forward. She was close to her first shift. I hoped she could hold out until we were back, safe and sound. The first shift was always the hardest. A moment where every bone in your body elongated and malformed. Muscles grew and changed. Tissues increased their elasticity. A moment of ultimate pleasure and death-defying pain. The screams of the young ones always made me shudder. Their first changes hard on their bodies as their inner wolves caressed their souls. But for Willa, she was a seventeen-year-old girl with a fragile frame. I was damned sure it would bloody hurt. I shuddered. The thought of her in so much pain made me tremble.

Mother was soothing Willa's tears as I stepped aside with Father, Alaric, Nicholas and Xander.

"It is time, my son," he said. His face stern, without reproach. "We must call on our allies, bring them here and offer them our gift. For those that take us up on it, we will teach and train them. "Now go! Get ready, take the packs and I will have them here for when you return!"

I nodded, turned, and took Willa in my arms. "Dry your tears, Princess. We are about to go to war!" She nodded, feigned a smile, and I kissed her hard.

Sleep was hard that night. We were both fraught with worry. Cleo was so young, sweet, and innocent. I did not know what Helas influence would do to her. We had a plan, though. It had to work.

Willa tossed and turned for the next few hours, by which time I gave up on sleep and gently left the bed, leaving her to sleep as much as she could. Sitting at my desk I went over the plans for tomorrow's act of all-out war. Technically, though, Hela struck first. She went below the belt on this one. No-one messes with my family!

Picking up the phone, I contacted Darius on his mobile. Updated him on the situation and he agreed to meet us there. No matter what happened, though, getting Willa out was a priority. She was too important to lose… both for me and the rest of the supernatural.

Morning rose as sunlight bled through the velvet curtains, and I realised I must have fallen asleep at my desk. Wiping away the drool from my arm, I got up and brushed my teeth. Returning to our bedroom to find Willa sat up, staring at one of my paintings.

"Is that it?" she asked, nodding at the painting. "Is that the battle?"

I smiled and sat beside her. "It was one of many, Princess. In our world, there is always some creature that wants to rule above all others."

"Do you?"

"What?"

"Do you want to rule above everyone else?"

I thought for a moment. "Honestly, no. I have enough problems being the Alpha of this pack."

She laughed.

"I don't know what you're laughing for. You're my Luna now. This all falls to you too."

"Crap." She groaned. I laughed, kissing her hard.

We got up, washed, and changed. Opting for a dark, inconspicuous look.

Grabbing the bags, we headed for the cars. The rest of the packs were already there, waiting. Tristan grinned. "Are you ready, lovebirds?"

I snarled, and Willa smirked.

"Let's get going!" I said. "It's time we showed Hela what we're made of!"

The packs roared. We entered the vehicles and set off on our journey to the palace.

Chapter Forty-three
Hela

Swirling and twirling around the room, I hugged one of the onyx pillars and sang. "Little tiny treacle tarts with blackened shadow hearts. My favourite little chew toys, my perfect little baby boys. They came with a gift, a tiny princess just… for… me." Black robes swished as I danced, picking up a squirmy little midget in my arms. Twirling and swirling around the onyx pillars, we toyed. Arm in arm with my cuddly teddy bear, I squeezed. Comforting my bosom on its weeny minor features. Smelling its strong odour of dirtied blood and gouged out tissue, my stomach rumbled. I needed this little ninja more than I needed anything right now, so I danced the dance of death as my fangs extended and I sunk down into the neck of the wriggly little beast, drinking it dry of all and any life it once lived.

"MARCUS!" I yelled, flinging its dead body across the room.

Two thick doors opened; Marcus stepped in. His amber skin alight as he sniffed the air, scenting out my mysterious little ninjas.

"Marcus! Clean that up!" I demanded, pointing to the dead midget on the floor.

He nodded, bowed, and ordered a man to rush in and remove the creature's body. I clapped. "Ooo Marcus! You didn't tell me we had a new servant!" I exclaimed, licking my lips.

"Yes, we do, my Queen. He is from the local village. Please don't kill this one."

I laughed. He was so funny, as if I would ever touch a strand of hair on my new toy's head. Walking over, I watched the man work. He was thin, scrappy looking. Probably held little blood in his body. I sighed. It wouldn't be worth the hassle. Walking back to the unconscious body of the little princess, I gushed. "My my, you are such a sweet little thing!"

I remembered back when I was merely a pup. Before everything changed and I became the almighty ruler, I am today! I beamed, stroking her wild black hair. I was this innocent once. She even looked like me. Well, perhaps if you squint with one eye shut, while looking through a frosted glass window. Then there would be a resemblance.

Tippy tapping my fingertips over her tiny jugular vein, circling it like a predator seeking its prey. Perhaps a small bite wouldn't hurt her tiny little body. Maybe a little of me would make her my own. She could be my own. Couldn't she?

I clapped, squealing out loud as my fangs protruded, joining in the dance. Sinking my teeth into her miniature neck, this child convulsed and contorted. Her body writhing under my grasp. Licking my lips, I pulled away, watching as the child screamed in pain. Biting my wrist, I poured my blood into her mouth. This one had better work, or so help me, I would slaughter every soulless creature in this vile place.

The blood dripped down her mouth, tickling her ear as she stilled her body, lying unconscious on the floor. "Well, that worked better than the last one!" I jumped up, wiping my mouth, and shimmied and skipped around the room, grasping at another miniature ninja to dance with me. One by one they poofed off, vanishing into the shadowy realm they came from. "No fun!" I yelled, tutting into the silent air. Marcus smiled, walked up, and offered his hand. Glowing amber skin wrapped around me as we danced until the clock struck noon. Twisting around, the dead body of one very young, very innocent little Princess Cleo.

"Cleo, is that what you called her?" I asked Marcus.

"Yes, my Queen." He smiled, bowed, and left the room, shutting the doors behind him.

So, Prince Ethan had a sister. Who knew! And now she's part of my new family. A family made especially by me, for me. She is a tad on the dead side right now. But she'll come round. I smirked, sitting down on the cold floor beside her. At least she didn't explode like the last hundred I'd tried turning. See that Ethan has a powerful family. One that will join me on my throne one day. I clapped, eager to see it. Cleo twitched. At least I think she did. Although it could have been me continuously nudging her with my foot.

"Cleo," I said in a creepy murderess voice. I cackled. I was going to have fun with this one!

"Little Cleo…." I sang, pulling back her eyelids as she blinked, then coughed and choked.

Awakening before me was the most glorious site. A wild child of my very own with silky black hair, a reformed pale face… to match me, of course, and the sharpest of baby fangs any vampire had ever seen. Although they'd never grow. She'd stay this little for all time. But I'm sure she will love spending eternity with me. Our new world will be both spectacular and splendid, all rolled into one fantastical, ferocious sandwich. I laughed. Cleo sat up, shaking her head. "Where am I?"

"Well now, isn't that the question of the day," I said, smirking. It was only hours ago Danica greeted me with the same line.

"You're in my Palace Princess." I smirked.

"I am!" she exclaimed, looking around. Her eyes were wide with intrigue. "How did I get here?"

"The mini men brought you my sweet cake."

"Oh, they were horrible!" she said, scrunching up her face.

I laughed. "I'm sure they will be much nicer to you now, my Cleo."

She smiled, baring her fangs, pricking her bottom lip. "Ouch!" she said, her hand feeling over her mouth. "What's happened to my teeth?"

I grinned, showing my own fantastical fangs. "Now we match!"

"How did they grow in my mouth?"

I squealed. She was so sweet I could eat her up!… but I won't… I'm sure I won't. "They grew when I changed you, Cleo. I've made you stronger, faster, and much more beautiful than you could have ever been. Much better than a mingy wolf."

Her eyes widened as she leant forward and touched my fangs with her delicate hand. "I have the same?"

I nodded, taking her hand and helping her up. "Do you want to see?"

She nodded, grinning from ear to ear.

"MARCUS!"

The double doors opened; Marcus walked in. His eyes widened when he saw my new hybrid child. "It worked!" he exclaimed, grinning.

"Yes, yes… bring me a mirror, Marcus. My Cleo wants to see her new fangs."

"Of course, my Queen!"

Cleo snapped round to face me. "You're a Queen?" I nodded, gleaming. "Can I be a Queen one day?"

I cackled. "You can be anything you want to be in my world, Cleo."

Her face lit up. "Can I show my family my fangs?"

I smirked. "Oh, I'm sure they will love to see your new fangs, my child. But for now, you must learn how to use them."

"What, like when Ethan showed me how to be a wolf?"

"Yes, quite like that."

Marcus entered, dragging in a large, long mirror. He placed it against one of the onyx pillars and bowed, leaving my throne room.

"Come here," I demanded. Cleo skipped across the room. Her eyes wide as she stared at her glorious new body, full of strength, allure, and intellect. "Do you see yourself?"

She nodded. "I look pretty!" she said, grinning.

I smirked. "You sure do. Can you see your fangs?" She nodded. "Do you know what they're for?"

"For biting people when they're naughty."

Laughter erupted from my body. "Yes… and for when you're hungry."

"But can't I eat sweets anymore?"

I laughed again, brushing back her silky black hair off of her beautiful pale face. "Yes, of course you can. But now you can eat naughty people too."

"Can I eat Danica?" she asked. "She was naughty to my brother."

I smirked. "In fact, Danica is here in this palace, too. Would you like to eat her?"

She nodded eagerly. I held out my hand. "Then come with me

and we'll take a trip through my palace so you can see Danica once again."

Taking my hand, Cleo smiled, her baby fangs protruding out from her lips. I smiled. I had a lot to teach her, she would absorb it like a sponge. This was going to be so much fun!

Chapter Forty-four
Hela

As the celebrations took hold, the ballroom was a display of magical enchantment. Edwina had done a marvel of a job with candles floating high above. The ceiling became a starry night sky while silks artists danced above, bringing an element of the circus to my celebration. Trapeze artists wandered and walked, riding bicycles across high ropes, every human gasping, shouting for more.

Fire eaters walked among us. The fantastical fires were devoured, adding to the amazement of every human in the room. Edwina smiled, Barnabus grinned. One, two, then three arrows burst through the air, caught by the immortal demon known as Abaddon. The Council knew him well. His devilish ways were to tease, torment and transfer the energy of his prey as he fed on their fear. But for now, he teased. A magnificent marvel of flames swirled and twirled through the air. Orange caressed burnt umber, giving way to the rampaging rouge as they entwined, encircling its audience.

Gasps of excitement, delight, and joy surrounded the demon. His grin grew, and the enchantment followed. Like the Pied Piper, he encapsulated every mortal in the room. Hungry grumbles filled every supernatural's stomach as Abaddon's hypnotic display led the mesmerised crowd through the ballroom, out the thick black doors and into the kitchen, where the chef stood, hatchet in hand.

Screams were heard, cries of pain and anguish. The Kane pack stood eagerly, waiting for their share. With every strike of the hatchet, each victim gurgled, choking on their blood as it fled freely from their bodies. The lower ranked vampires interceded, cleaning up the floor as they suckled on the remains of man, woman, and child. It was a glorious display of power, hunger, and thirst. Abaddon continues to play, trapping every human with his hypnotic dance of devilish desire.

On the dance floor, three more joined him. The three succubae known as Sarlissa, Keloriya and Jenasia weaving their wilds around Abaddon's enchanting body. Six hands caressed his skin, sensual and sexual. The sisters danced, delighting in every person, both human and supernatural, watching their rhythmic display in awe. Sarlissa twirled her body, snaking her way across the audience. Fiery red hair bloomed as she enchanted a young human man with blond hair and blue eyes. Her kiss is a melody in its own right, her breath falsified with the allure of a lover's mate when they reach that point of unadulterated ecstasy.

Sarlissa's body was a beauty, every shape made to draw in her prey. Lips entwined as the man's life force drained before her. His body groaned as he orgasmed through her dance of death. Finishing, she laughed, dropping him, her silky hair cushioning his fall. Dried up, dead and rotten, his corpse starred up, a darkened expression as he realised the mistake he had made. But too late was the label for everyone who ever crossed their paths. Then for the finale, her sisters took the lead, both finding their own victims, taking their beauty, their energy and ultimately their life forever more.

I clapped over the moon with the celebratory dance before me. I almost wished I could join them, but knew I'd tire of the games and eat every mortal in the palace. Smirking, I sat up, the cold onyx throne holding my spectacular body for all to see.

I was the reason they came, whether through love or fear, it didn't matter to me. This display of affection before me would not release the rage I felt deep down. They hadn't replied to my invite. Even after I'd threatened their very existence. It all came down to my tiny ninjas, and their ability to infiltrate any hovel and bring back what was rightly mine.

This time it had been Cleo, my Cleo. The first hybrid I could ever make. Bubbles of callous cackles ripped from my throat. Marcus turned around, bowed, then went back to the tempting display of scantily clad women before him.

Abaddon had disappeared. Made his way to the kitchen to help the Chef behead the rest of the mortals. I nearly kept one too. A young little girl with bright green eyes and blond hair. She was an absolute picture... especially when she saw her mother murdered before her eyes. The look of fear that governed her face is a memory I wish to treasure. There is nothing more honest than a fearful child. But then it wore off, that pale-faced look, and the screams began. I groaned. I grew tired of the screams. Chef took her head at that point... too much of a disturbance... interfering with my spectacular celebrations. I yawned, growing tired of watching the sister's dance.

Standing up, I ushered them off. The room fell silent. Every remaining mortal stood fearful and tearful. Every supernatural being eager for their turn to feast. But right now... it was my turn.

Swirling and twirling around the room, I danced. My body coiled around each spectator as I made my way to Harold, the local bar keep. I'd met him a few times, a few times more than he should have lived. But what can I say… he knew how to pour the perfect pint.

Dancing around him, I grinned, coming up behind and crushing my mouth onto his thick neck. Fangs protruded. The humans gasped, and I guzzled a few pints from the fat man. Kicking him to the floor, I clapped, and the buzzards took hold. Vampires pulled him limb from limb. Demons twisted and toyed with his mind. He was in the best company right now.

Smiling, I wiped my mouth on Marcus's sleeve. He smirked, staring down at Harold's cellulite and intestines strewn across the floor.

"Let the dancing begin!" I yelled, meaning it was a free for all in the ballroom.

Heads bounced, bodies slumped, blood, guts, and gore splattered across the room. It was a slaughterhouse, and I was their queen watching them play. Taking a deep breath, I sat down, encouraging the dance to continue.

There was one person I'd missed. Unheard of the infernal cries in the ballroom. A little girl with raven black hair. She was standing in the corner, her eyes wide, jaw dropped. I could tell the miracle of food developing before her eyes astonished her. I watched, waited. It wouldn't be long before her cravings took hold. Even after Danica, she would still feel the hunger of a new-born vampire. Let alone the fact she shared the same hybrid blood as me.

Moments later, my lips curled upwards. Her expression had darkened. Her little feet had catapulted her into the air, landing her on top of a farmer from back down in the village. She grabbed him from behind, claws dug in as he carried her like a backpack in the rain. Blood rain. I grinned as she toyed with him. Hand on my heart, I felt like a proud mummy right there and then. She was a quick learner, and the fact that she could hide her vampish appearance was a bonus. I'm sure that would come in handy. I grinned, liking my fingers.

Taking a deep breath, I called Marcus over.

"Marcus, move their remains to the side. It is time we dance off these calories, don't you think?"

He smiled, nodded, and ordered a group of human waiters in. Growls and grins cast over my supernatural ensemble. Marcus ushered them back as the waiters pushed the bloodied bodies to the side. The band played again, and I joined Barnabus for our all-time favourite waltz, gliding over the bloody floor, swirling, and twirling in his arms till the music came to a halt, and the next song began.

Continuing to dance I glided from person to person, lost in a memory of enormous dresses, fans and beautiful brides. Even without the guests of honour, this celebration was turning out to be one of the best yet. I smiled, quenching my thirst on a new-born baby a mother had left behind.

Chapter Forty-five
Willa

The sun had already set when we arrived. The journey tiresome. A car journey wasn't exactly hard on the body, but my worry for Cleo was hard on my heart. I still felt it was my fault. Although I knew Ethan never blamed me. He equally took the blame, feeling he should have protected us both. We'd talked about it on the way. We'd cried. Well, I did... he sniffled.

The last twenty-four hours had been an emotional rollercoaster for us both. My brothers had come back into the picture. I was nearly decapitated, and now Cleo had been kidnapped.

I sighed. I knew my brothers would be at the palace, and that stirred some hope within me. They'd look out for Cleo, see where she's being held. Darius had said he'd promised our father they'd be back in time for the celebrations to begin. Was I ready to see him again? My father? I know he did what he thought was best for me, but knowing how I'd been treated, you would have thought he'd have intervened. Then again, did anyone besides those that lived in the manor house know how I was treated? Nora had always made sure they dressed me as a princess every time we ventured outside. I guess in some respects, no-one saw the need to question it. I groaned. Seeing my father wasn't something I was looking forward to. Darius had told me he had grown quite cold since he joined the Council.

Ethan gripped tighter on my hand as the car slowed to a stop. The driver slid open the window. "We're here," he said. The other cars pulled up behind us.

Ethan nodded as Alaric opened the door. "Alpha, we're a mile away. We can hide the cars here," he said, pointing to the overgrown forest beside us.

I stared out of the open door. The evening sun shone down on us, casting its last shadow across the land. "So, where is the Palace?"

Alaric pointed up and in the distance. Ethan stepped out, pulling me up and out to join him. My feet squelched on the fallen rotten leaves that littered our path. In the distance, and on the top of a hill, was a large, black crystal palace overlooking the nightmarish landscape before us. The forest looked ragged. Autumn had been and gone, skeletal trees stood tall with bare claw-like branches gripping the environment.

"They're bound to see us coming from up there!" I said, pointing at the palace.

"Yes, maybe we should have tried your Google Maps before we ventured out here." Ethan said, scratching his head.

I laughed. "Have you ever even been on the Internet, Ethan?"

He shook his head. "I don't really see the point of it."

I smirked. He was missing out on so much! "I'll show you when we get back. If you ever get Wi-Fi in that Castle of yours!"

"Of ours," he corrected. I smiled, snuggling up to his arm.

"Cold?" he asked, offering me his coat.

"Thank you," I smiled. Leaning up to kiss him hard on the lips. My tongue searching his mouth, tasting him, needing him.

"Aww get a room!" Nic said, gagging.

I laughed when Ethan groaned, slapping him on the back of the head. Nic smirked.

Taking my hand, Ethan smiled. "Come on, we've got a way to go yet."

I nodded, walking hand in hand into the darkened forest ahead.

"Alaric, take Xander and Aaden and scout the way ahead." He nodded, took off his top and trousers, and shifted into wolf form. Xander and Aaden did the same.

I ran over and picked up their clothes. Ethan smirked. "What? They'll need them later!"

Placing them in my backpack, I carried on trekking across the landscape. Ethan's mother had packed light for me. Basically, a glitzy dress and a silver pair of shoes to match. The problem was she hadn't exactly packed me into a changing room to hide in. I chuckled under my breath.

"What?" Ethan asked, staring into my eyes.

"I was wondering where I'll get changed."

He growled. Clearly, he hadn't thought of this. "Hmm. Don't worry. The packs will not dare to watch you," he said.

Tristan ran past, "I can't say for certain that my pack won't." He continued running, laughing to himself as Ethan growled.

I laughed at Ethan's clear jealousy. "It'll be fine."

"They had better not watch you!" he growled.

"Ethan quit growling; you sound like an old man that smoked forty a day all his life."

He flashed me a look, narrowing his eyes. I smirked, turning his face towards me and leaning up to kiss him.

He groaned, holding my body to his. Pulling back, his eyes narrowed. "Just remember you're mine Willa Rose!"

I laughed. "Always Ethan James."

We continued to walk hand in hand. Aaden reported back that the path was clearly ahead, and we sat on a fallen tree, picnicking under the moonlight.

Ethan bought me a ham sandwich, pork pie, sausage rolls, and a bottle of juice. "Thanks," I said and smiled.

"Don't thank me. The chef arranged it."

"Who carried it, though?"

"The packs split it between them"

I nodded. Taking a bite of the sandwich, I watched as Ethan and Tristan talked tactics. They were good together, those two. Brothers from another mother. I smirked, thinking about where the heck that phrase had come from. Must have been another book or perhaps an old film I'd watched.

It was nice to see the calm before the storm, though. I wasn't sure what awaited me at the palace, but I was bloody sure I was going to fight to take down every one of those blasted Council members. Hela had a horrific childhood; I could say that for certain. But that was no excuse for her to turn into the monster she was today. Heck, I hadn't had the rosiest childhood either, but you don't see me massacring entire races.

We can win though, right? My lips pursed, breathing faltered. We had to. Cleo's life depended on it. Ethan walked over as I finished my food. "You were hungry!" he said, then smiled.

I laughed. "Famished!"

"Please remind me to feed you sooner next time." He grinned, lifting me off the branch and taking a walk with me.

"I will indeed, Mr Bane. You have no right to starve me!"

He chuckled and gripped my hand tighter. "Come here!" he said, pushing me down to the ground. Pulling at my top, he slid his tongue over my stomach, unzipping my jeans with his teeth. Feeling for my panties, he slowly slid them down. His thumb caressing my lip as he placed butterfly kisses on the inside of my thigh. Biting my bottom lip, I groaned.

He kissed and nipped his way up and over my body, positioning himself, growling. His eyes eager for more. I pulled his lips to mine and tasted him. A hot, passionate kiss. One where our tongues collided, tastes intermingled, and our arousal exploded. Hell, I needed him! Pulling him closer, I pulled his jeans over his buttocks, freeing his hard cock. Taking a sharp breath, I curled my legs over him, taking him inside me as he mounted me right there and then. Holding my arms above my head, he moved up and down, slowly at first, speeding up as the friction kissed my clit repeatedly. Nails dug in, panting hard as we were in the throes of passion. Toes curled, body tense, I screamed out, tightening my inner walls around him. His body arched, tensed as he groaned, biting down on my mark, intensifying the pleasure as we orgasmed together. Hot. Sweaty and Happy.

"You two finished?" Nic asked, bounding in, sitting beside us.

"NIC!" I yelled, pulling up my jeans and fixing my top.

"What? It's not like the entire pack didn't hear you!"

Ethan chuckled. "You were very loud."

My face flushed. He laughed, rubbing his thumb along my cheekbone.

"My Luna," he said, standing up. I smiled, taking the hand he offered. He rested his arm around me, held me close, and we joined the rest of the two packs. There were a few sniggers when we joined them. Ethan growled, and they soon stopped.

An hour later, we reached the middle of the forest, staring up at the crystal palace on the hill. Ethan stopped. "Okay, time to get changed. Make yourselves scarce," he said.

Ethan faced me. Tristan, Alaric, and Nic faced away as they formed a circle around me. I frowned.

"There you go, now no-one will see you."

"This is weird, Ethan," I said, brow furrowed.

He chuckled. "They won't turn around."

I groaned. "Fine!" I took the dress out from my bag, pulled off my boots, jeans and top, and Ethan helped me slide into it.

"You look gorgeous Princess!"

Nic coughed. "Can we turn around yet?"

I grinned, "yes, thank you."

They turned around and stood silently, staring at me.

"What?"

Ethan growled. Tristan held up his hands. "What, you can't blame me mate, look at her!"

"Bloody unmated wolves!" he said, growling.

I laughed.

"Want a hand with your shoes?" Nic asked. Ethan growled again.

"Yes, that would be lovely, thank you Nic."

Nic stuck his tongue out at Ethan and buckled both shoes for me.

Ethan narrowed his eyes and swatted him afterwards. Alaric laughed, picked up the backpack, and carried it for me. I smiled, thanking him.

Three steps forward, and I must have looked like a penguin on ice as Ethan picked me up and carried me the rest of the way. I smiled, staring at his chiselled jaw, stubble, and ocean blue eyes. Taking a long, deep breath, I rested in his arms, content in the moment.

Chapter Forty-six
Willa

We arrived at the gates. Ethan placed me down on the path and pulled out a shirt, switching up his black inconspicuous top for a deep blue slim fitted one. His muscles were on show. I rolled my eyes. Of course they were. But damn, he looked good.

"Right, Betas, you're in charge of the packs. Tristan, you're with me. Make sure my Luna is safe at all times." Tristan nodded and patted me on the shoulder. "Everyone ready?" The pack Betas nodded and ordered the packs into hiding. Tristan pulled on a shirt, and we walked along the gravel path to the iridescent black palace before us.

Two guards were stationed at the gate. "NAMES" they boomed. Ethan growled and Tristan gave our names. There was no use in hiding it. She would catch our scent a mile off.

The doors opened, and they directed us along a glass corridor, across the hall, to the right and toward the sounds of screams, laughter, anguish, and joy. Every step we took, I trembled more. How could my brothers live here? I feared for them, felt sorrow at the lives they must have lived. The crystal palace was beautiful, but it was born from darkness, and no matter how far you ran from it, the darkness would always seep inside. This place was cursed.

I held my breath when we arrived. Ethan's grip tightened on my hand. Two tall, black wooden doors lay closed in front of us. "Breathe Willa!" Ethan said, looking alarmed.

I gasped for breath.

"Are you okay?" he asked. I nodded. Tristan stood watching me. "If you want to leave, we can right now," he said.

"I can't. We need to find Cleo!"

Ethan sighed; his expression saddened. He nodded.

Tristan placed a hand on my shoulder. "Ready?" he said.

I took a deep breath in and exhaled. "Ready" I said, nodding.

Tristan pushed open the doors, and all hell broke loose.

No-one seemed to notice our arrival. They were too preoccupied with the massacre unravelling before us. It was a sight of complete devastation. A horrific scene expected from the likes of Hannibal Lector in Silence of the Lambs. Monsters bathed in the blood of the innocent. Wolves wore the pelts of their fallen comrades, and Shifters delighted in their ability to remove the skin off the dead, wearing their faces as masks at a masquerade ball.

In the centre of it all danced a deadly viper, a fanged foe with a porcelain face and jet-black hair. She was covered in blood, trails of which began at her mouth. Hela swayed her body around every living person in the room. They chanted her name, sang her song, and danced in the delight of her presence. Her audience was besotted with her, and through all the chaos, pain, and dismay, I could not see why. This life was not one any sane person would want to live. So why would they? Perhaps they had lost their humanity as she did. Maybe they fight for the ability to feel again. Could the only way they feel be one of pain, fear, and anguish that they delivered to their victims?

The three of us were stone silent. There were simply no words. Ethan gripped my hand and pulled me backwards. His fear for my life engulfed my senses.

"You can't be here!" he said to me, his eyes wide with fright.

I took a deep breath. "I have to be," I said, letting go of his hand and stepping into the room.

Two vampires snarled in the corner, spotting us as we arrived. Behind us footsteps ran down the glass corridor. "Willa!" a voice yelled. I spin around as Ethan pulls me back. Darius!

My brothers catch up with us. Darius keeps his distance, not wanting anyone to discover we were related. "Willa. We have to go in."

"Don't!" I plead, taking his hand. He pulls it back and looks around.

"We have to Willa; they'll suspect something's wrong if we don't."

Adam stepped forward. "Do you want us to announce you?"

I gulped. Tristan nods, whereas Ethan still grips my hand tight.

Darius nods and my brothers enter the room, heading off to the side, out of sight.

I watch as Adam whispers to an amber skinned man. He claps and draws Helas attention. She turns, the music stops, and every eye in the room is directed straight at us.

"Shit." Tristan says.

Hela jumps up and down in glee. "Come in. Come in!" She sings in a high-pitched voice.

I swallow back my fear. Waiters walk past us and pull the remaining limbs from the room. Dead bodies trail blood down the corridor.

"There, look," she squeals. "It's all pretty again. Come in! Come in!"

I step forward, but Ethan holds me back. "We have to, Ethan!" He growls, then nods. Hela squeals, clapping her hands.

Taking a deep breath, we all walk in together.

"Come, come," let me look at your bride Prince Ethan!"

I walk forward with Ethan. Around me vampires snarl, wolf's growl and shifters laugh. Even the odd red demon parades across the room. The scene was a setting from a darkened version of Alice in Wonderland, where the Red Queen was actually Hela in disguise. She certainly appeared that way. After all, they'd displayed the heads of her previous victims on spikes around the room. Gulping, I looked at every one of them. One familiar head screamed out during his last moments. Lucius Daventry. I nudged Ethan, and he looked over and nodded. It was. So where was Danica? Thankfully, though, I couldn't see Cleo on display with them, so I had to have hope!

We reached the throne and Hela stepped down; her slinky body jingled with all the beads she wore over her body. At least we'd hear her coming, I thought, smirking. Shit. We're dead anyway. A little humour can at least lighten that fact.

"Ethan!" she says, running her hands over his back and chest as she stalks around him.

"Hello Hella," he says, his voice cold and angered.

"Oh, how I've missed you!"

His brow furrowed; expression darkened. "We've never met Hela,"

"No, but I feel like I know everything about you," she exclaimed, squealing, squeezing him.

"Danica, I presume?"

"Now, how did you guess?"

"It wasn't hard."

"Took you four years though, didn't it," she squealed, clapping her hands. His eyes narrowed. "And if this little minx here hadn't stolen your gaze, you'd be a member of my Council by now!"

"I doubt that," he said. I smirked.

"Oh, Princess Willa, aren't you a rare flower."

"Why thank you, Hela," I said with a sarcastic undertone.

Hela pauses, looks at me, then bursts into laughter. "Oh, I like this one!" she exclaims. "MUSIC!" she yells, clapping her hands. Taking Ethan's other hand, she pulls him towards her, and we lose grip on one another. In mere seconds the room filled with all manner of creatures dancing around. Hand's grip on my own, spinning me around and around until I fall to the floor, dizzy and confused. My heart pounds, sweat beads on my brow. Where is Ethan! I stand up, searching the room, but he's vanished. Tristan is on the other side, looking around. "TRISTAN!" I yell, waving at him. He nods and sees me, just as a vampire pushes me to the ground.

Amongst all the legs, shoes, and footsteps, I'm lost, trapped in a never-ending dance of despair. Panic radiates through me, my chest tightens, breathing speeds up. Ready to scream, cry or claw my way out, I push myself up, coming face to face with a wild, madly grinning Hela. "Care to dance?" she says, grabbing my hand. I'm pulled around, twirled and spun from person to person. The darkness of the room encapsulates my vision, faces merge, creature's laugh and chant around me. No matter how much I try, I cannot stop the migraine from forming within. Vision blurred, heart palpating. I gag at the swirling despair before my eyes.

Hela grabs me and pulls me up into her arms. She grins, drops me down on her knee, then kisses me. Ice stiff lips steam against my own, and in the moonlight's glimmer that glares through the window, I see her garter knife pulled free. A shimmering, sharpened blade rises above me. She squeals. A sadistic smile fills her face as she slams it down to my chest. Cheers emanate across the room. I wince, bracing for impact. The final moments of my life flashing before my eyes. But the pain never strikes. The sharpened blade never touches my skin, and I am hurtled across the room, flying into the arms of my brothers.

"Willa!" Darius yells, picking me up. An old man beside him looks at me, his face familiar. My father. "Go Willa, run!" he screams.

A moment of madness escaped me as I turned to see it was Tristan's wolf who pushed me free. Hela was sitting on top of him, plunging the knife in over and over again. His body convulsing, his mouth choking on the blood.

"TRISTAN!" I yell, trying to save him. Darius and my father pull me back.

Hela cackles as she pulls his head clean off. I scream, pushing to reach him.

"He's gone Willa! You must run! Take Ethan and run!"

My heart sinks, tears streaming from my face. "Where is Ethan?"

Darius points to see Hela laughing. Ethan shifts, slicing her face open and knocking her backwards. She jumps on his back, grips his chest, squeezing him with all her might. Ethan yelps. Adam runs forward, but Hela bats him away. My brothers pile on as I stand there, silent, frozen in the moment. Ethan's eyes turn from ocean blue to silver, fading before my eyes. He was dying. His body shakes as she squeezes the air right out of him.

Fists pummelled, body tense, I scream. "YOU WILL NOT HAVE MY MATE!" My body convulses, pain ignites my core, and every bone in my fragile frame distorts, crying out to change. Tissue moulds over me, muscles tear and reform. The agony I felt was excruciating. Teeth extend and my face grows out as I roar so loud the candles flicker out, and darkness reigns over the room.

Silence. In that moment, not a soul spoke. Darkness cast a spell across the room. Not a proper spell, but a jaw-dropping silence of magnificent proportion. Padding forwards, I caught my reflection in the mirror. Reflecting back at me was the face of a crimson wolf, a deep red snarling beast whose fur was alight with flame. I was larger than any who stood before me. Grander than any that ever lived. I had shifted for the first time, and every person in the room was in shock from it.

Ethan let out a gasp of air as he freed himself from the vices of a very shocked hybrid Hela.

Hela shook herself, growling. Her hands turned to claws as she swiped Ethan across the back. I growled, stepping forward, looming above her, her little body wide eyed below me. My fur was on fire as she backed away, screaming for her guests to do something.

Ethan shifts back, walks towards me "Willa?" he asks. I look over at him. My green eyes soften, and I nod.

"We must go, Princess." I nod again, turn away from him, facing the crowd and roar, every creature silenced in fear.

Ethan picks Tristan's body up and we run from the room, my brothers in tow. Feet pad the glass floor as we run as quickly as we can, pounding through the palace, escaping as our packs jump in to join us.

Alaric stopped dead, staring up at me. "Alaric take Tristan!" Ethan says, passing him Tristan's body. He whimpers when he looks down.

Ethan took a deep breath, faced me, and rubbed his hand over my flaming fur. It didn't burn him. For that I was amazed, but thankful for. "Willa, you need to change back. You won't be able to blend in amongst the trees."

Nic stepped forward, holding an unconscious Cleo in his arms. "Aww kitty, you'd stand out like a sore thumb in there!" I growled at him, and he stepped back, wide eyed.

Taking a deep breath, I stand there, relaxing every part of my body, willing it to shift back.

"Relax Willa!" Ethan says.

What do you think I'm doing! I growl at him.

Once again, I relax each part of myself. Shaking my body as I begin the shift back to my human form. Going backwards wasn't so bad. It made me feel sick though, like someone was washing up in your stomach. Bile wretched as I fully transformed, falling to the floor. Ethan picked me up, and we ran from the palace.

Even through the pounding of Ethan's feet on the gravel path, I could hear Helas screams behind us. "GET THEM!" she yelled, as she screamed so much that her crystal palace cracked, shattering around her.

Chapter Forty-seven
Willa

The journey home was a silent one. Ethan and I sat with Tristan's body on the seat opposite. We'd tried to cover him up as best we could. But his bloody hand hung down, bouncing around with every bump or turn the driver made.

Why did Tristan do this? Why sacrifice himself for me? Ethan would be lost without him. I know he jumped in front to save me. But it had cost him his life. Hela had ripped his head clean off his wolfed-out body. He'd shifted back to his headless form, blood squirting everywhere. The packs had gone mad at that point. Understandably so!

Ethan was raging, ready to turn on every person in the place, and he would have done. But Hela was fast. We never realised how powerful she was. She had Ethan in her deadly grip within seconds. It was only me changing into the flaming red wolf that averted her eyes.

The entire event was a shit show from the beginning, and now our friend had paid dearly for it.

Tears welled in my eyes. It was so close! Too close! Why hadn't I attacked her, I had her there below me, stunned into silence. I could have ripped her head from her body if I'd tried. Why didn't I try?

Ethan pulled me close, held me tight. I pulled back, shaking my head. None of it made sense. But through it all, we'd saved Cleo. I sighed. Ethan kissed my forehead, sat back, and I leant into him. At least I think we'd saved Cleo. She was clearly delusional, spurting all kinds of rubbish as Nic pulled her away. I shook my head; I hate to think what torture she endured in that psychopaths' hands. She looked pale too, cold skinned, saddened. Her body had become the opposite of what she used to be, and I could tell it'd take a long while to get her back to us.

Leaning my head on Ethan's shoulder, I closed my eyes. We still had a few hours left to go, and I couldn't bear looking at Tristan's corpse any longer. Ethan kissed my head, his hand stroking my hair as a tear dropped onto my face. He was crying. It wasn't something I expected to see. But he needed this. He needed to live through his grief and heal one emotion at a time.

Gripping his hand tighter, his body shook. He buried his head in mine and let out the pain she'd caused us all. Shaking violently, he coughed, choking on his tears as he regained control.

"Are you okay?" I asked, sitting up and wiping the tears from his face. I could have kicked myself though… What a stupid bloody question.

He took a deep breath, regaining control. "I will be," he said with a faint smile. He lent forward, took Tristan's hand, and covered it over. I nodded, taking a sharp breath. Thank God he'd hidden it away. It almost made the journey more bearable again.

"Do you want to talk about it?" I asked.

He shook his head. "No, what I want is revenge," he growled. "What I want is her head on a block… and what I will do is destroy every single one of her followers." He growled deeper. "When I'm finished with her, there will be nothing left. No Council. No palace and no more pain."

I nodded; lips curled upwards. He was a tad scary right now. I grinned, licking my lips. I liked it.

Turning to face him, I pulled his head around and our eyes met. He growled, gripping my neck. Pulling my face to his. Lips crashing together, we kissed hard. He groaned, pulling my body on to his.

"We can't do this," I said, panting, looking towards Tristan's body. "Not here."

He nodded, yelled for the driver to stop. Got out. Picked me up and raced over to one of the other vehicles.

Opening the door, four faces looked stunned. "Get out!" He yelled. They fled, even the driver left rather quickly.

Pushing me on to the back seat, he jumped in, closed the door, and ripped off my clothes. Lying bare on the cool leather, I groaned as he felt down below. Growling louder, he kissed my body all over. Ravaging every inch of me, as if his life depended on it. I wasn't complaining, though. It was quite the opposite. I'd already reached my peak by the time he thrust himself into me. Our sweaty bodies moved together in pure ecstasy. He needed this, heck; I needed this. It was a release of pleasure in a purely painful time. Arching upwards we came, every part of me screaming out in joy. Ethan stiffened, growled loud and slumped down beside me, exhausted.

Sweaty lips met when he kissed me. His tongue searched deep inside. Holding his head, I kissed him hard. Pulled away and kissed him again.

He smiled, "you are so fucking sweet Willa, I could devour every inch of you!"

I laughed. "I think you've already done that, Ethan!" He grinned.

Searching the floor of the car, I found my underwear ripped into pieces. Same as the rest of my clothes. I smirked.

"It looks like you owe me a shopping trip," I grinned, holding up half a tee shirt.

He grinned. "I'd have you wear nothing all day if I could Willa. But I'd be pretty pissed if anyone else laid eyes on your scrumptious ass."

My eyes narrowed, and I pouted. "Can I borrow your tee shirt? Otherwise, the entire world will see my sweet ass," I said, then laughed.

He smirked. "Yes, wait… I'll get Alaric to get your bag for you."

I nodded.

"Alaric, Get Willa's bag, it's in our car."

"Yes Alpha, I've already got it… thought you might need it after the clothes ripping started."

My face flushed, and I buried myself deeper into the car seat. Shit. They heard everything. I swear I'm never going to get used to their heightened senses!

Ethan laughed, opened the door a little, blocking my body from view, and took the bag.

I rummaged around, pulled out jeans, underwear, and another tee shirt. "Please don't ruin this one, I kinda like it."

He grinned. "You can continue to wear my top if it makes you feel better?"

I smiled and nodded. His tee shirt had his scent on. An aroma I could lap up at any second of the day. One I could easily get lost in.

Ethan grinned when he saw me sniffing at his top. "It looks like your wolf abilities are taking form."

I chuckled. He had a point. Everything seemed stronger around me, my eyes more focused, hearing on point, and of course my sense of smell was more than intact and meant I'd easily be able to track Ethan's scent should I ever need to.

In fact, I had the entire pack's scents stored in my mind. I could tell exactly who was outside the car and even hear as they complained about their hunger.

They had a point, though. My stomach grumbled and I could surely eat for a week right now.

Ethan smiled, looking at my stomach. "Your first shift takes its toll. You could do with some food."

"I think we all could," I said, nodding towards the men outside.

He laughed. "They're always hungry."

"I can see why!" I laughed.

He grinned, opened the door, and held out his hand. I took it as he pulled me out of the car into his arms.

"Let's get some food, shall we?"

Alaric nodded. "The driver says there's a fast-food drive through right down the road beside Kappers Barn."

Ethan nodded. "Sounds good to me. Alaric orders for everyone and takes Xander to collect it."

Alaric nodded, and the four of them got back in their car and drove off. Ethan smiled, "are you okay with travelling in the same car as Tristan?" he asked.

I took a deep breath and nodded. I would not stop him saying goodbye to his friend, now was I.

We drove off and pulled up in the car park of the fast-food restaurant. Alaric was already there with bags of food. He passed us ours through the window and we both delved in.

"Where's Nic and Cleo?" Ethan asked, noticing a car missing

from our fleet.

    I shrugged, but alarm bells rang inside me.

    Where were they?

Chapter Forty-eight
Ethan

Where the fuck was Cleo?

Fists pummelled, heart pounding. Shit.

"They could have stopped for a pee," Alaric said, as hopeful as ever. "You know Nic will protect her."

I growled, getting out of the car. Willa stood next to me and nodded, thanking Alaric. "Ethan, give him a break, they're going out to look for them now." My eyes narrowed; teeth bared. Argh! If it were anyone but Willa, I'd have ripped into them for saying that. Hot damn, she had me wrapped around her little finger! Gripping her waist, I closed the gap between us, staring deep into her eyes. Lips crushing together, hungry for more.

She groaned, nipples hard against my tee shirt.

Pulling away I licked my lips. She tasted so sweet!

"I can't contact them," Alaric said, concerned.

"They must be out of range," Darius said, walking over. Great, that's all I need!

"Darius," I said, nodding.

Darius nodded back and spoke to Willa. "What's wrong?"

"Nic and Cleo are missing," she said.

"Maybe they drove off earlier… couldn't be bothered to listen to you two making out." Willa's face flushed.

"Crap. Did you hear that?"

"Yeah, little sister, as did the rest of the pack." She groaned.

I smirked, pulling Willa in close. She looked at me and snarled.

"What?" I said,

"I'll take Adam and Xander," Alaric said. I pulled back from Willa, kissed her forehead, and nodded. Willa sat on the car bonnet and delved into the food, grabbing a burger and fries for herself, and handing the rest over to me. Darius continued chatting with her, talking about the prophecy by the sounds of it. But I couldn't concentrate. Nic and Cleo were still missing. I sighed. My stomach grumbled. I hadn't eaten for well over twenty-four hours and for a wolf, that's not a good thing. No wonder I was over the edge today. Then again, Tristan's corpse may have something to do with that!

Alaric jumped in one car, turned on the ignition and pulled away when a ragged black Mercedes pulled into the car park. They were here! Alaric jumped out and ran over. The front tyre was shot. Blown out by the looks of it.

Nic stepped out and ran past us, straight to the food. I smirked. He was easily pleased. Cleo stepped out and held her hand up against the sunlight. She shuddered and sat back in the dark car.

Willa looked at me, frowning. "What?"

She smiled. "I'll see how she is."

I nodded, taking a bite from my burger.

Willa jumped off the car, picked up another burger and headed over to Cleo, getting in next to her in the car.

Nic strode over. "How's Cleo?" I asked.

"She's messed up, man!" He said, spinning his finger round by his head. "Completely cuckoo!"

I frowned. "Why? What did she say?"

"That's just it. She hasn't!"

My eyes widened.

"She's been silent the whole journey, staring at me, licking her lips… it's weird!"

"Maybe the burger will help?"

He shrugged. "Whatever is going on in that head of hers, it's not good!"

"She'll feel better when she's home."

Nic nodded. At least I hoped she would.

Willa came back from the car, frowning.

"How is she?"

Her lips pursed; eyes narrowed. "Honestly, I don't know. But she was definitely hungry. She devoured that burger within seconds of me giving it to her." I nodded. That could be it. Women, even little ones… they get hangry.

Willa narrowed her eyes at me. Shit, did I say that aloud? I smiled "what?"

"You've got that look on you…"

"What look?"

"The one when you're plotting something."

Technically, I wasn't. I was pointing out the obvious. Although, "I think she needs more food and a good night's rest at home."

Nic nodded, grabbed a large bag of food, inhaled a burger, then headed back to the car. That should keep her hunger at bay. Hela must have starved her! The poor kid!

Xander cleaned up, and we all went back to the cars. We had several hours left to travel and would need to be well rested by the time we reached our home. The next few days would be lost to plotting, planning, and scheming. We would avenge Tristan and honour his sacrifice, if it was the last thing I did.

But first. First, I needed to talk about baby werewolves with Willa. If father's plan were in play, we would soon have an army of humans ready to turn into wolves, and most of those would be from Willa's adopted family. She needed to know.

Sitting back down, Willa rested her head on my shoulder. The last few days had been exhausting for her. The talk could wait. At least for an hour or two. She needed rest. I closed my eyes and breathed in her scent of roses and lavender. Relaxing, I lay my head on hers, steady breathing, slower heart rate. I drifted off into a land of dreams. One where all was right with the world again. Willa was by my side. Tristan was alive. Hela was dead. Life was perfect. Completely and utterly perfect.

Chapter Forty-nine
Hela

What utter tragedy has befallen me? Since when did a child of human descent shift into a flaming red wolf before my eyes? I staggered backwards, recalling the event. To say it simply exposed me to the depths of her darkness was an understatement. She didn't just wolf out. She went full prophecy on me. I cackled callously. And here I am sitting on my glorious throne as Queen of all things peculiar and yet I never saw that coming. I sighed, tip tapping my fingers on the edge of the onyx throne.

"MARCUS!"

The double doors flew open, and my amber skinned madman walked in.

"Yes, my Queen?"

"Did you know that the primped-up princess was, in fact, the flaming red wolf from the prophecy Edwina loved to talk about?"

He shook his head, lips pursed. "No, my Queen!"

"Huh, well that makes two of us then!" I shrugged. "So where did the delight that is Willa go?"

"I don't know my Queen."

I stood up, tutting, and shaking my finger.

"Did you even check in the hallway?"

"I did my Queen."

"What about in the linen cupboard?"

"No, she is not in there either."

"Hmm… she's a tricky one she is."

"Indeed, my Queen."

I swirled my hand over the shiny onyx pillar. It was so cold, so… I took a deep breath; so, exhilarating. Unlike my disaster of a celebration last night.

How could Prince Ethan even hope to bed his wife if she were too busy fulfilling this pathetic prophecy! Well, attempting to at least. And those soldiers of mine. The Amber Rose clan. Why did they crowd her and help her escape? What were they even thinking? I screamed. Marcus jumped. It just wasn't right! None of it was! Had there been traitors in my midst for all this time? Hadn't I given them a home, love, and a family? What more did they want from me?

I ushered Marcus out of the throne room. "Go bring Henrick to me. The brothers too. Oh, and those pretty little ladies I married off. Bring them too."

"Yes, my Queen." He bowed and walked out of the room.

Moments later, two of my guards dragged in Alpha Henrick of the Amber Rose pack, forcing him down to his knees.

"Oh, Henrick my sweet. Did you not think I would find out about your betrayal?"

"No, your majesty. It was not a betrayal. We simply did not want to dirty your ranks with a human child."

Explosions of cataclysmic cackles erupted out of me. "So, she was in fact your blood born daughter?"

He nodded. "Yes, but she was a mistake. Nothing more."

"A mistake that cost me dearly!" I sat back on the throne after kicking him hard in the gut.

He coughed and spluttered. I smiled from ear to ear. It bought me comfort seeing him wobble like that.

Perhaps I should take comfort in the fact I needed comfort?

So up I stood, running for the head of the man. Kicking it up high as it rose, flying across the room.

"GOAL!" I yelled, squealing.

Marcus chuckled. "Amazing shot my Queen!" He said, clapping.

A trail of blood splattered across the floor. I jumped and danced, swirling and twirling. I couldn't help the ecstasy I felt at that moment. Sinister smiles, callous cackles. I was in awe of my right foot right now and in love with the ultimate power I possessed with it.

Henricks head rolled across the floor. His limp body spurting blood from the gigantic hole where his head used to be. I'm not saying that he had an enormous head… but he kinda did!

Panting hard, I danced my devilish way over to my throne. Taking in the sights of the dead wolf before me. The head of the clan. Dead. Cold and Bloody. I loved it!

***

The following day I arose from my slumber. A nightmare of dreams had segregated my sleep pattern. I yawned, stretching from my tippy toes to my fingertips. I'd slept well. Like the dead, some might say. Chuckles escaped my lips.

It was a bright, sunny day. Not the best for one with vampirism in their blood. But still I loved to see the sunshine, even if it did burn a little. Thankfully though, as a hybrid I healed pretty quick, so I never suffered. Not that I'd mind suffering. It's all part of the journey of life, after all. Or death in my case. Well, perhaps not death. Maybe an in between. To be completely honest, I wasn't sure at what state of living I was in. Granted, I breathed. Had a faint pulse… very faint, mind you. But I'd lost all colour when he changed me. Daddy dearest wasn't that keen on having a tanned wolf daughter. No, he wanted it all. Thus, the birth of the one and only hybrid… well, until now.

I closed my eyes again, picturing her silky black hair. She was so young. So sweet. Perfect almost. My new and only hybrid child, and she was all mine. I know. I know. They had taken her. But I had a teeny-weeny devilish plan up my sleeves and my Cleo had a large role to play in that.

I got up, stretched again, and splashed my absolutely gorgeous face with water. Hmm… what to do today?

So, if I recall from Marcus's ranting last night. The vampire named Vivian is bringing Henricks daughter Myra to the Palace to play. I clapped, swirling around, my arms wide and reaching.

It would be spectacular. I knew it would be! And looking at the clock, she would be here just after breakfast. Hmm. Presuming they could enter through the front door. I groaned. Me and my screamy mouth. Now I had a tower to rebuild and crystals to fix. Huffing, I made a mental note to get Marcus to hire more townies to fix my shattered tower.

Now it's time for breakfast. It was one of my many favourite meals of the day. It involved the latest local human with a dashing of pastries on the side. Granted, I might be a vampire, but my wolf's side still craved a Danish every now and again… the pastry type, not the person. My eyes narrowed. In fact, I've never really had a

Danish human before. I wonder if they're a delicacy. Mental note… ask Marcus to find me a Danish human!

Okay, so breakfast came and went, as scrumptious as a homeless woman could be. Why I was fed the scraps of the streets, I do not know. I certainly wasn't keen on the sordid nature of it! It felt like my teeth needed a good brushing! Burgh! I sat on my throne, thinking. I was never too keen on the whole blood farming thing; it sounded hard work, but maybe that was the answer? But this was as bad as drinking from rats in the sewer, and I certainly didn't fancy that again. Ooo, maybe that's exactly what I need! A blood farm! "MARCUS!"

"Yes, my Queen."

"We need a blood farm."

"Pardon?"

"A blood farm, Marcus… do I need to spell it out?"

"Perhaps, my Queen."

"Find a farm, put healthy humans in, and slowly drain their blood. If you do it slowly enough, they'll replenish and provide the perfect food source."

"But won't we have to care for them too, my Queen?"

"Really? But why?" I frowned; lips pursed.

"Otherwise, they will die and no longer be able to deliver blood for you."

"Hmm." I taped my fingers on the handle of the throne. "Yes. Then you can feed them. Water too… that makes them produce more blood."

"We will need security as well, my Queen."

I nodded, eyes wide. "Yes! We must keep them safe."

"And to stop them running away my Queen!"

"Why would they run away?" I puzzled; brow furrowed.

Marcus winced. "They may not like donating blood?"

I sat back; jaw dropped. "They do it all the time in those little baggies with the needles. What's the difference?"

He shrugged. "We could call it a national blood drive. Every citizen must donate to save tiny humans in caves or something?" Marcus smirked. "What? Those humans will believe anything."

He nodded. "Okay my Queen, I'll have Pippa look into it."

"Yes, yes… she's good at all that organising stuff."

He smiled. Bowed graceful and backed out of the throne room, closing the double doors behind him.

In entered Vivian, the smartest Vampire teen, this side of the block. Well, at least he thought he was.

"Vivian! It's been too long!" I exclaimed. Not long enough, more like! He walked towards me, took my hand and kissed it, leaving a saliva trail right in the centre. I gagged, wiping my hand on my robe.

"Now, Vivian, where is that gorgeous nephew of mine?" I grinned ear to ear.

In walked a very ragged brunette, Myra. She'd lost a good four stone since I last saw her, practically skin and bone. Holding her hand was her three-year-old little boy, Joey. His blond curls and pale skin reminded me of Vivian. It was only his eyes that matched Myra's. Joey was my one and only nephew. Well, he wasn't, really. But he was all the same. Little Joey had the blood of a werewolf in his veins. An Amber Rose one, in fact. I smirked. But he also had the vampiric nature of Vivian. One of my first turned vampires after daddy dearest turned me into the most powerful hybrid in the World. Well, until little Joey was born. He came naturally to this pair. He practically bit his ferocious way out of Myra, but somehow this mini miracle survived.

Little Joey saw me, let go of his mother's hand, and ran over.

"Auntie Helly!" he yelled, hugging my legs. I bent down, picked him up, and planted butterfly kisses all over his belly. He squirmed and wriggled.

"Hello, my little man. How are you doing?"

"I'm good Auntie Helly. Daddy says I'm growing big and strong!" he said, showing his muscles.

I laughed. "You sure are!"

"Myra," I said, calling her over. She looked worse than that homeless woman from earlier. "Come here Myra," I ordered. Myra walked over. "I have a fun day planned for us all." She smiled. I turned to Little Joey. "Do you want to know what we're going to do?"

He nodded, jumping up and down. "We're going to make a movie!"

Myra shuddered. Little Joey squealed.

"What's we doing in it?" he asked, jumping from foot to foot.

"We're playing headball. Have you heard of it?" He shook his little head. Vivian smirked. I nodded to him, and he grabbed Myra by the throat.

"Kneel before your Queen!" he demanded. She winced at his grip. Eyes watering in pain. Little Joey stood silent, brow furrowed, watching as his father pushed his mother to the floor.

"KNEEL!" Vivian yelled, kicking Myra's legs from under her. She knelt. Tears streaming down her dirtied, sullen face.

Marcus strode in with a phone. "Would you like me to start now, my Queen?" I nodded. He stood behind me, videoing Myra, Little Joey, and Vivian. I strode in front of the camera and blew it a kiss, smirking.

"Now, Little Joey, this is your mother, isn't it?"

"Yes, Auntie Helly. Mummy is right there with Daddy."

Myra squirmed under Vivian's grasp. He held her hair taught, pushing her body to the ground. Vivian lent down and dug his fangs into her bony neck. Myra screamed. I clapped.

"Joey, did you want to have a go with Daddy?" I asked, ushering him over to them. Joey looked concerned. "What's wrong Joey?"

"I don't want to hurt Mummy," he said, his head lowered to the floor.

"Oh Joey, Mummy is poorly, and this will help her heal and go on to the next special place."

"But will she be gone then?"

I nodded.

"Don't listen to them, Joey!" Myra shouted. Vivian slapped her to the floor. Marcus gasped behind the camera.

I knelt down beside Joey. "Your mummy is very sick. She doesn't know what she is saying anymore, and we are afraid she might try to hurt you." Joey's bottom lip wobbled.

Myra sobbed, and Vivian hit her again.

"Come here, little Joey," I said, giving him the biggest cuddle. He cried in my arms, pulled away, and nodded.

"Okay, I help her get better?"

"It's okay, Joey, you're not strong enough for headball yet. But I can show you if you'd like. Then you can help the rest of Myra's family."

"Really! Can I see them?"

"Of course you can. I'm sure they would love to see you."

"And I can help them too?"

I nodded, placing him on the floor and stretching, striking a pose. "Are you ready?"

Vivian nodded. Little Joey clapped. I walked backwards. Vivian pulled Myra up to a sitting position, gripping her hair. She braced herself for the inevitable, holding her eyes shut tight.

"Ready… steady… go!" I yelled, running forward and kicking Myra in the head as hard as I could. Her head flew from her neck, Joey gasped. Blood trailed across the room as Myra's shocked head crashed through the window and out into the forest below."

"GOAL!"

Vivian jumped up, still holding a clump of Myra's hair in his hand, scalp attached.

Joey looked over as his mother's dead body twitched on the floor, blood flowing freely from it. He licked his lips. Vivian took his hand and pulled him towards her.

Marcus walked around, zoomed in on the corpse, then into Vivian and finally Little Joey, as they feasted on her free-flowing blood. I sat back on my throne and smiled.

Chapter Fifty
Ethan

"There's got to be another way, Ethan!" Willa said as she slumped down in the chair. The early evening sun cascaded through the library windows. We'd spent the day talking, going over our plans for the war ahead. Dust scattered across the room as Willa huffed. I sighed. "It's just... they don't know what they're getting into."

"I know. But who do you think Hela will come after when she's finished with us?"

Willa looked down at the floor. "I didn't think of that."

Sitting beside her I took her hand. She looked at me. "We will give them the choice."

"They won't believe us Ethan... You've never met my stepsister."

"I'm sure they will when we shift in front of them."

"Wait what?"

"It's the only way!"

"I thought you avoided shifting in front of humans."

I smiled. She was right. Before Willa, I purposely avoided humans at all costs. They're tendency to dramatize everything really grated on me."

"We do. FALCON doesn't take too kindly to it. But this calls for all the rules to be broken."

She nodded. "Will they come after us?"

"Who FALCON?" she nodded. "Probably."

"So, we're trading one enemy for another?"

"Yeah. I guess so…" I frowned. "But Nic and Alaric are en route to London right now. I'm hoping they find Nathaniel and smooth things over with FALCON."

"Jeez, I hope so!" She took a deep breath. "But who's Nathaniel?"

I smiled. "Nathaniel Night is an old friend. He's a unique wolf," I grinned.

"Like me?"

I laughed. "No, nothing like you. He remains in his human form when he shifts."

"What does that mean?"

Smiling, I explained, "he looks human, but with fur, sharp teeth and claws."

"So, what is he, then?"

"A genetic mutation," I said. She frowned. I nodded.

"Okay, that sounds like a whole other story right there!"

Grinning, I stood up and pulled her into my arms. "Oh, it is Princess, and it's one worth telling. But I'll let Nathaniel share that one with you."

She smiled, and I leaned in, kissing her hot lips, delving deep within her as she groaned. Gripping her head, our bodies pushed together. I growled, pulling away. Hot damn, she made me horny!

"What was that for?" she asked, smiling, taking a deep breath.

Lips pursed, I pushed her onto the sofa. She squealed, grabbing my arm. Kneeling over her, our lips crashed together, strong, hot, sexy kisses followed. Deep, breathless, and hungry for more, I gripped her bra.

"Wait!" she said, giggling, unhooking it properly. "I'll have no clothes left at this rate!"

I smirked, waited impatiently as she undressed beneath me. She laughed when I growled deep inside. Thick, muscular arms held her body in place. Ripping my top off and unbuttoning my jeans, I pulled her pants clean off, ripping them in two. Her eyes narrowed as she tutted, then smirked, leaning up to kiss me. Hot, hungry kisses cemented my arousal.

Finding her clit, I played, kissing her, and tracing my tongue over her naked body, suckling her nipples.

Aroused and groaning with pleasure, she arched. My wet fingertips delved inside, finding her g-spot, making her moan in pleasure. She tasted so damn sweet. I growled, needing more.

Sliding back up her body, I pushed my cock deep inside, grinding back and forth. Her nails gripped my back, drawing blood, legs wrapped around my buttocks. Faster and deeper. Stronger and harder we pushed. Sex never felt so good! Willa arched, tensed, and screamed out. Her walls closed in, squeezing me as I pushed for more. Losing all control as the pleasure of orgasmic ecstasy rode over me. Body tensing, growls escaping, and finally shivering with satisfaction, I withdrew. Willa smiled. Her naked body flushed and dripping with sweat. Sitting up, we kissed, our tongues exploring each other's mouths.

I sighed, relaxed, and kissed her again.

Taking my tee-shirt, Willa covered herself over. She smiled. "I'd like to come with you when you talk to my adopted family."

I nodded. "I was counting on it."

"Well, handsome," she grinned. "I'm going for a shower. Care to join me?"

I smirked. "Do you even have to ask?"

She wandered into the bathroom, left the door open and turned on the shower, sliding herself inside. I growled, watching as she washed herself. Handprints appeared on the glass as she relaxed under the water. Eager for more, I joined her. The warmth of hot water washed over me. I groaned, my hands sliding down her body as she showered. Soap suds lathered over her breasts. Her hands strained against the tiles. I kissed her neck, bit down on her mark, her legs trembling below me. Moaning, she arched her hips up, panting for more. I pushed myself deep inside, gripping her hips, pushing harder, deeper still. Willa was my addiction and right now. I was sailing as high as a kite. Groaning in harmony, she buckled under the pressure. Holding her up, we reached our crescendo. Igniting the raw hunger inside us both.

"Bloody heck Ethan. I can't anymore!" she screamed.

Laughing, I pulled back. Exhausted and holding her tight. Relaxing into my arms, Willa smiled, turning off the water. Her stomach rumbled. "Worked up quite the appetite, have we?" I grinned. She smirked, pushing me out the door.

"Just a bit!" She smirked.

Grinning, I chucked on my black pyjama bottoms, kissed her forehead, and headed to the kitchen. As I closed the door, the cold air hit me. Castles weren't the warmest of places. Even with central heating!

Walking down the corridor I found Cleo sat in the corner rocking herself back and forth.

I frowned, knelt in front of her, and touched her knee. She growled. Eyes wide, I jumped back. "Cleo?" I asked, studying her. What was going on with her?

She narrowed her eyes. Growled, then stood up and ran off. I watched her go. Clearly, she wasn't in the mood for any type of conversation right now! Damn!

Mother walked past. "Ethan... have you seen Cleo?"

"Yeah, she's acting a little psycho right now." Mother sighed. "But she went that way." I pointed. She nodded.

Damn, the drama in this place was reaching epic proportions! The kitchen was quiet. They must be on their break. I grabbed the essentials... a few cans of cola, a selection of pastries, fruit, and chocolate. Then picked out a rose from the vase in the hallway. Every man knows the way to a woman's heart is with flowers and chocolates. I smiled, heading back to our room.

Upon entering, I saw Willa dressed in a modest black dress. She smiled, then turned away from me, handing me a brush and a ribbon. Taking them, I brushed her gorgeous red hair, pulled it back and tied it in a ponytail with a black ribbon. She looked in the mirror. "You've done that before," she said. Grinning.

"Cleo," I said, laughing. "Just don't tell anyone." I winked.

She laughed, "your secrets safe with me... after all, a macho Alpha like you playing dress up with your kid sister," she smirked. "It might not go down so well!"

I growled, grabbed her waist, pulled her in close, and kissed her hard.

Willa placed on her heels and did a twirl for me. My heart faced. She looked damn sexy in those heels. "Wow!" I said. She laughed as I picked up my jaw. "You look beautiful!"

"Why thank you," she said, smirking.

"Too hot damn beautiful," I growled, placing the food and flower on the desk. My inner wolf pushed for more. Stepping forward, I reach out, closing the space between us. Growls erupted as my lips crashed into hers. She kissed me back. Hard. Then pulled back, flustered.

"Now Now Prince Ethan, I'd rather keep this outfit intact."

Growling, I pulled her back to me. "I wouldn't!"

She laughed, kissing me again and walking over to the desk. "Later Ethan. Later." She smirked. I sulked. "Is this for me?" she asked, picking up the rose.

"Of course." I grinned, catching her arm and holding her close. Roses and lavender caressed my senses. "Mmm!"

Willa smiled, took a deep breath, and said, "Ethan, you need to get ready."

Reality hit at that moment. Waves of grief crashed above me, forcing me to withdraw. I made my way to the desk, took a selection of pastries, and sat on the edge of the bed to eat.

Willa placed her hand on my shoulder and kissed my forehead. "I'll be with you," she said. I smiled, continuing to eat. Willa did the same, choosing the pain au chocolat over anything else.

As the sun waned, I knew it was time. She was right. I had to face what was coming and say goodbye to my best friend. Tristan. Tristan had always been there for me. We'd shared a life together and were closer than any brother or pack member I'd ever had. When his parents died, he was lost, broken and helpless. I saw myself in him. The responsibility I knew I would one day inherit, and I did. He inherited that from a young age. An Alpha throughout most of his teenage years. He was a natural, too. Granted, he screwed up so many times, I'd lost count. But he always corrected his mistakes, owned up to his flaws, and the way he handled his pack was inspiring. I'd taken his lead and learnt through him for so many years. I'm not sure how I can handle this on my own. Head down, I sighed.

"Are you okay?" Willa asked.

"I will be," I said, taking a deep breath.

She smiled. "I'm always here for you, you know."

I smiled and nodded. I knew she was. She was a miracle. I hoped that one day she would see herself as I see her. Perhaps she would. When she stood there leading everyone to victory. Perhaps then she will realise just how far she's come. It's my turn to teach now. The ropes have passed down, and I will teach her everything I know. Everything Tristan taught me.

Chapter Fifty-one
Willa

The funeral was not one I had ever witnessed before. It reminded me of a Viking funeral. Where their loved ones cleaned the body, dressed them, and pushed out to sea, then lit with a flaming arrow by a loved one. This was down to Ethan. His hands shook slightly as he took in the sight of his dead friend before him. He whispered in his ear, then pushed the boat out into the lake. Taking a deep breath, stepping back and firing a flaming arrow into the pyre before him.

Tristan's body lay in that inferno. Sent off as a warrior to the cause. He had stepped in and saved my life. I was the reason he lay there, burning. Taking a long, deep breath, I shuddered. Stretching out myself limb from limb. I needed to get through the pain of guilt. Remember, he made his own choice. Not me. But even knowing that wouldn't quiet the darkness growing inside of me.

Ethan feigned a smile and walked over. I took his hand and held it tight. He squeezed mine back, watching as every pack member nodded to him as they walked by. Some tearful, some solemn. Many laughing through the good times of Tristan's life. But far to the side, I spotted my brothers. All seven stood with their heads lowered in respect for the dead. I smiled and kissed Ethan on the cheek. "Go, be with your pack. I will be there shortly." I said, nodding over to my brothers.

Ethan nodded, kissed me, and caught up with his pack. Laughter erupted as he recalled a story or two about Tristan's comical personality.

Smiling, my brothers walked over to me. "How did it go?" Adam asked.

"As well as expected," I said.

"Do you think he'll be okay with what's coming?" Darius said.

I nodded. "He will be. He just needs a little time to come to terms with losing his best friend." I sighed, smiling. Darius nodded.

"Well, we will be at the campsite when you're ready."

I smiled. "It would be good if you were at the castle?"

He took a deep breath. "How about we let the dust settle first?"

I nodded, smirking.

Stefan smirked. "Too soon, Willa, too soon!" he grinned.

I laughed. "But surely you'd like to sleep in an actual bed?"

Stefan laughed. "Yes… when I know your Prince won't murder us in our sleep!"

We all laughed, but yet I felt there was some truth to that statement. I always saw Ethan as my partner, my mate. But to them, he's still the most powerful Alpha out there. They had every right to fear him!

"Okay, well, I had better catch up with Ethan." Darius nodded. "I'll see you soon!"

I waved as I walked away. "You could always text!" Stefan yelled.

I turned and laughed as he had his phone in his hand, waving it around. "I would, but there's no signal at the castle!"

"Well, that sucks!" he said, frowning.

Laughing, I waved again and ran off to catch up with Ethan.

Ethan was sitting on the steps in the courtyard. His pack was all gathered around him.

"How are you all?" I asked, unsure of their temperament.

Ethan looked up and smiled, and as he did, he sniffled. "I'm good. We're all good, in fact. But I tell you one thing Princess…"

"What's that?"

"We all need a bloody good drink!"

I laughed. "That can be arranged!"

Ethan stood up. "Let's go to the Crescent Bar. It's where Tristan and I would go all the time."

"Oh, so that's where you were hiding?" I joked.

"Maybe." He grinned.

Heading down to the bar, we held hands. To any other couple, we looked like two humans in a normal, happy relationship. Little did they know the dirty details of it all. A werewolf mated to a human. That human shifting into a wolf. A witch with her spells and a Prince who lost four years of his life to the perverse seductress named Danica Daventry. I sighed, remembering the journey we had been on. Biting my bottom lip, I gripped Ethan's hand tighter. He turned and smiled. I smiled back. I wonder if she's still alive. Danica, I mean. Shuddering, I shook it off. Do I even care if she is? Shrugging, my mind continued to wander as we walked to the bar. Ethan really has been through Hell and back with her, and now to have lost his best friend too. If there is a God, he has really got it out for us!

There must be, though. A god I mean. After all, there are demons out there. I saw one of the sneaky little assholes at Helas messed up a celebratory dance. Bright red, point tail, horned head. The works. It was almost comical to see. Except I guessed that nasty little thing would surely pack a punch!

What other supernaturals were out there, though? Ethan had said Hela had wiped out many of the lower races. But surely, she didn't wipe out all of them? After all, I saw some strange-looking ones in the palace. Abaddon, for example. Who even is that? I made a mental note to ask Ethan later. I sighed.

Reaching the bar, I took a seat and a gulp of gin. Ethan was right. We all needed a damn drink right now. Staring into my glass, the pink gin swirled around the sides, mixing around the ice cubes. Ethan carried on telling tales about Tristan and all the mishaps he got into. I smiled, listening. Well, until my mind wandered again. The problem with alcohol, sadness, is that your thoughts can go to a dark place if you're not careful, and on the day of a loved one's funeral, they steer towards the depths of dismay. It didn't help that I had no clue how to be this almighty prophecy wolf, let alone how to even shift into one. Wasn't there like a manual on this kinda thing? Perhaps that's it. Perhaps I needed to write a manual for all the newbie werewolves out there. Sketch out a map of the basics, like shifting, hunger and the need for sex repeatedly. I laughed. Ethan looked at me and smiled. I was really hoping that wasn't a serious part of the conversation I laughed at! He nodded. I smiled back. Then he continued to talk to the pack.

Ok so maybe the sex thing was all me, rather than a 'wolf' thing. Hell, I don't have a clue, really! But I was sure as hell going to take notes so I could pass them on to this army we're about to create.

Ethan downed the rest of his pint when a horrendous howl shattered the silence throughout the bar. Human folk choked on their drinks, many wary, afraid and unsure. Ethan stood up. "Wait here!" he said, leaving the bar.

Two of his pack members followed him. I groaned. As if I was going to wait there. Something was happening, and I was a part of it. So, downing my drink, because you know… gin cannot be wasted. I stood up and left the bar, entering out into the evening sky to see a sight of seven saddened wolves before me.

Chapter Fifty-two
Darius

Every one of us heard that all telling chime from our phones. Marcus had sent a message. Why had Marcus messaged us? He never did.

Stylan's expression darkened. His jaw dropped. One by one, my brothers looked at their phones. Each one of them a display of emotion. Anger. Upset. Pain. Betrayal.

I picked up my phone. Saw the message and opened it. I wish I hadn't. Because there, displayed in 4k, was my beautiful little sister Myra's slaughter.

Her tiny, frail body looked drawn in and old. Ragged clothes covered with blood. Pale skin, lifeless eyes. She stared up at me from that screen and begged for mercy. But none was given.

I gagged as Hela took Myra's son, my nephew, and destroyed his life, killing his mother in front of him. I didn't even know I had a nephew. Why didn't I know that? Hela had manipulated him to do her bidding. It was so fucking wrong, and I was so angry I could scream. Gripping the phone harder, I watched. Eyes wide. Panicked and pained. She did it, kicked Myra in the face, severing her beautiful bright head from her lifeless, pained body. I gasped, choking back the tears, vomited into the undergrowth beside me.

Stylan was in floods of tears. A brave faced Adam was comforting him. They and Myra were always so close to growing up. Each of them watched out for each other. It helped that they were both close in age. He'd been born after the twins. Shit! What about Lorena? Is she next?

I wiped my mouth and comforted my brothers. Harper was shouting blasphemy, kicking the shit out of a tree. While Stefan, who was usually the most hopeful of us all, was sitting alone beside a tree, staring at the phone in shock. I didn't know where to turn. The fact that Hela knew of our betrayal, or that she used it to murder our sister in cold blood. And Joey, who even was Joey? We hadn't seen Myra for over three years; ever since Hela married her off to Vivian, the teenage vampire with a tendency to love the ladies. But what… she had a kid and never told us? We should have pushed harder. Stayed in touch. How did I not know the pain she had lived through? Three years with this wife beater. I growled at the thought of it. He'd pay. I'd feed every part of his cold, rotting corpse to him before he died. He'd eat himself to death, and I'd fucking enjoy watching every second. Neither of them would survive this. I'd make damned sure they didn't, even if it was the last thing I did.

Crushing the phone in the palm of my hand, I threw it at a tree and growled, shifting into my wolf. My brothers followed suit. Each of them shifting, every one of us running through the pain. Faster and faster, we ran, sliding through the Vale as though our lives depended on it. I didn't know where we were heading until we ended up behind the Crescent Bar, scenting Willa inside. I howled as loud as I could. Ethan came out looking puzzled. His eyes still red from the loss of his friend Tristan.

"Now's not a good time," he said as a few of his pack members followed him out. Beers in hand.

I nodded and growled, padding the floor. Willa came out and smiled when she saw us. Seeing her brought even more pain to my heart. I howled low and saddened. Willa's brow furrowed as she came to me. Her delicate hand resting on my grey fur.

Ethan watched; his eyes narrowed. "What's wrong?" he asked. I howled in pain again. Ethan nodded, turned to Willa. "Stay here Princess," he said.

She didn't look impressed. "I don't think so. If something has happened, I'm coming too."

Ethan growled. "Can you shift?"

She shook her head. "I haven't figured out how I did it yet."

He smiled, took her hand, and whispered in her ear. She smiled. He undressed, handed her his clothes, and shifted. She jumped on his back, following us back to our camp.

The ride was fast, heavy, and hard. Each of my brothers whimpered as we ran.

When we arrived, it pained me to see the remains of my phone scattered over the campsite. Willa jumped off Ethan and walked over to me, picking up the piece. "What happened?" she asked, her face filled with concern. I howled in pain, head lowered, eyes tinged with tears. Willa stepped back into Ethan as he shifted. He grabbed on to her, held her tight. Her face was full of anguish as she felt the pain of our hearts breaking.

"What's happened, Ethan?" she asked.

"I don't know Princess. Come here, you're shivering," he said, wrapping his naked arms around her tighter.

"More like you'll be freezing!" she said, handing him his clothes. Ethan changed while I shifted back, grabbed some clothes from my tent. My brothers did the same. Adam lit the campfire, gave Willa a blanket, and offered her a seat beside him on the log. He would probably be the best to tell her. I wasn't exactly the most level-headed right now. I sighed; fists pummelled. If I could just get that last image of her pleading face out of my head. "ARGH!" I yelled, kicking the old rotten leaves across the camp.

"What is going on?" Ethan demanded, sitting beside Willa.

I took a deep breath. "Adam… show them."

He looked up; eyes narrowed. "Are you sure you want her to see it?"

I sighed.

"See what?" Willa asked, brow furrowed.

"It's not something you'll ever unsee Willa," Stylan said as he placed his hand on her shoulder.

"Perhaps Ethan should see it first," Adam said.

"No. We're all in this together," Willa said, huffing.

"Okay," I sighed, nodding to Adam to show her the video. "But I'm sorry you have to meet her this way."

Willa frowned, took the phone from Adam and pressed play. Both Willa and Ethan's faces paled. Willa gripped the phone harder. Ethan swallowed hard; his jaw dropped with disbelief. Tears welled in Willa's eyes, her face full of shock, fear, and pain. My heart sank for them, knowing full well the pain they were enduring. Willa's hands shook so much she dropped the phone. Her heart breaking as she sobbed, sliding off the log to her knees. Ethan picked up the phone and threw it to the side. His face red with anger. Growls erupted from him, loud, piercing growls. His inner wolf was urging to snap, rip their limbs from their bodies, just as we had wanted to.

Myra and Ethan knew each other well as children. They were as close as Ethan and I were as children. Myra and Lorena were both younger but looked up to him as little sisters would. We'd all been close back then. I missed it. Closing the gap between Willa and me. I picked her up off the ground and held her tight. Her tears fell on my chest. She was heartbroken, as was I. We'd lost our sister, and poor Willa never had the chance to know her, not like I did. Willa's body shook in my arms. Cries wailed from her innocent breath as Adam talked Ethan down and ushered him to Willa's arms. Backing away, I watched as they held each other. Mates soothed by one another's touch.

Sitting down, I stayed silent. Lost in the thousand memories I had of my sister, Myra. How could I have been so stupid? Why did I ever let Hela marry her off to that monster? But then father said it was the best. If Myra hadn't had agreed she would have been no use to Hela, and those that were no use were disposed of. Much like we would all be soon.

I knew this was a warning. A sick, twisted evil warning. But a warning all the same. Hela was gunning for each of us. One thing I knew for certain was that we'd meet her on the battlefield. We'd tear her apart. Destroy everything she stood for. And at the head of that battle would be our red-haired flaming beauty. Our sister Willa Rose. The prophecy will stand. We will survive and we will save every bloody supernatural we could on the way.

Chapter Fifty-Three
Willa

"Darius…" I said, eyes stinging from all the tears. He feigned a smile. Patting the bench next to him, I sat down.

I took a deep breath. Whatever sadistic games Hela was playing, it wouldn't last long. I'd make damn sure of that. I sighed, wiping my face. With every war there's casualty's, I know that. But this was my sister! I never knew her. Tears threatened to spill again. She looked so sad, so tired and worn down. That vicious dead thing would pay for what he did! I sighed. I wanted, no needed vengeance. But now wasn't the time. There was still an innocent child's life at stake, and we couldn't let him be caught up in the middle of it all. He was Myra's, after all. My nephew. "We must save Joey," I said, laying my head on his shoulder.

Darius tensed up, took a few deep breaths, then exhaled. "Yes, you're right." I sighed with relief. "I dread to think what he has endured with having that vampire as a father!" I shuddered and sat up. Ethan sat beside us. "We will have an army, Darius. But we will need help training them."

Darius's brow furrowed. Adam joined us and sat on the log beside Darius.

"What army?" Darius asked.

"My adopted family. Hela will come for them too. Ethan will offer them the choice to take the risk and become a wolf, fighting by our side."

Adam narrowed his eyes. "But how will you get them to believe you?"

"He's going to shift in front of them," I said, eyes wide, nodding as Adam gulped.

Ethan sighed. "What? It's not like any of you ever followed the rules before now!"

Darius smirked. "He has a point."

"So, when do we start? Actually, don't we need a leader?" he asked, brow furrowed, looking at Darius.

Darius shrugged. "Don't look at me! I have enough with you lot!"

Stylan feigned a broken heart as he came over, listening in. I laughed.

Ethan sat forward. "We already have a leader, and we will strike down every fucked up supernatural in that place."

"What you?" Darius spat.

"Shit. Don't look so horrified! I am the all-powerful Alpha," he grinned. Darius shot him a dirty look. I smirked. "But no, not me. There's another wolf more powerful than me here."

My eyes narrowed as everyone looked at me. "What?" leader?"

Ethan laughed. "It's you Willa! The prophecy says it's always been you!"

I coughed, choking on my saliva. Has he hit his head? "Are you being serious?"

"As serious as ever, Princess," he smiled.

"But I can't even shift?"

"You've done it once; you'll do it again."

Adam smiled. "We will help teach you Willa," he said. "That's what big brothers are for!"

I smiled, thanking him. "But that still doesn't mean I'm capable of what the prophecy says!"

Stylan sat upright and smiled. "Oh, you are, baby sister. Didn't you see yourself in there?"

My brow furrowed. "No? Why? What did I miss?"

Ethan laughed. "When you shifted you had the flaming red aura surrounding you."

"The what?"

He laughed again. "Your fur was on fire!"

"Shit! Really?" he nodded. "I just thought it glowed a bit." I said, puzzled. "But wait, it didn't hurt," I said, brow furrowed. "Why didn't it hurt?"

Darius smirked, put his arm around me, and ruffled my hair. "You've got a lot to learn, little sister!" He laughed.

Ethan smirked, stood up, and held out his hand. "And the first lesson for today is how to endure being ridiculed by your brothers."

I laughed, took his hand, and stood up.

"Right. On that note," I yawned. "I think I need sleep."

Ethan grinned. "Your first shift really did a number on you, didn't it?"

"Ah ha," I said, stifling another yawn.

"Come on Princess, let's get you home."

Darius stood up and hugged me. All of my brothers did. Waving them off, I couldn't help but feel the sadness in their hearts. Myra wasn't a sister I had the chance to get to know. But she was family and family stuck together, no matter what.

Jumping on the back of Ethan, I stroked the back of his neck, snuggled into his fur, and whispered in his ear. "I love you, Ethan James Bane." He howled and rubbed his head against mine.

"I love you too, Princess," his voice echoed through my mind. Smiling, I leant into him, letting him carry me home, safe and secure, knowing that tomorrow would be a new day. A special day and a day worth living. For tomorrow I train. I learn and tomorrow, we go to war.

THE END.

Other books by Annalee Adams

In this universe:

The Resurgence series:
The Midnight Rose
The Heart of the Phoenix
The Rise of the Vampire Kng
The Fall of the Immortals

The Fire Wolf Prophecies:
Crimson Bride
Crimson Army (out 2023)

The Shop Series:
Stake Sandwich
The Devil Made Me Do It

Other books not in this universe:

The Celestial Rose Series:
Eternal Entity
Eternal Creation
Eternal Devastation
Eternal Ending

Gruesome Fairy Tales:
Gretel
Hansel

ABOUT ANNALEE

Annalee Adams lives in England with her Husband, two children and a zoo worth of animals. She loves a good strong cup of tea or coffee, plenty of chocolate and binge watching her shows on Netflix.

Annalee began her career with the Celestial Rose series while at University. She spent much of her childhood engrossed in fictional stories, starting with teenage point horror books and moving up to the works of Stephen King and Dean Koontz. However, her all-time favourite book is Lewis Carroll's, Alice in Wonderland -which explains her mindset quite well.

CONNECT WITH ANNALEE

Join Annalee on social media. She is regularly posting videos and updates for her next books on TikTok and Facebook.

Join Annalee in her Facebook group:
Annalee Adams Bookworms & Bibliophiles.

Also, subscribe to Annalees newsletter through her website - for free books, sales, sneak previews and much more.
Subscribe at www.AnnaleeAdams.biz

TikTok: @author_annaleeadams

Website: www.AnnaleeAdams.biz

Email: AuthorAnnaleeAdams@gmail.com

Twitter: https://twitter.com/AuthorAnnalee

Facebook: https://www.facebook.com/authorannaleeadams/

Made in the USA
Columbia, SC
23 January 2023

a29e5994-675e-4fb1-9d32-549d9cae7b7eR01